THE ARCHMAGE

A *Just Cause Universe* Novel

IAN THOMAS HEALY

Local Hero Press

The Archmage: A Just Cause Universe Novel
Published by Local Hero Press, LLC
http://localheropress.ianthealy.com

1st Printing
Local Hero Press: trade paperback, September 1, 2012
2nd Printing
Local Hero Press, LLC: trade paperback, May 1, 2014

ISBN-13: 9781971445021

Cover art by S. Bell
Book design by Ian Thomas Healy

This is a work of fiction. Names, characters, places, and incidents are either the product of the author's imagination or used fictitiously. Any resemblance to actual events, locales, or persons, living or dead, is entirely coincidental.

Books by Local Hero Press

The *Just Cause Universe*
Just Cause
The Archmage
Day of the Destroyer
Deep Six
Jackrabbit
Champion
Castles
The Lion and the Five Deadly
Serpents
Tusks
The Neighborhood Watch
Jackrabbit: Big In Japan
Arena
Hero Academy
The Path
Cinco de Mayo
Search and Rescue
Rooftops
Plague
Soldiers of Fortune
Just Cause Universe Compendium
Destroyer of Earth
Flint and Steel
The Club
Jackrabbit: Rinse and Repeat
Posse
Extinction Event
Rain Must Fall

Pariah of Verigo
Pariah's Moon
Pariah's War

Three Flavors of Tacos
The Guitarist
Making the Cut
The Scene Stealers

Collections
Airship Lies
High Contrast
The Good Fight
The Good Fight 3: Sidekicks
The Good Fight 4: Homefront
The Good Fight 5: The Golden Age
Muddy Creek Tales
Caped

Other Novels
Assassin
Blood on the Ice
Funeral Games
Hope and Undead Elvis
Horde
The Murder Squad (2026)
Roast Wyvern (and Other Recipes)
Starf*cker
Strings
The Oilman's Daughter
Troubleshooters

Nonfiction
Action! Writing Better Action
Using Cinematic Techniques

Praise for *Just Cause*

"Ian Healy's *Just Cause* is a slam-bang good superhero story: part *JLA*, part *Young Romance*, with some splashes of *Our Army at War* to keep you on your toes. I thoroughly enjoyed Mustang Sally's adventure and look forward to reading more of Healy's work."

—Rob Rogers, author of *Devil's Cape*

~~~

"Ian Healy's *Just Cause* is solid, serious superhero action in the classic tradition, with tons of interesting characters, extremely well-crafted action scenes, and real depth. Highly recommended."

—Van Allen Plexico, author of *The Sentinels*

~~~

"The best thing about Ian Healy's books is the accessibility of their worlds and characters. He welcomes us in and takes us for a fun and memorable ride, and unlike other superhero universes, we never feel like the understanding of an entire mythology is out of our grasp—or would take thousands of reading hours to accomplish."

—Allison M. Dickson, author of *The Last Supper*

"Ian T. Healy's fun, engrossing, and thoroughly-realized *Just Cause* universe will make you want to break out your own cape and cowl."

—Jeff Hebert, creator of the *HeroMachine*

~~~

"Mr. Healy clearly loves superhero fiction. He has taken tried and true superhero tropes, made them his own, and crafted an excellent world, story, and characters. I highly recommend."

—Corey L. Bishop, *Creative Commoners* podcast

~~~

"Ian Healy's *Just Cause* is a great superhero book because it creates a world that is so close to our own we almost think that maybe these things did/are really happening, it's just that we don't live in the right city, and don't maybe have that special brick touch pattern to get us to Diagon Alley."

—Jenn Zuko, *Nerds in Babeland*

~~~

"It almost feels like you're watching a movie instead of reading a book when the superheroes are battling the villains."

—Megan Bostic, author of *Never Eighteen*

AUTHOR'S NOTE

I am greatly indebted to Allison M. Dickson, my dearest friend and best editor, for helping to make this tale far better than I could have done on my own. Many thanks to my parents Tom and Erin for their ongoing support, to my wife Richelle for indulging my writerly madness, and to my children Patrick, Caitlin, and Zachary for proudly introducing me to everyone as their *Dad who writes books*. You have no idea how much that means to me. Thanks, and much love to you all.

PROLOGUE

"My official stance on magic? There's no such thing."

-Dr. Grace Devereaux
Scientific American
April 1990

April, 2004
Tokyo, Japan

"More sake, *Wiru-san?*"

Deep in thought, Will Kramer looked down at his clay mug, still half-full of the warm alcohol. *Or half-empty,* he thought. *After all, I'm a pessimist.* Nevertheless, he turned and smiled at his hostess, Kanayo Saito. She was petite, even for a Japanese woman, and had aged so gracefully that she didn't look anywhere near her age of eighty. Only the deep wrinkles around her eyes and the skin of her hands gave any indication of her many decades of life. She was wrapped in a traditional kimono, delicate red with cherry blossoms printed on it. Her husband, a tall reedy man named Hotaka, sat at the low table and sipped from his own mug. He had two of his crickets out of their gilded cage and watched them frolic on a mat, if such a term as *frolic* could be applied to insects. Nevertheless, their shiny black carapaces almost glowed as they crawled back and forth across the *tatami* mat.

"No thank you, Kanayo-san, but it is very good sake." Will bowed. His tall purple mohawk bobbed forward with the motion. In parahuman circles, he was called Stratocaster, the superhero from America's Lucky Seven team. He played a brilliant white custom guitar made for him by the oldest, most-skilled craftsman at the Fender company. He endorsed their products and they allowed him to use *Stratocaster* as his super identity. His powers, diverse and mysterious, could only be accessed when he played his instrument. He called it magic, and others laughed, because everyone believed there was no such thing.

Only a few people knew the truth: magic was real, and he was part of the very small fraternity of wizards and witches who could bend the mystical power to their wills.

Like Will, the Saitos were also mages. The couple had spent more than half a century in the study of magic and how to control it. Will suspected they were the most powerful mages on the planet, but for all that ability, they rarely called upon the power to do their bidding. The Saitos subscribed to the philosophy that power corrupts, and the more of it they acquired through their studies, original research, and practical application, the less they actually chose to use it. Sometimes they argued—good-naturedly, as they weren't the sort of people to foment conflict—with Will about his persistence in continuing to put the power to use.

Will loved using magic, whether in the service of the Lucky Seven, or simply to make aspects of his daily life simpler. For him, the thrill of the power flowing through him came on like a runner's high. The feeling of magic as it flowed through his fingers into the guitar beat any narcotic, and Will had tried a good number of them as part of his rock-and-roll lifestyle. He carried his sake in one hand and his guitar in the other, and walked over to the window to look out upon the lights of Tokyo, smothered in pollution and drizzling rain.

There weren't many mages left in the world. Once, when civilizations were young, there had been hundreds, perhaps thousands, but they'd been mere dabblers and charlatans. According to the Saitos, the amount of magical energy in the world remained constant, like the mass of the universe. It could never be created anew nor destroyed; it could only be controlled by those who knew the secrets of it. As the number of mages decreased, those who remained could control a proportionately larger piece of the whole.

And now there were seven fewer.

Hotaka had looked stoic and impassive, his cheekbones standing out in sharp relief from his tightly-clenched jaw. Kanayo's eyes had filled with tears and she'd bitten a knuckle to keep from crying out when Will told them the news. Seven of their fellow mages had been slain in less than two months. Their names still echoed through his head: Gendarme and Rousseau in France; the Spaniard Gomez; Turko in Finland; Shostakovich in Russia; Vishnawas in India, and Sujin in Singapore.

Someone or something was hunting down the mages of the world.

"Surely you don't believe it's a coincidence, Hotaka--san?" asked Will. "Seven of us dead in as many weeks?"

"It is no coincidence, *Wiru-san*," said the elder mage at length. Neither he nor his wife could pronounce *Will*; *Wiru* was the closest they could manage. "I had hoped not to encounter an Archmage in my lifetime, but history and prophecy are against me."

Will sat down across the table from Hotaka, crossed his legs and laid his guitar across his lap. "I know the word, but what does it mean in this context?"

"According to the histories, every thousand years a single mage will absorb all available magic, stealing it from those who possess it. His or her power will become virtually absolute." Mages acted as batteries for magic, and released those energies upon death. A nearby mage could absorb those energies into his own body and become that much more powerful instead of letting the energies dissipate throughout the world or remain in isolated pockets until found by future mages.

"So you think that it's a mage who killed the others?"

"I do." Kanayo hunkered down next to her husband and placed a loving hand on his shoulder. He smiled at her, sad but full of love. "And I fear he will come for us."

"Who is it? Is it Banks? Or maybe Williamson? I never trusted him very much." Stirred by his strong emotions, a ghostly whine of harmonics echoed from the strings of the guitar.

"No. Attend." Hotaka pulled a small pouch from inside his robe and poured a sparkling powder onto the table before him. He muttered some ancient words and the powder streamed into the air before him as if guided by invisible breezes. It shaped itself into glyphs which Will couldn't translate. He marveled at the relaxed ease with which Hotaka channeled the power. "I believe his name is . . . I apologize, it is a difficult name. *Wufegane Feraziare*."

"*Wufegane . . .*" said Will thoughtfully. "Wolfgang?"

The older man smiled in relief. "Yes, that is correct."

"I don't recognize the name."

"He has been hidden," said Kanayo softly. "Shielded, certainly, by dark magics. Only now has he begun to draw the power to him. Surely you have noticed the pull on your own powers."

Will took another sip of his sake. He had indeed felt something tugging on him, like a magnet. He hadn't understood what it meant until the Kanayo explained it. He could sense it even now, like a voice that whispered in his ear like a seductive lover. "Yes," he said. "You said he's coming for us?"

Hotaka's face became impassive, but a single tear tracked down Kanayo's face. "He comes for all of us. He means to become the only magic user in the world. The Archmage. He can only succeed by eliminating all rivals."

"Meaning us." A squeal of feedback from the guitar punctuated Will's remark. "Can we stop him?"

"I do not know, *Wiru-san*. We are very old. We may not have the strength to battle him, and he is already very powerful."

Kanayo laid her head on her husband's shoulder. "You may be our best hope to stop him, *Wiru-san*."

Will choked on the mouthful of sake he'd just taken and spluttered. He wiped his mouth with the back of his hand. His eyes watered as the alcohol found its way into his sinuses. "Excuse me?"

"My wife speaks the truth. You are not like other mages, *Wiru-san*. Your powers follow neither convention nor form. You can achieve amazing results with your instrument, and yet cannot perform the simplest incantation without it. It is this . . . *flouting* of magical standards that may prove to be the key to defeating this man."

"How can you say that, Hotaka-san?" Will felt a cold sweat break across his forehead. "I've never had any formal training. I hardly even know what I'm doing. I just kind of make things up as I go along and hope to hell it works."

"And that makes you unpredictable. It is as if you can think in three dimensions when the rest of us only think in two," said Kanayo.

"Okay, I'll give you that. Suppose that I am such a brilliant, unpredictable mage—which I don't believe for a second—how am I supposed to defeat someone who's taken the magic from seven other mages? That makes him seven times as powerful as before, right?"

"Unfortunately you are correct," said Hotaka. "I did not say your task would be easy."

"There is one way we could give you our power, to make you stronger," said Kanayo, her mouth a razor-thin line.

Will sprang to his feet. "You mean die? Commit suicide or *seppuku* or whatever you call it? Or have me kill you? No way." He flung his guitar strap over his shoulder angrily and prepared to strike the power chord that would send him away in a flash of purple light.

"Please, *Wiru-san*. No offense was meant. Do not leave in anger." Hotaka's voice was calm and quiet, and yet it sliced through Will's hot anger like an icy blade.

Will bowed his head. "I'm sorry, Hotaka-san. I know you meant well. I am honored that you would offer your lives to me, but I am not worthy of such a gift."

Hotaka carefully lifted his crickets in the palm of his hand and whispered to them. He opened the door of the little pagoda-shaped cage to allow the crickets to walk into it where they joined several of their brethren. One began to chirp. After a moment, another joined in and soon their ghostly chorus echoed through the large apartment. It was a peaceful sound, reminiscent of Will's childhood in rural Illinois. He felt the tension wash away from him.

It returned a moment later full force when Kanayo spoke. "He approaches, husband. I sense him."

"Yes," said Hotaka with a deep, worldly sadness. "*Wiru-san*, this does not yet have to be your fight. If you wish, you may leave to rejoin your friends now."

"No way, Hotaka-san." Will checked the tuning of his guitar. "I'm not about to let some asshole come in here and . . . and do as he pleases."

"You must swear an oath to us," urged Kanayo. "Right here and now, or we shall bar you from this place. Certain things must never come to pass so long as you live."

"Anything you like." Will's skin prickled. He spun all his tone and volume pots to maximum and was rewarded with a gentle whine of feedback from the air around him. His guitar produced amplified sound even though it wasn't connected to anything, as if the very air itself became his speaker.

"Swear that you will not let him take our power. If our defeat is inevitable, you must take our power for yourself. It is your only chance to survive."

"What?" Will couldn't believe his ears. "Come on, you can't be serious."

Hotaka set his cricket cage on a high shelf so it would be out of danger. His ancient paper-thin skin took on a hardened, shiny appearance. The fabric of Kanayo's clothing moved to reshape itself around her as if it were alive.

"Swear, or I shall banish you from this place forever. You know I have the power to do so, Wiru-san." Hotaka raised a hand surrounded by a glowing nimbus of energy.

"Okay, I swear," Will grumbled.

He had never before seen the Saitos use their magic in great quantities. Hotaka stood straighter, and somehow taller and more massive than before, as if his legs and body had lengthened. His skin transformed to shiny, black chitin, and horny blades pushed out of his arms and legs. *He looks like a cricket*, thought Will as he noticed the long antennae sprouting from Hotaka's forehead.

Meanwhile, the layers of her clothing had reshaped around Kanayo to form an approximation of ancient samurai armor. A sash whipped out, straight and hard, and she grasped it like a *katana* sword. Magic crackled off both of them like static electricity. They seemed almost young and vibrant as the power flowed through them.

Lightning flared outside the windows, and thunder boomed instantly along with it. Will saw a dark figure floating in the air, backlit by the storm. He had just opened his mouth to shout a warning when all the windows facing east shattered inward. Razor-sharp slivers of glass whirled through the apartment. The shards deflected off Hotaka's insectile armor and only cut a few threads on Kanayo's fabric. Will barely managed to strum a chord in time to create a screen of force in front of him to keep from getting shredded.

Will squinted through the rain that blew into the room. The figure drifted closer to the building face, illuminated by the room lighting. He was in his mid-thirties, with a slender frame and gaunt face. Male-pattern baldness had begun to show through his short black hair and gray hairs streaked his neatly-trimmed beard. Although he floated in the rain, not a drop reached his skin or his fashionable clothing. No costumes for this fellow; he wore designer jeans, a white Oxford shirt, black leather jacket, and alligator skin boots. He gazed into the Saitos' apartment with interest.

"How nice," he said. "You have company. Saves me a trip. I'm Wolfgang Frazier and I'll be killing you all this evening." His voice was husky, as if he smoked a couple packs a day, but carried subsonic power in it that made Will's stomach churn.

Kanayo raised her hands and a mass of sashes and ribbons shot forth like serpentine missiles. They raced through the air toward the man as if they were alive. The man countered with a spell of his own that caused the fabric to blacken and crumble into ash as it touched him.

He stepped out of the air through a broken pane of glass, and Will let him have it with a massive, crunchy power chord from way down on the neck. The blast of sound turned the remaining glass shards in the room into powder. Frazier flew backwards from the impact and tumbled out of the window.

Will turned to face the Saitos with a smile and a shrug. "That didn't seem so hard."

Eldritch flames spurted into the sky as Frazier rose again, borne on a column of flame. "Simpleton," he hissed through magical amplification that parroted Will's. "Did you really think I would be so easily defeated by the likes of you?"

"I was sort of hoping, yeah."

Kanayo and Hotaka stepped in front of him and assumed fighting stances. "You shall not have him, monster," rasped Hotaka through jaws better-suited to tearing steel than starting conversations.

Will's jaw dropped. "What are you doing?"

"Oh, please," Frazier snarled. "You think a couple of fossils like you can stop me?"

Hotaka rasped his forearms together with a sound like swords being sharpened. Fabric flowed around Kanayo like living water. "Coward." Kanayo's voice sounded like that of a young woman, smooth and silky.

"Fancy a melee, do you? Fine. It should be quite amusing." Frazier extended his hands and a pair of glowing swords grew out of them. Each blade sparked and spat flames. He held one in front of him vertically, and lifted the other over his head in a mock salute. "Come on, then. I haven't got all night." Smoky Western-style armor appeared around his body and glowed dim purple in the gathering darkness.

Will started to play his best speed metal attack riff. The steel girders of the high-rise vibrated in sympathetic harmony. A single word of power passed from Frazier's lips and suddenly Will couldn't feel his fingers. The sounds of his guitar changed from mellifluous to jarring and dissonant, and his magic became erratic and uncontrolled.

Hotaka and Kanayo rushed the intruder. Frazier moved in a blur and used his magic to counter theirs. Hotaka's chitin blades flashed as Frazier deflected them with his own swords. Kanayo used her magic to make her curtains constrict him. He struggled to move against fabric as unyielding as steel. As Hotaka closed in on him, a cloud of pitch darkness filled the room. Frazier's swords flared hot and orange in the unnatural darkness.

Will closed his eyes against the black and concentrated on finding his fingers again. He knew they were still there; his body had the memory. He just needed to reestablish the paths of his nerves. Magic coursed down his arms and overcame the spell which held his fingers fast. He began to play once more. A pinched harmonic on the high E string dissipated the darkness as quickly as Frazier had created it.

Hotaka and Kanayo fought on full defense, hard-pressed by Frazier's attacks. Fresh gouges in Hotaka's armor smoked where the would-be Archmage's flaming blades had cut it. What seemed like several acres of cloth swatches were strewn across the floor, their edges charred. A deep cut in Kanayo's side stained her fabric armor with her blood. Frazier appeared unharmed, and even seemed to be enjoying himself.

Will swore that if nothing else, he would wipe that stupid grin off Frazier's face.

His fingers danced over the frets as he wove magical energies in a storm to compete with nature's own pyrotechnics outside. His force interposed itself between Frazier and the Saitos to protect them from his flaming swords. Then it gently lifted them over and behind him. They might not be out of harm's reach, but at least he'd moved them out of melee range.

Frazier's smile fell as his kills were robbed from him. He snarled and his swords vanished. He drew power into him in preparation for the incantation which would destroy Will. Will could feel it draining from the very air around him.

Will compressed as much of the magical force around Frazier as he could and shoved him once again out into the rainstorm outside. He pulled off a difficult two-handed arpeggio up and down the neck of his guitar and built up to a climax which should crush Frazier into powder.

A sparkling shield emerged from within the enemy mage and pushed back against Will's energies. Even though he worked hard to defend himself, Frazier still found enough power to go on the offensive. He released a glowing yellow cloud that drifted through the air, unaffected by wind or rain. Will changed tactics from technical prowess to sheer balls-to-the-wall speed metal. The cloud broke apart and flowed past him in thin yellow streamers.

The Saitos! Will realized.

He whirled around just in time to see the yellow cloud envelop the two elder mages.

"No!" screamed Will as he tried to find the right chord to fling the poison away from them.

Hotaka took his wife's hand in his own and smiled even as blood began to trickle from the corner of his mouth. She in turn nodded at Will before she closed her eyes. They both pitched forward to crumple into heaps which decomposed into dust.

And their energies poured into Will.

"No, it was supposed to be mine! Mine, you bastard!" shrieked Frazier.

Between them, the Saitos had nearly two hundred years to absorb magic, and those energies flowed out of their remains like water from a fire hose. If the power had been lightning, it would have sought the ground. But this was magic, and it sought the nearest conduit of eldritch ability.

It sought Will.

Brilliant white light surrounded him. He stopped playing; he couldn't have continued even had he wanted to. His body went completely numb. The concentrated power protected him from Frazier's sneak attack, a bolt of power which rebounded away to dissolve a large hole in the apartment's wall.

The landlord's gonna be pissed, thought Will, drunk on the power as it coursed through his body. He immediately understood the appeal of becoming an Archmage, if it felt like this all the time. He turned, only dimly aware that his feet hovered several inches over the floor.

"No matter," grumbled Frazier. "I'll get their power when I kill you."

Options poured through Will's mind like sand through a sieve. There were so many new things he knew he could do with the fresh influx of pure power: invocations, evocations, transformations. Choices overwhelmed him and he floated, helpless, unable to decide on one. Another of Frazier's power bolts blasted against Will and shattered the magical shield between them.

At last, Will understood discretion was the better part of valor. His mind latched onto a spell he hadn't known before. His fingers flexed on the guitar to form the chord to unlock the power. *Might as well look good doing it*, he laughed to himself. "You'll have to find me first," he mocked.

He pointed the neck of the guitar straight up in the best stadium rock tradition and struck the chord.

When the swirling purple energies around him dissipated, he found himself back in his studio in the Lucky Seven's Chicago headquarters. Frazier's scream of fury still echoed in his ears. The incantation seemed to have worked properly, since Will had been transported to a place of safety. Furthermore, he was masked from Frazier's magic, and effectively invisible to magical detection.

So many new ideas ran through his head that his legs grew wobbly and he had to sit down. Maybe there really was something to all the book learning that most mages followed. *Nah*, he decided. Studying was for the birds. Satisfied with that rationale for now, and secure and comfortable in his studio, Will began to play again. This time he played not for the magic, but for the music.

The magic simply happened anyway.

CHAPTER ONE

"One of the myths about superhero teams that perpetuates is that we're always busy fighting the so-called Forces of Evil. The truth is that there is far more down time than action. It can actually be pretty boring."

-Jack "Crackerjack" Raymond
The Late Show With David Letterman
August 28, 1998

May, 2004
Denver, Colorado
Just Cause Headquarters

Jason's alarm chirped. Sally groaned, rolled over, and felt around for the clock as she tried to avoid opening her eyes. After a minute or so, she still hadn't found the elusive alarm, so she cracked open one eyelid and tried to resolve the blurry images into something familiar. He'd moved his clock again, the sneaky jerk. It mocked her, just far enough out of her reach that she'd have to get out of bed to shut it off. He knew her proclivity for sleeping in, and had moved it before he'd left for his shift in the control center.

"Dammit, Jason." She grumbled as she got to her feet and trudged across the room to shut it off. Shenanigans like this would irritate her to no end if it had been anyone else but Jason doing them. She wouldn't let something this trivial get her all riled up, especially now they were sort of living together. Sally stripped off Jason's oversized t-shirt which served her as a nightgown and headed for the bathroom.

A splash of red and yellow made her glance toward his computer. His screensaver showed the picture they'd had taken together the day she'd been inducted into Just Cause. He mugged for the camera in his brown and gray costume, blond hair flopped over his face, chin unshaven, while she smiled from behind her goggles. Her slender form, wrapped in her bright red and yellow speed suit, contrasted with his thick muscles and earth tones, like a hummingbird beside a bear. She rarely noticed how much smaller she was than him except when she saw that picture. She was a third of his weight, and only reached up to his shoulder if she stood on tiptoes.

He treated her as gently as if she were made of delicate porcelain. When they made love, he took great care not to crush her. To that end, they'd started to experiment with some different positions they'd found on a website. A couple of them made Sally blush just thinking about them, although she liked the one called the *cowgirl*. It made her think she ought to get a special hat to complete the experience.

She decided she'd better wash her hair since it had been a couple days. Conventional wisdom for super--speedsters was to keep hair short. She rejected that trope, and kept hers long enough to touch the small of her back, in spite of the hassle. Super speed presented its own unique hair-care concerns: split ends to give beauticians nightmares, thatched tangles like birds' nests, and the ever-present danger of catching it on something and turning her head into a 500-mile- -per-hour tetherball. She went through conditioner as fast as she did tread on her boots. More than once she'd considered cutting it all off and going with something short, cute, and sexy. But Jason loved her long hair, and when he ran his fingers through it, it gave her the best kind of shivers.

She shut off the water, dried herself, and dressed in a short-sleeved hoodie and shorts. She slipped out of Jason's room barefoot and with her hair still dripping, and headed up the hall to her own quarters. She paused by Sondra's door and considered whether to knock, but Jack had just come off monitor duty and they were probably occupied with one another. Jack and Sondra, known respectively as Crackerjack and Desert Eagle in parahuman circles, were her two best friends.

She let herself into her quarters and wrinkled her nose at the slight stuffiness. Just Cause members rated their own private suites as nice as any in an upscale hotel, but the windows weren't designed to open except in an emergency. She hadn't known this and had set off a general alarm the first time she propped hers open. Team commander Juice had been very nice about the whole thing, but dropped a thinly-veiled suggestion that perhaps as the newest member of the team she might *read* her book of rules and regulations. All she'd wanted was to feel the spring breeze and to air out her suite.

She slipped on her knobby-soled trainers, grabbed her costume goggles, and headed for the nearest exit. Most people took showers *after* they ran, but Sally wouldn't be working hard enough to even break a sweat. She mostly just did it to dry her hair. A couple of laps around the Just Cause compound at a nice, easy sixty miles per hour would take about as long as fighting with a blow dryer, plus she'd get a tan.

She slipped the goggles over her eyes as she stepped onto the pavement outside the dormitory and took off. Cool air blew against her bare legs and helped wake her up a bit more. She needed to do anything she could to wake up. Between Control Center shifts, training, public relations, volunteering, and the occasional date with Jason, it felt like she never got enough sleep. And when the need arose, Just Cause heroes responded no matter where they were, or how much sleep they'd had.

Sally kept well inside the perimeter fence for her morning jog. She had once thought the locals in Denver would be used to parahumans with Just Cause Headquarters and the Hero Academy both in the metro area, and had gone to run along a bike path. Then some morning commuter caught a glimpse of Sally as she ran twice as fast as traffic, spilled his coffee, and rear-ended the car in front of him. They all had a good laugh about it at a subsequent staff meeting.

When it happened a second time, it wasn't nearly as funny and Juice called her into his office for an explanation. Since then, she tried to be a lot more careful about using her powers out of uniform and off-duty. It seemed she'd spent more time in Juice's office than out of it ever since becoming a full-time member of the team. She wondered if everyone new got into as much trouble as it seemed she had.

She reached her first marker, near the northwest corner of the compound property, and turned to the east to run toward the morning sun. The heat on her face reminded her of Phoenix, where she'd grown up. Her hair streamed behind her like a blonde flag and flapped itself dry. Speed beckoned to her with its tempting call, but the winter had been mild and the spring dry, and most of the land on which the Just Compound sat was covered with prairie grasses and weeds. If she stepped carelessly on a stone and it glanced off something the wrong way, it could spark and ignite a grassfire. Over time, she'd worn a clean track from her daily runs, but kept her speed down just to be safe.

Her phone beeped from its clip on the back of her shorts. She sighed and skidded to a stop in the dust. Never *really* off-duty. "Sally, go ahead."

"Good morning, beautiful," replied Jason's voice. "Enjoying your run?"

"Well, I was until you interrupted me. You couldn't have waited another ten minutes?"

"Hey, you're a speedster. I figured you'd be done already." He laughed.

"Liar," said Sally as she bent down and touched her toes to keep herself limber. "You're probably watching me from the satellite feed right now."

"Uh, no I'm not," stuttered Jason, and she grinned with the knowledge she'd caught him.

"Oh, good. What's on your mind, sweetie?"

"Juice asked if you could stop by his office when you're done this morning."

"Am I in trouble?" she asked. Going to see the boss during downtime was never a good sign. It usually meant a reprimand of some sort.

"No, he said he wanted to ask you about a couple paras you might know."

"And his fingers are broken so he couldn't call me himself?" She turned to walk back toward the headquarters building, some five miles away from her current location. She could have covered the distance in seconds, but she wouldn't be able to talk and run at the same time, and she didn't mind making Juice wait so she could keep talking to Jason.

"He seemed pretty busy. Bustled through the Command Center and barely even said hello. I suppose maybe he thought you'd rather talk to me than him?"

Sally laughed. "Well, he's right about that. Anything you want to chat about, Jase?"

"Not really. Just grumpy about monitor duty on opposite hours of you."

"I could always start sleeping really late."

Now it was Jason's turn to laugh. "More than you already do, you mean? I think you'd sleep for twenty hours a day if you could."

"Yes, please. It's my metabolism. Super-speed is a rough power to use. It really wears you out."

"Nice try, babe. I almost bought that."

Sally giggled. "Yeah, pretty convincing, wasn't it? I almost believed it myself. Oh!" She caught her foot on a rock which protruded from the ground. Her lightning-fast reflexes saved her from a tumble. She caught her phone before it hit the ground. Like most Just Cause equipment, the phones were made from pretty durable construction, but they still had the unfortunate luck to always land on a fracture point.

"Are you all right?"

"Yeah, I just tripped. Hang on." Sally checked around to see which rock was the offending culprit. It had to be the odd-shaped dirty gray one. She blinked at it. It didn't look like a rock; it looked more like the end of a bone sticking out of the ground. Curious, she crouched down for a closer examination.

It had to be a leg bone because of the ball-shaped knob on one end. She wondered if it was from one of the deer that ran wild across the territory. She looked around and found a sturdy stick and scratched away the hard dirt around the bone. After a few minutes of rapid scraping, she had the bone exhumed. The shape looked familiar; she didn't think it was from a deer any longer. She held it up against her own leg for comparison. It matched in length. "Hey, Jason?"

"Yeah?"

"See if Jack's busy or if he wants to play amateur archaeologist with me. I think I've found a dead person. *Really* dead. Like maybe for decades."

"You found a body?"

"No, not a body. Just a bone, but I think it's human. You'd better mark this spot on the map for reference."

"I'm buzzing Jack now," said Jason. Sally scratched around in the dirt a little more.

"Sally?" Jack's voice came over the phone. "What's this about you finding a body?"

"I didn't find a body, I found a bone." Her stick uncovered what she thought was a tibia and fibula. "Make that bones."

"Well don't disturb them. It could be a crime scene," said Jason.

Sally looked at the stick in her hand with sudden guilt. "Uh, okay."

"Let me get some gear together and I'll be right out. Mind if Sondra comes along?"

"Of course not."

Ten minutes later, Sally heard the sound of an engine and saw Jack ride an ATV up over a hillock. His brown hair, starting to gray at the temples, flopped in the breeze behind his yellow-tinted tactical glasses. Sally could see his grin the second he came into view. She must have interrupted paperwork or some other thankless misery with her find. Sondra wheeled overhead with her large brown wings spread wide. The full-blooded Apache woman wore cutoff jean shorts and a string bikini top, one of the few things that she could wear easily over the huge brown and white wings that sprouted from her muscular back. She fluttered lightly to the ground and flexed her primary feathers before she tucked her wings against her back. Sally hugged them both.

"Hey, now . . . people are going to talk." Jack sounded pleased. He opened the tool box strapped to the rack of the ATV and rummaged through a haphazard lot of tools. "I didn't know what all I'd need, so I grabbed everything," he said.

Sondra examined the bone Sally had unearthed. "Well, I don't think this is a crime scene. Or if it is, it's only of anecdotal interest. This is really old."

"We can take a sample back to the lab guys and let them carbon date them." Jack staked out the site. Since he was invulnerable to physical harm, he just held the stakes on top and hit his hand with the hammer, which made both Sondra and Sally cringe and wince.

"I hate it when you do stuff like that," grouched Sondra as she looked away.

Jack grinned. "I know. You suppose this is like an Indian burial ground or something? Maybe we're going to get swamped by angry ghosts. *You moved the gravestones but you didn't move the bodies!*" Jack whisper-screamed the last, a quote from the movie *Poltergeist*. He was a movie buff, and tended to spout off lines at opportune moments.

"Last I checked, dear, we were still calling ourselves Native Americans." Sondra shook out her raven-black hair and punched him in the shoulder.

"I'm speaking with forked tongue, you know," said Jack, and laughed. "Check this out. Subsurface radar set." He held it up with all the fervor of a kid showing off a new toy. He fiddled with the set for several minutes after he hooked it to his laptop and ran what looked like a high-tech ping pong paddle across the ground.

"Do you know what you're doing?" asked Sally.

"*Back off, man. I'm a scientist,*" retorted Jack.

"*Ghostbusters,*" said Sally. "You quote that movie all the time."

"Good lines in that one." He ran the colorful images through filter after filter on the laptop. "Far as I can tell, there's all or most of a body down there."

"I could have just dug for awhile and told you the same thing," Sally grumbled.

"But this is much more fun," said Jack.

Sondra sighed. "Boys and their toys. So should we exhume it?"

Jack shrugged. "I don't see why not. At the very least, it makes for an interesting scientific find. At the most, it could be enough of a mystery to be a refreshing change from the everyday drudgery of our dull and wasted lives." He pulled a couple of shovels and a pick from the back of the ATV and passed them out.

"What's with him? He's acting like Mr. Discovery Channel." Sally raised an eyebrow at Jack as he attacked the dirt with fervor.

"He's been frustrated," said Sondra. "All his investigations into that German guy who was working with Destroyer in Guatemala turned up nothing. He needs something to take his mind off all the dead ends."

Four months ago, Just Cause and several other allied teams had faced off against the deadly villain Destroyer and an army of artificially-created parahumans. Destroyer had been plaguing Just Cause since the late Seventies and showed no signs of slowing down as he reached middle age. His silent partner in the parahuman-creation operation in Guatemala had been a mysterious German man known only as Heinrich Kaiser. Both Just Cause and the CIA had launched independent investigations of the man, but nobody had turned up any information on him. Jack had taken the investigation very personally because Destroyer and Kaiser had killed two Just Cause members, tortured another, and nearly killed Sally as well.

The two women watched Jack work for awhile, then shrugged and began to help. Sally could work much faster than either of the other two, but she had to be careful not to dig so quickly that she threw away small bone fragments. Jack had Sally switch from a shovel to a brush and she dusted away loose dirt from the bones. They uncovered a pelvis, then vertebrae and ribs. "Indiana Jones makes archaeology seem a lot more exciting," she said, fussing with the brush.

"Hollywood makes *everything* seem a lot more exciting," said Jack. "Maybe we can find some Nazis to shoot at us while we're digging. Uh oh." He knelt down and picked something out of the rib cage. "Looks like this answers some of our questions." Sondra and Sally crowded in to see what he held: a triangular piece of stone worked into a sharp blade.

"Is that an arrowhead?" asked Sally.

"Yes." He turned the stone around in his hand. "See the edges? How they've been sharpened?"

Sally nodded.

"Well, it's definitely foul play," Jack continued. "But this is one heck of a cold case. I guess we can leave this one for the historians to solve." He sighed and looked a little glum.

Sondra stepped over to him and ruffled his curly hair. "Hey, it was fun for a few minutes at any rate. Come on back. I'll make coffee."

Jack made a face. "Thanks, love, but no thanks. I've *had* your coffee."

Sally laughed.

"Oh well," he grumbled. "Sally, you want a lift back to headquarters?" He jammed his shovel into the ground.

"No, I'm going to finish my run first. Then Juice wants to see me so I ought to at least clean up. I'm a mess." Dust and dirt caked her sweatshirt, arms, and legs—and probably her face, too—from her rapid digging. Sondra stuck her shovel into the ground like Jack, but when she did so they heard the unmistakable *clink* of metal on metal. The heroes looked at each other in surprise.

"I suppose . . . a little more digging wouldn't hurt?" asked Sally.

"Sure. Maybe it's an old six-shooter or something. That would be cool." Jack retrieved his shovel and they started the excavation anew.

After a few minutes, they retrieved the culprit. Jack laughed when he saw it. It was a horseshoe, caked with rust. "Here you go, Sally." He offered it to her. "You can start a collection. Or maybe keep it as a replacement in case you ever lose one of the others." Sally had inherited a pair of horseshoes that her grandmother had wielded like brass knuckles back in the '40s when she fought crime as the hero Colt for Just Cause's precursor team *American Justice*.

She took the shoe with a hint of distaste. "Thanks . . . I think."

"Don't mention it." Jack grinned. "Let's pack this fellow up. We'll shoot an email over to the Colorado Historical Society and let them know what we've found. They'll probably want to take a look at his bits and pieces. Good opportunity for some PR." Jack was Just Cause's official Public Relations manager, and looked at everything from a promotional angle.

Jack marked the boundaries of their dig in case an archaeology team wanted to do any further digging. Sally helped he and Sondra pack the bones back onto the ATV. She grimaced at just how dirty she'd gotten from a bit of digging. "I'm going to need to take another shower."

"Too bad Jason's on duty today or he could scrub your back," Sondra whispered to Sally.

"No kidding. I hate monitor duty."

"It's got to be worse for you." Sondra flapped her wings to snap the accumulated dust from her feathers. "Since you're a speedster, time's got to pass a lot slower . . . especially when you're bored."

"You got that right."

"Well, ladies," said Jack. "I'm all finished up here with the packing. I hope I'm not interrupting your conversation or anything."

"Oh, sorry, Jack." Sally smiled and hefted the horseshoe. "Thanks for this, anyway. Maybe I'll try to clean it up."

When she got back to her room, she left the horseshoe on her desk by the two from her grandmother. She took a five-minute shower and scrubbed herself pink. She sighed in discontent at her mass of once-again-wet hair. She did her best to towel-dry it and then worked it into her customary twin braids.

She made her way through the headquarters building toward his office. It seemed much emptier since both Forcestar and Glimmer had died in Guatemala, leaving the team two members short.

Juice's real name was James Forsythe, but he was one of those rare superheroes whose alter ego seemed to fit better than his given name. Almost nobody called him James; even his wife tended to call him *Juice, honey.* He bent over his desk, locked in mortal combat with a stack of paperwork that could choke an industrial shredder. A fine film of sweat shone on his clean-shaven brown head.

Sally rapped her knuckles against the door frame. "You wanted to see me?"

He smiled, took off his reading glasses, and set them on top of the paperwork, all of which bore official Department of Homeland Security or Just Cause logos. "Sally, what's this about you finding a body today?"

She sighed inwardly. News traveled faster than she could outrun it when Jack was involved. "Not exactly a body. More like some bones that are probably a hundred years old or more."

Juice chuckled. "You know, we're sitting on some seventeen thousand acres out here and I'll bet that in sixty years nobody has done any kind of serious surveying. They used to manufacture chemical weapons and pesticides here way back when. I doubt they ever looked around all that much. Who knows what else is out there, just waiting for you to trip over it?"

"I don't know."

"Rhetorical question, Sally. Sit down. Don't worry," he said as he saw the look of concern on her face. "You're not in trouble or anything. We're getting two new team members. One is temporary, the other might be permanent. Do you know about a psi by the name of Switchboard?"

"Isn't he on the Second Team?" Just Cause had a second unit based in Richmond, Virginia.

"Yes. They're going to loan him to us for awhile. I've got my eye on a promising kid in the Academy, but we're looking at a minimum of thirteen months before we can bring him aboard even as an intern." Juice closed a file folder on his desk. "Switchboard is a better telepath than Glimmer was, but unfortunately he doesn't have such a wide range of other abilities like Glimmer did. It's too bad psionics are the rarest of parahuman powers. They're just so darn useful to have around." He leaned back in his oversized chair, which creaked under his weight.

"Yes sir." She wondered where Juice was going with all this.

"His name's Chris . . . he's a good guy and should fit in fine here. However, the other para we're being assigned I don't know anything about. And you do."

"Who is it?"

"Shannon Tokugawa, also known as Vapor. What can you tell me about her?" Juice cracked his knuckles with a sound like boards snapping.

Slut. Bitch. The words came unbidden to Sally's mind and she clamped down on her tongue lest they escape between her lips. "She's nice," she lied.

CHAPTER TWO

"There are probably more independent parahumans now than there are on teams, which is actually a pretty sobering notion when you really think about it."

-John Stone
Hardball with Chris Matthews
February 19, 2001

May, 2004
Denver, Colorado
Just Cause Headquarters

"Shannon—" Jason's brow furrowed.

"Tokugawa," said Sally. "She was in my class at the Academy, you big dumb jock."

Jason rolled onto his back and put his hands behind his head. Sally had stayed up late so she could spend some time with him after his duty shift was over at midnight. She laid her head on his chest and toyed with the whorls of fine blond hair that dotted it.

"Yeah, I know who she is."

"Oh?" A twinge of jealousy spiked in Sally's mind.

"We, uh, we went out a couple of times."

"I see." Her voice took on a frosty tone.

"Hey, that was like two years ago." Jason lifted his head so he could look into Sally's eyes. "I haven't talked to her at all since I graduated."

She tried to push away her sudden possessiveness. "I'm sorry, Jase. I know I'm not your first girlfriend. You were honest with me about that. I just get a little crazy thinking about you . . . you know, hooking up with anyone else."

Jason's cheeks colored. "Who said anything about her and me hooking up?"

You don't have to, she thought. *Your face tells the story.* "Anyway, she and the guy from the Second Team are supposed to be here tomorrow. Guess who gets to give them the grand tour?"

"Tomorrow? You mean later this morning." He looked at the bedside clock and chuckled. "Hope it's not too early."

"No," laughed Sally. "I'll get plenty of beauty sleep. Eventually." She winked.

"You're insatiable, you know." His eyes sparkled in that way that turned her insides warm and glowing.

She kissed his stomach and enjoyed the feeling of an abdominal muscle as it fluttered under her lips. "Can't help it. You bring out the best in me."

Jason casually kicked the covers off the bed. "Well . . . it's been a long day in the command center. You know, saving the world and stuff. But I think I can find the energy to satisfy you yet once more tonight." He started to sit up but she pushed him back down. Rather, he allowed her to push him back down; with his strength, very few people could push him around. She straddled his chest, leaned down, and kissed him hard. If she accomplished anything at all tonight, she thought, it would be to drive any stray thoughts of Shannon Tokugawa from his mind.

The next morning came far earlier than Sally would have liked. She rolled over and kissed Jason, who had just started to stir. "You're amazing," she whispered. That had become one of their rituals ever since the first time she spent the night with him.

By the time Jason stumbled into the bathroom, Sally had finished up in the shower. "Morning," she said, bright and cheerful.

He grunted.

She stepped out of the shower and wrapped a towel around herself while Jason brushed his teeth. His shoulder-length hair stuck out in random directions and made him look like a sleepy, overgrown toddler. She stepped up onto the toilet so she was high enough to lean over and kiss the side of his neck. "You know what? I think I'm in love with you."

Jason choked on his mouthful of toothpaste and struggled for a moment before he managed to spit most of it into the sink. "Really?" he said as he wiped his mouth on a towel.

During the ensuing pause, Sally felt her ire start to rise. She forced it back into the dark recesses of her mind. She whispered in his ear, "When someone tells you that, you're supposed to say the same thing back to them."

"Oh. Duh." Jason's familiar grin returned. "I'm falling for you too."

Sally sighed. That was probably the best he could manage before caffeination. She decided she'd better ease him into the morning after her bombshell. "Are you guys practicing tonight?" She referred to Jason's band, *Velma's Glasses*. He played guitar and sang.

He nodded. "Yeah. We've got a big performance coming up in two weeks—we're the headline act at Bart's." Bart's Basement was the first place Sally had seen the band perform; it had been their first date.

"Cool. I'll be there. Gotta run. Noobs will be here pretty soon." She decided to dispense with her braids, wrapped her hair up into a sloppy bun, and shoved a couple of chopsticks through it to hold it in place. She dressed quickly and headed out the door.

Jack was on duty in the command center, and Juice was on a conference call with Homeland Security, so only Sondra and Doublecharge, Juice's second-in--command, sat in the cafeteria. They were paging through file folders and talking quietly when Sally walked up to them with a bowl of yogurt, some fruit, and toast in one hand and a full cup of heavily sweetened, caramel-and-whipped-cream-drizzled coffee in the other. She'd learned to love coffee after a year on the team, even though super-speed jitters were no laughing matter. "Morning," she said. "What's up?"

"Looking over the new members' files." Doublecharge didn't smile, but she almost never did.

"Want a look-see?" Sondra slid a folder over to Sally.

"Absolutely." She took a sip of her drink and debated whether it needed just one more sugar or if it was actually sweet enough. She lifted Shannon Tokugawa's file to the top and started to page through it. She told herself it was just good practice, getting to know a new teammate via her file. Shannon wasn't the competition.

Surely not.

Although Sally had been in the Academy with Shannon, they hadn't talked much. Sally didn't really know much about her besides her midnight visits to the boys' dorm, which she'd bragged about to the other girls. Her parapowers of invisibility and insubstantiality had proved to be a great boon to sneakiness. After graduating from the Academy, Shannon had declined to do an internship with any of the existing teams. She seemed to have dropped out of the superhero business altogether. Instead, she'd chosen to attend George Washington University with a major in Political Science.

"I don't get it . . ." Sally speared a piece of melon. "Why go to all the trouble to go to the Hero Academy at all if you're not going to do anything with your powers?"

Sondra shrugged and took a piece of bacon. "Maybe she decided it wasn't for her after all."

"Then why's she coming back?"

"You have to read between the lines somewhat," said Doublecharge. "She didn't volunteer herself. She's being sent by Homeland Security. That means she works for the government in some capacity."

"You think she's a . . . a covert operative?" asked Sally in surprise.

"You watch too many spy movies." Doublecharge nearly smiled, which was enough to make Sally hold her breath in case the world was about to end. "I suspect that she's just another employee of Homeland Security like you and I, except she's not attached to any team."

"But not covertly? The girl can become invisible and insubstantial. Any dirty tricks agency like the CIA or NSA would turn cartwheels to get her on their payroll. Hell, I suspect even Homeland Security would like to have her checking out the suspects on their watch lists." Sondra finished the sludge that was her coffee and set the cup back on her tray. "Maybe she's being sent to spy on us."

Doublecharge snorted. "I'm sure Homeland Security has more important things to do than keep tabs on its parapowered operational arm. You're reading way too much into this."

Sally's phone beeped. "Morning, Sally. Are you up yet?" asked Jack from the Command Center.

She raised the phone up to her mouth. "You know very well I'm sitting here in the cafeteria." She looked up at the nearest security camera and made kissy-lips toward it.

"Stop, you're breaking my heart. Anyway, our new teammates have arrived and are waiting for you in Juice's office."

"Has he already given them the welcome speech?"

"He's doing that now. Oh," said Jack suddenly. "Thought you might be interested . . . the lab places those bones between a hundred twenty and a hundred forty years old. Congratulations, you're officially part of Colorado history."

"Like the *Wild Wild West*, right?"

"Frontier days," agreed Jack.

"Pretty cool. Okay, I guess I'll go meet the fresh meat." Sally pushed back her chair from the table.

"Be nice," warned Sondra. "You were the fresh meat five months ago."

"I know, and I will." She left the cafeteria and made her way to Juice's office, where the team leader was just wrapping up his welcome speech.

She took a moment to examine them through the glass before knocking. Chris—Switchboard—wasn't a typical reedy psi. He was built like an Olympic wrestler, with shoulders like cantaloupes stuffed inside his polo shirt and a jaw like a lantern. He wore his brown hair in a short, athletic cut, and seemed very much at ease with Juice.

Shannon, on the other hand, appeared much more nervous the way she shuffled her feet and looked around her. Sally remembered feeling that way at her initial meeting with Juice. And pretty much every time since then, she had to admit to herself. Shannon's dark hair was cut short in a bob. Her face looked mostly Japanese after her father, but her skin was fair with a sprinkle of freckles across her nose courtesy of her mother. She looked natural in her business suit, as if she wore one most days.

Juice wrapped up his introductory speech and motioned for Sally to enter the office. She put on her best smile and strolled in with all the confidence she could muster. Shannon's face lit up with what Sally imagined was false pleasure. "Sally, I'm so happy it's you going to show us around."

"Shannon, it's great to see you too." Sally smiled and suffered a hug from her classmate. Shannon's business attire concealed a body hardened by many hours of training; to Sally, her muscles felt like steel rods coated with velvet. Sally wondered if the Political Science major was just a cover.

"Hi Sally, I'm Chris Ryerson. Switchboard. Pleased to meet you." Switchboard extended his hand and shook Sally's. His muscles looked like Jason's.

"You're the biggest psi I've ever seen," she said.

Both Switchboard and Juice broke out in laughter.

Switchboard wiped his eyes. "I thought I'd break tradition and spend some time working on my frail body instead of being reedy and mysterious like all the other psis in the world."

"Sally, if you'll give them the tour, I'll see about getting together a dinner meeting tonight." Juice touched a few keys on his computer.

Sally made a face at that. "Staff meetings are unhealthy. We ran across the Antimatter Woman at *my* first meeting." Nevertheless, she led them through the main offices and headed in the general direction of the Command Center. "So what have you been doing with yourself since the Academy, Shannon? You're not affiliated with any teams, are you?"

"No, I'm more interested in politics. I'm majoring in it at George Washington."

Sally showed them the Command Center from the doorway. "Mission control, right here. You'll both get your turns at monitor duty like the rest of us." She led them onward and looked sidelong at Shannon. "I'd think it would be pretty tough to be elected if you're a parahuman. There are a lot of people who don't trust us."

"Oh, I'm not planning to run for office or anything. I thought I might look into being a campaign advisor or manager or something. I figure to work more . . . behind the scenes."

"I'm sure," said Sally. She led them through the cafeteria towards the dormitory with a desperate hope that they wouldn't run across Jason. "These are the apartments. Our supply master, Harris, is getting each of you set up in your own place. After the tour, he'll hook you up with all the appropriate credentials and passes."

"Pretty luxurious surroundings." Switchboard looked over the well-appointed recreation room as Sally ushered them through. "I'm not going to want to go back to Virginia after this."

Sally noticed with satisfaction that Switchboard had been assigned the empty room next to Jason's, while Shannon was in the one at the end of the hall, a few doors down. She showed them the cafeteria, conference rooms, and offices; all the boring but necessary part of the bureaucratic infrastructure required to keep Just Cause running smoothly so the heroes could be free to do hero stuff. Eventually she took them to the underground training center, nicknamed The Bunker.

And that was where they ran into Jason.

Sally could have kicked herself for not realizing he'd most likely been working out. She was just taking Switchboard and Shannon into the weight room when she saw him and brought herself up short. Jason worked on one of the specialized machines which only he and Juice could operate, doing a two-ton bench press. He wore only a pair of biker shorts, his cross-trainers, and a sweat-soaked bandanna tied around his head to hold back his damp blond locks. His chest muscles quivered and creaked with his effort against the massive resistance on the machine. Not an ounce of fat resided on his powerful frame, which Sally knew because she'd spent many nights exploring every inch of him. Her breath caught in her throat at just how good he looked. If she'd been alone, she'd have jumped him right then and there.

She heard Shannon's quiet exhalation through pursed lips. How dare she almost-whistle at him?

Jason's shaking arms folded with a ground-shaking crash as the heavy-duty springs snapped back into place. In a surge of panic, she turned to escort the others as far away from *her Jason* as possible. His voice froze her in her tracks.

"Hey, babe, what's up?"

"Oh, hi." Sally swallowed a sudden lump in her throat. "Just showing the noobs around. We didn't mean to interrupt you. We're leaving."

"Jason?" Shannon stepped past Sally. "Wow, look at you. You look great."

"Hey, uh, Shannon," said Jason, aware of Sally's venomous expression. "Good to see you."

"What's it been . . . two years?"

"Uh, yeah. Something like that."

Sally grimaced. She felt like an awkward teenager all over again next to the professionally-dressed, cool and confident girl who might have been the same biological age but seemed years older. In a blur, Sally interposed herself between Shannon and Jason and planted a quick kiss on his lips. "We'll let you get back to your workout, babycakes. I'll see you later, okay?"

"Yeah, ok." Jason blushed.

"Come on . . ." Sally stepped past Shannon without so much as a glance. "I'll show you guys the Bunker. You'll love it."

The Bunker was a miracle of post-modern technology. Microscopic robots housed there could configure raw materials into any setting in which the team could train. The nanomachines built it up molecule by molecule. Just Cause heroes could train there at full power without concerns about collateral damage. Switchboard found the Bunker especially fascinating. The Second Team couldn't utilize the nanomachine technology because of local zoning regulations, so they had to train in a heavily-reinforced warehouse instead.

Eventually Sally dragged the muscular psi away from the observation deck. Down below in a cavern the size of a dome stadium, several floors of a high rise were taking shape. It was like watching claymation in slow motion. Sally hated the scenarios which took place inside buildings. She couldn't ever make the most of her speed in the enclosed corridors. But since Just Cause often had no control over the location of a potential battlefield, they had to prepare for whatever they could.

At last, she passed Switchboard and Shannon off to Harris, the little rodent-like man who handled supply details for the team. As he began to interview them about their needs for costumes and gear, Sally made a hasty excuse and ran back to her room. Once safely behind her own door, she flopped into her desk chair and rested her cheek on her folded arms. She didn't cry, but felt like she should.

She knew Shannon had hooked up with Jason. She'd been his first, and now she'd returned like a perpetrator to the scene of a crime, and Sally felt threatened. Was she overreacting, or had she seen the spark of interest in Jason's face when he'd seen his ex? Did Shannon already have designs on the boy Sally had admitted that she loved?

Sometime between when they'd begun dating and now, her affection for him had deepened into something she could only describe as love. Her mother, of course, would say that was ridiculous. Sally was eighteen. What could a moonstruck teen possibly know about love? Never mind the fact that her mother had been only fifteen when she'd started dating her father.

Sally had never known her father. He'd died shortly before she'd been born. The psychopathic villain Destroyer had attacked Just Cause at a funeral for one of their own and her father had been one of the casualties. Sally looked at the carefully-framed picture of the man who looked so much like her on her desk. She'd inherited his thick blond hair and sparkling blue eyes. In a way, Jason reminded her of her father. Maybe that was why she loved him.

Her hands searched for something to keep themselves busy and began to toy with the horseshoe Jack had found amid the bones. It could have been an identical twin to her grandmother's, which she now carried. She wondered idly if it had come from the same manufacturer. The remarkable similarity carried even down to the notch along the back of one arm.

Sally frowned. Why would that notch be there? She'd knocked a chip off one of her own horseshoes when she'd jammed it into Destroyer's armor, short-circuiting it and avenging her father's death. She lifted her own horseshoe and looked at it for comparison. The notch looked *identical.*

Impossible!

In a flash she sped across the building to Harris's offices. He was in the middle of explaining the security procedures to Switchboard and Shannon when Sally burst in on him.

"Help you, Salena?"

"Sorry to interrupt you, Harris. I need a wire brush."

He stepped over to a cabinet and held one up for display. "Like this one here?"

"Thanks, Harris." Sally snatched the brush out of his hand and sped away.

"Anytime," his voice floated down the hall after her.

Back in her room, she took the horseshoe to the kitchenette sink and earnestly scrubbed away at decades of accumulated rust. Working at a superspeed pace cleared the rust quickly. She washed the last bit of rust down the sink and patted the horseshoe dry with a paper towel. Then she took it into her bathroom, which had the brightest lights in her suite, to compare it to her current horseshoe.

As near as she could tell, it was almost perfectly identical. Scars on the metal occurred in the same place on each shoe, slightly more worn on the one that had been buried with the body, but otherwise nearly exact. The sliver of metal which had been chipped away in the fight with Destroyer was missing from each shoe.

Sally sat on the floor in her bathroom for a very long time and stared at two identical horseshoes, one of which had been found with a body that was over a hundred years deceased.

CHAPTER THREE

From: Juice

Fewer than ten percent of the artificially-created parahumans from Guatemala are currently accounted for. Homeland Security advises us to be aware in case some of them show up in the U.S., as they represent an unknown variable. As if we need to be told. —J

- Just Cause Internal Memo #03012004-009
March 1, 2004

May, 2004
Denver, Colorado
Just Cause Headquarters

"Time travel," repeated Jack around a mouthful of the Reuben sandwich he'd ordered for lunch.

"Yes," said Sally. She had dark circles under her eyes that would have shamed a raccoon. She'd barely slept for the past three nights between her fear that Shannon would move in on her relationship with Jason and her irrational uneasiness that the body she had found might have somehow been herself. She'd tossed and turned so much last night Jason had finally gone to sleep on the couch.

"I've never heard of such a thing outside of the scope of science fiction movies."

Jason sat down with them, his tray piled high with enough sandwiches to feed a high-school football team's offensive line. "Talk some sense into her, Jack. She's becoming impossible to live with."

"Oh, really?" Sally's voice dripped with sarcasm.

"Hey, babe, relax." Jason bent down and kissed the top of her head. "I'll manage." Then he winked at Jack. "She fidgets at super-speed. It's like having Magic Fingers built into my bed."

Jack laughed. "Seriously, Sally. As far as I know, time travel violates the laws of physics, and *ye canna change the laws of physics.*" He finished with a passable impression of Star Trek's Scotty.

"Oh?" said a new voice. Shannon sat down on the other side of Jason with a small chef salad and bottle of spring water on her tray. Sally glanced at her own tray, which was loaded down with pasta, breadsticks, and cookies. It was all carb-heavy comfort food, and wished she'd chosen something more healthy to eat in front of Jason. Not that he would have noticed what she was eating until she stopped, at which point he'd ask if she wanted him to finish what she hadn't. "Most parahuman abilities regularly violate physical laws. Doublecharge is a textbook example. Remember the law that says energy cannot be created or destroyed but only changed? So where do her lightning bolts come from then?"

Jack groaned. "You're giving me a headache. I flunked physics."

"I thought you were majoring in political science," said Sally in a slight accusatory tone.

Shannon shrugged. "I like to learn a little bit of everything. Never know when it'll come in useful."

Sally snuggled up a little closer to Jason.

"Babe," he said, "I'm eating here."

"Oh, right. Sorry." Jason took his food intake very seriously. Nobody who sat near him had lost any fingers yet, but it was a running joke on the team someone would sooner or later.

"Listen, Sally . . ." Jack wiped his mouth with his napkin. "If it'll make you feel more comfortable, we can have the lab try to pull genetic information from those bones. It might take awhile, though. I think they're already off the base. I'm sure we can get them back with a phone call." Just Cause had donated the human remains Sally had found to the Colorado Historical Society.

"Sure," said Sally. "What else do I have to do but wait?" She sighed and poked at her food without much interest.

Just at that moment all their cell phones broad cast the emergency callout signal. Red lights in the corners of the room lit up and spun, and a warning klaxon sounded.

"Well, you could respond to the alert," said Jack.

"All available Just Cause personnel report to the launch pad," ordered the Command Center over the base's loudspeakers. "We have a Code Alpha situation at the Denver Mint."

Sally's mouth dropped open in surprise. A Code Alpha meant actively hostile parahumans with immediate threats to civilian lives. It was Just Cause's equivalent of a lights-and-sirens response for a police department.

"Why would someone attack the Mint?" asked Jason as he disentangled himself from the table and hurried after the others toward the exit.

"Couldn't be because there are piles of cash lying around, could it?" Jack snickered.

"No, not that. Don't they just make coins?"

"Maybe it's the Vending Machine Mafia," said Jack with perfect timing, making Sally giggle in spite of her general malaise with life.

"I think what he means is why someone would choose to attack it here, right in the shadow of Just Cause," said Shannon.

"The dons of the Vending Machine Mafia aren't known for their smarts. All that junk food and sugar is ruining their brainpower," said Jack.

"Jack, if you don't knock it off, you're going to be riffing to an empty room," said Sally. "But I'm sure you're familiar with that sensation. I'll meet you guys at the pad. My boots are in my room." She stepped lithely around Jack and sped down the hallway to the dormitory to retrieve her expensive, custom footwear. She took a few seconds to change into her costume. In a moment, she was garbed in her tight-fitting red bodysuit with the stylized yellow chess knight emblem. She pulled on her breathing mask and let it dangle at her throat, then stuck her goggles up onto her forehead where they'd be ready at a moment's notice. Once she got moving faster than seventy or eighty miles per hour, she needed them to protect her face from windburn and airborne particulates. She saw the three horseshoes on her desk and hesitated. She was being silly, she told herself. Ridiculous. Time travel. She grabbed her two horseshoes and left the imposter behind.

The team's custom jet taxied out of its hangar. The *Bettie* resembled a wide-bodied, heavily-armed and armored Learjet. Its engines could rotate downward to allow it to take off vertically and hover like a helicopter.

Most of the team had already assembled inside the jet except Sondra, who was on Command Center duty and wouldn't leave it unless the team required her assistance. Juice was at a Homeland Security meeting in Dallas and wouldn't be back until the next day. Doublecharge made final adjustments to her black and white costume with its stylized lightning borders. She would command the mission in Juice's absence.

"Everyone's aboard, Reed. Launch as soon as you're ready," said Doublecharge.

The former Alaskan bush pilot at the controls acknowledged over the cabin speakers. "Roger, ma'am. Taking off now. Everyone hold on . . ." The *Bettie*'s engines rose in pitch and intensity as the jet lifted straight up from the launch pad.

Sally could see Shannon's eyes, lids half lowered, as they constantly strayed back toward Jason. Being a speedster, she didn't build up to a slow burn; her anger and temper were quick to ignite and inside she blazed furious.

"Okay," said Doublecharge as she held a headset up to one ear. "We've got at least six, possibly seven unknown parahumans apparently intent upon robbing the Denver Mint."

Jack chuckled. "Such asshattery. Words fail me."

"All right," said Doublecharge over his interruption. "I don't want this to turn into a free-for-all since the Mint is right in the middle of downtown. Police are trying to evacuate the area, but I suspect we won't have that much time."

"Doesn't the Mint here just make coins? Not much profit in robbing that." Switchboard looked out the window at the city rolling by underneath them.

"I already said that," said Jason, looking goofy and proud. "Who's the dumb jock now?"

"Nobody called you a dumb jock," said Shannon.

Sally felt like sinking into her seat, knowing she'd uttered those very words only the day before. She hadn't meant them in a hurtful way, but bringing that up would only drive more of a wedge between her and Jason, and Shannon was like a shark circling a tired swimmer.

"They also store some gold and silver bullion," added Shannon. "And there will be printing dies there as well. They could print more money."

Insufferable know-it-all, thought Sally.

"If everyone is finished with their extracurriculars, I'll get on with this briefing, since we're almost there already." Doublecharge glared around the cabin, and a tiny lightning bolt crackled between her eyes. Everyone shut up. "Speed's of the essence, here, so let's try to keep this from degenerating into either a slugfest or a running battle. Teams of two: Jack and Sally, Jason and

Shannon, and Switchboard with me. Take down your nearest opponent. If you can't, call in another team and tag out. We'll start from the outside and work our way in. Reed will give us a single flyby pass before landing. Switchboard and I will deploy out the lock then. The rest of you follow upon set-down. Standard public protocol from here on out."

Standard public protocol meant they were only to refer to one another by their alternate identities: Crackerjack and Mustang Sally, Mastiff and Vapor, Switchboard and Doublecharge.

"We're over the Mint now," came Reed's voice over the cabin speakers. "I got two hostiles standing guard over, uh, some horses."

"Horses?" repeated Doublecharge.

"Yes ma'am. Only . . . they look like they're armored or mechanical or something."

"Get a camera on them and feed it in here, Reed. Stand by for airlock deployment."

In a moment, the cabin's viewscreens showed a group of seven entities. They might have been armored horses. Or, like Reed said, they might have been mechanical devices. Two men in SWAT-level battle armor and cowboy hats stood guard over the mounts. They also had neckerchiefs, chaps, and spurs.

Jack burst out laughing. "*Morons! I've got morons on my team!*"

"*Butch Cassidy and the Sundance Kid*," retorted Sally. "It's been on the Westerns Channel all month."

"Saw that, did you?" Jack rolled his eyes. In the five months Sally had been with Just Cause, he had yet to stump her with a movie quote.

"Switchboard, move out," said Doublecharge. The two headed for the back of the *Bettie*, where a special airlock allowed the flying members of the team to enter or exit while the jet was airborne. "Crackerjack, call the ball for the team when it's on the ground."

"Yeth thir, Captain Doublecharge, ma'am." Jack kicked his heels together, crossed his eyes, and saluted.

Sally heard thumps from the rear of the jet as the airlock opened. Reed whipped the *Bettie* around to kill its forward momentum. Switchboard and Doublecharge dove toward the cowboys. Electricity crackled around Doublecharge's hands as she ordered the two men to lie on the ground with their hands on their heads.

Sally's stomach leaped into her throat as Reed dropped the *Bettie* down to the pavement below and grounded the jet right in the middle of the street. The bomb bay doors opened and Jack ordered everyone out. "Reed, stay on the ground on hot standby unless you start taking fire."

"Roger that," replied the pilot.

The two cowboys' eyes bugged out when the *Bettie* landed. Sally saw they looked terrified by the appearance of Just Cause on the scene. *What did they expect*, she wondered as her perceptions sped into high gear to give her plenty of subjective time for consideration and internal commentary. *It's not like we'd just stand by and let them get away with it.*

The pudgier cowboy raised his hands. At first Sally thought he was surrendering, but in a moment ribbons of energy flowed from them. The ribbons broadened to form a shimmering hemisphere over the robotic horses and the cowboys. The second man pulled a Nextel phone from his belt and shouted rapid-fire Spanish into it.

Sally waited, impatient for Jack to catch up with her. She disliked being partnered with anyone, because she always felt like she wasted time when she had to operate at "normal" speeds. And she was steamed because Doublecharge partnered Jason with *Shannon*. Sally stamped her feet like a racehorse chomping at the bit. Everyone seemed to move through the air as if it were as thick as molasses. She couldn't stand it any more and made herself slow down enough to speak to

Jack on a comprehensible level. "I'm going to scout inside real quick. Be back before you miss me."

She zipped away as Jack said "Wait, what?" She'd leave the others to take care of the two cowboys outside. The fat one had force fields, which meant he'd be a little harder to take down. Or maybe not; Switchboard could probably put the man to sleep with his psionic powers.

Chaos reigned inside of the Mint. Despite heightened security measures implemented since 9/11, nobody had really ever expected terrorists to try to rob the Mint. Security had been arranged to minimize the risk of demolition, not robbery. Public tours of the Mint by were no longer permitted, but plenty of employees remained inside the building. A Mexican standoff had developed on the main printing floor. Three more cowboys—one actually a cowgirl—had taken some employees hostage and were using them as human shields against the armed Treasury guards.

Two more perpetrators dressed like the others were breaking apart machinery for the plates and dies inside. One of them had appropriated an entire roll of paper. Sally had to give them a little more credit than Jack had. He'd thought they were common bank robbers, especially given their whole Wild West motif. They weren't bothering with the gold or silver bullion in deep storage; they were stealing the materials with which to print their own money, and the false bills would appear perfect to anyone except a Treasury agent.

Doublecharge had said speed was of the essence, and nobody was faster than Sally.

Nobody.

She ran down the line of guards and pushed clip releases with one hand while she popped the chambered rounds out of the slides with the other. She'd practiced the technique for hours until she could perform it faster than even a seasoned gunman like

Jack could pull a trigger. In spite of her speed, one guard got a surprised round off. Sally cursed and changed direction instantly, something she could do no matter how fast she was running. She could see the bullet spiraling through the air right toward a hostage. She slapped it aside with one of her horseshoes to send it toward a wall.

She paused in front of the guard who'd fired just long enough to disable his gun and waggle a reproachful finger in his face. Then she sped away and headed for the three villains who held civilian hostages. One of them twitched suddenly in her direction faster than anyone should have been able to with a motion almost a blur even to Sally.

Something wrapped around her legs, constricted, and she skidded hard into a printing press. Her goggles cracked with the impact. *At least it wasn't my skull*, she thought in a daze. Blotchy stars danced in her visions from the force of the impact. *What the hell was that?* She looked down toward her feet. A sinuous ribbon of ruby-colored energy wrapped around her ankles and held them fast. The end of the ribbon curled away to end in the fist of a tall, reedy cowboy with a real soup-strainer of a mustache.

"*Usted la ha conseguido, Azote?*" shouted the cowgirl to the man holding the energy whip.

"*Sí, ella no puede escaparse,*" said Azote in satisfaction. He twitched the whip and jerked Sally sideways.

"*Hay más de ellos afuera,*" shouted another villain.

"There are more of us in here too, asshole," called a familiar voice from high above. Sally glanced up and saw Jack perched in a high window, a pistol in each hand. "*Hablo español. Usted entiende inglés?* Let the hostages go and let's go outside and talk this over."

The woman glared up at him. She held something Sally thought was a ball bearing. Upon further examination afforded by her accelerated perceptions, she could see the woman had similar metallic spheres all over her costume. The way the woman brandished it, the little ball was obviously some kind of weapon. "No chance, *Americano*. Drop your weapons, or we start killing hostages."

The energy ribbon around Sally wound further around her and constricted like a serpent. She gasped for breath and struggled against the crimson force.

Jack didn't move. "Come on, this isn't the way you want this to go. You've seen the movies . . . you know how it ends when you take hostages."

"We're walking out of here," called the woman. "And you can't stop us or we start killing them, starting with your friend."

"Let's make a deal," called Jack. "You release all the hostages and you can take me instead."

"No deal," she said.

"Come on," said Jack in his most convincing voice. "My team isn't going to attack you if you're holding me. Let's just let you guys get out of here with a minimum of fuss and bother and let these poor people get back to their loved ones."

The big man holding the roll of paper looked nervous. "*Él tiene quizá razón, Pistola.*"

"Shut up, *Cañón*," hissed Pistola, not taking her eyes off Jack for a second. "I know what I'm doing."

"You guys know who I am?" Jack called to the security guards in English. "I can't really reach my badge just at the moment."

"Yes, sir," replied one of the Treasury guards.

"Then you know I have the authority to order you guys to get the fuck out of here. Clear out. As of right now, this incident is under the jurisdiction of Just Cause and Homeland Security. You're complicating things and people are going to die."

The guards paused, uncertain what to do.

"Move it!"

One of the guards made a decision. "Okay, guys. You heard the man. We ain't getting paid to stop supervillains."

"But, Chuck . . ." started one of the men who plainly wanted to play hero.

"Shut up, Joe. I want to live to get my pension."

The other man shrugged. "Good point." The guards backed out through the doors to leave the printing floor vacant except for Jack, the cowboys, and their hostages.

"All right," called Jack. "Now are you guys going to play ball or what?"

Sally twitched a little as she tried to find some weak spot in the energy ribbon binding her, but it held her so tight she could barely breathe. Nobody had ever managed to snare her when she was running at speed before. For the first time in her life, she'd found someone faster than her, and she was scared.

Pistola came to a decision. "All right, mister. You come down here and surrender and we'll let these people go. Drop your weapons."

Jack leaped down to the printing floor. Another man might have broken his legs in the drop, but Jack's invulnerability protected him from harm. He set his guns on the ground and kicked them gently aside, then undid the clasps on his combat harness and let it fall to the floor. He smiled, put his hands on his head, and took a couple of steps forward. "Let the hostages go."

"I don't know, Pistola. He's got something planned. I don't trust him." One of the cowboys was actually another cow*girl*, Sally realized, but with a butch haircut and square jaw.

"Quiet, Espada. I've got it under control."

Jack waited patiently as Azote extended another energy ribbon around him and soon he lay on the ground next to Sally, trussed up like a rodeo calf. "How are you?" he whispered.

"Hurt."

A worried expression crossed Jack's face. "You going to be all right, kiddo?"

"I don't know." She was glad her goggles were cracked so Jack wouldn't be able to see her tears of fear and frustration.

"You shouldn't have run off like that," he chastized.

"I'm a speedster. Running off is what I do best."

"Good point. So what's the plan?"

"What do you mean, *what's the plan*? Don't you have a plan?"

"No." Jack gave her his best infectious grin. "Do you?"

"Idiot." Sally grumbled. In spite of her dismay, Jack's indomitable spirit made it difficult for her to remain miserable.

"You people get out of here right now," Pistola shouted at the hostages. The hostages, stunned, looked around helplessly. "*Mierda, tengo que tirarlos para hacer que entienden?* Move it before you get shot, dumbshits!"

The prisoners headed for the exit, first tentative, then in a mad panicky rush. Pistola watched them go, and then turned to look critically at her new hostages. "*Llévelos, Puño. Vayamos a los caballos.*" Pistola slipped some printing dies into her belt.

The largest of the cowboys easily lifted both Sally and Jack under his arms as if they were no more than bags of charcoal. Jack looked up at him pleasantly. "Hi, handsome. In town long?"

"*Qué? No . . . no entiendo,*" stammered the huge man.

"*No hable con él, Puño,*" ordered Pistola. "*Consiga listo para luchar.* Get ready to fight."

The five robbers activated their various parapowers. Ball bearings whizzed around Pistola like miniature planets. Fresh ribbons of red energy crackled from Azote's hands. The bonds he'd laid around Sally and Jack showed no signs of weakening. Sally wondered how many ribbons he could maintain before his control started to waver. Espada's forearms lengthened and stiffened into bony, razor-sharp blades. Puño's hands were full of Sally and Jack, but he was probably just as tough as he was strong and wouldn't shirk from fighting when it erupted. Cañón, who was almost as big as Puño, hefted the large roll of paper as easily as if it had been a balloon.

"Going to just ride off into the sunset while the closing credits roll?" asked Jack. "Retire to Bolivia and have a whole flock of little pistoleros?"

"Shut up!" Pistola screamed.

"Are they outside?" Sally mouthed to Jack. He winked back.

"Do you see anything?" Espada whispered to Pistola as she scanned the street outside.

"No . . . that's what worries me. Escudo and Cuchillo are gone. So are the horses."

A cool breeze played across Sally's face. She didn't think much of it until she also saw a trail of mist float past as well. Jack's smile grew wider as he saw it as well. "Well I sure hope nothing bad happens to you guys." He spoke with emphatic clarity. "*Especially* to the guy holding the red energy whips."

Sally got the hint and gathered herself for a quick getaway. Even tucked under Puño's meaty arm, she could still shake herself free of his grasp by shifting her weight at top speed. All she needed was a moment of freedom from Azote's bonds. She knew Shannon was in the room with them; an ace in the hole, but without any offensive powers. All she could do was become invisible and insubstantial. Sally didn't see how Shannon could possibly be any use, or what Jason could see in the little slut for that matter. Her temper rose quickly through the dull roar in her head.

Shannon materialized suddenly to one side of Azote. She faded into vision and solidity, already spinning around in midair, one leg tucked underneath her and the other whipping around toward Azote's head. She caught him by surprise before he could react with his whips. Shannon's foot connected with his jaw. It sounded like a baseball bat striking a punching bag. Azote's eyes rolled back in his head as he tumbled to the floor, unconscious or maybe dead. Sally caught a glimpse of a superior grin on Shannon's face before she faded from view again, just as one of Espada's arm-blades cut through the space in which she'd stood.

"Wow," said Jack, just their bonds faded into nothingness. Sally shook herself free at super-speed. For Puño it would have felt like trying to hold onto a jackhammer. She dropped to the ground and immediately ran to the far end of the lobby to get her bearings. Her head still buzzed from her collision with the printing press. With a crash of glass, Jason smashed through one of the arched windows into the lobby. Sally smiled. He loved to break stuff and lived for good brawls. From the look of excited anticipation on his face, he was ready to go toe to toe with whoever dared stand up to him.

Doublecharge flew in through the broken window. Electricity spat and crackled off her hands. "Just Cause," she announced. "Surrender now."

"*Entrega, amigo,*" suggested Jack to Puño. "*Usted lo sentirá si usted no hace.* Give it up, dude."

"We can take them, Vaqueros," cried Pistola.

Shannon appeared right behind her, one of Jack's guns touching the back of Pistola's head. "I'd reconsider if I were you," she said.

Puño released Jack and put up his hands. "Don' shoot, I give up!" he managed in heavily accented English. Espada and Cañón realized they were outnumbered and outpowered and likewise surrendered.

Pistola spat on the floor in fury and put up her own hands in surly surrender.

"Babe," said Jack with a cheerful lilt, "You should have just stayed in bed."

Several minutes later, Switchboard supervised the administration of sleeper sets to the would-be bank robbers. Sleeper sets were a safe way of keeping parapowered prisoners unconscious. They transmitted a signal into the wearer's brain that induced a coma. The bandits would be kept safely asleep until a Deep Six transport could collect them and take them to the prison where they would await their trials.

Sally sat off to one side and suffered a paramedic's examination. He checked to make sure she hadn't suffered any overt ill effects from Azote's powers or her hard collision with the printing press. As he worked, she watched as Jack recounted Shannon's takedown of the energy whip-wielding villain to Jason. Jason shared in conspiratorial laughter with Shannon and Jack. Each guffaw felt like an icy dagger in Sally's heart.

"Well, miss, you took quite a knock on the head," said the paramedic as he shut his diagnosis case. "I'm calling it a mild concussion. Have you ever had one before?"

"Yeah," she replied. "A few months ago."

"You need to follow up with your own doctor. Multiple concussions can get pretty severe over time. You might think about wearing a helmet and mouth guard to reduce the risk of further traumatic impacts."

"Okay." She had no intention of doing any such thing, but the paramedic didn't need to know that; he was only doing his job.

"I can't find any injuries related to the . . . whatever you called them. Energy whips?"

She nodded. Her broken goggles dangled loosely from nerveless fingers.

"But if you notice any kind of ill effects," he continued, "you make sure to check in with your own medical staff."

"Thanks," mumbled Sally.

A shadow fell across her face. She looked up to see Doublecharge standing over her. The older woman glared through her mask. "Okay, let's have it," she said without preamble.

Insolence rose up in Sally. She tried to keep control of her ire. Shannon's attention to Jason and his apparent reciprocation had her so angry she almost couldn't see straight. "You said speed was of the essence."

"I assigned you to a team." Doublecharge's voice was icy calm.

"But nobody got hurt," said Sally, "and somebody might have if I hadn't gone in. One of the guards fired his gun."

"Yes, and it seems to have worked out well, but that doesn't change the fact that you disobeyed an order."

"I ordered Sally to go inside and scope out the situation," said Jack from behind Doublecharge. "I was worried about the possibility of hostages."

"I don't recall hearing you give that order," said Doublecharge, folding her arms.

"My headset is damaged," said Jack as he held up a frayed wire for evidence. "I didn't notice until after our cowboy friends surrendered and I got my gear back."

Doublecharge considered Jack's story. Sally could see she didn't believe a word of it. "Very well," she said. "I'll include that in my report. See to the loading of the horse things."

Sally nodded. Jack flashed one of his famous radiant grins. "Of course."

Doublecharge headed for the *Bettie* to supervise Switchboard and Jason as they loaded the comatose prisoners for transport to Deep Six.

"Why'd you do that?" Sally asked Jack in a low voice as they went over to where the robotic horses still stood.

"Didn't figure you'd want to be in Juice's office again so soon," he replied. "What's on your mind, sweetheart? You're hardly your usual chipper self." He walked around one of the horses and examined it from all angles.

"I'm just . . . dealing with some issues." She wished Sondra was off-duty; Sally could talk to her about anything. *Especially* Jason.

Jack whistled at the engineering of the horse. "I wonder how those zeroes got hold of these, and where they're from anyway?"

"I don't know." She watched as a Just Cause semi pulled up. They would load the horses onto it so technicians could examine them back on the base.

"I wouldn't expect you to. It was a rhetorical question." Jack stepped up next to her and put his arm around her shoulders. Sally swallowed hard to keep from breaking down, but a single tear managed to escape onto her cheek nevertheless.

Jack, for once, didn't seem to have anything to say.

CHAPTER FOUR

"Love is a perky elf dancing a merry little jig and then suddenly he turns on you with a miniature machine gun."

-Matt Groening
Love Is Hell
1994

May, 2004
Denver, Colorado
Just Cause Headquarters

"I'm not sure, but it certainly looks like the same technology," said John Stone as he straightened up after peering into the inner workings of one of the robotic horses. The man who looked like a granite statue come to life leaned on a heavy titanium steel cane. Although his mind was as sharp as ever, sixty years of fighting against gravity in a body which weighed seven hundred pounds had taken its toll. He had been a heavy hitter for Just Cause back in the Sixties and Seventies and was now the Vice Principal of the Hero Academy.

"You think these came from the same place that built the Steel Soldier?" asked Jack. The robotic horses were tethered in one of the hangars. They stood calmly where they'd been tied; indeed, they'd barely even moved when Jack and a couple of technicians had removed some of the plating from one of them to expose the internal machinery.

"Possibly." John Stone readjusted his hat, a fedora which had been his affectation and trademark for decades. "The technology is similar, but the components look brand new. It might be someone who worked on the Soldier program or had access to the blueprints. I suppose someone could have reverse-engineered the technology from the wreckage, except all the Soldier's remains were lost on 9/11."

"Or someone who'd seen the Soldier close-up," prompted Sally, who'd tagged along with Jack. Normally she'd have been hanging out with Sondra, but after a long stretch in the Command Center, the winged woman had begged off for a nap. On one hand, Sally dreaded letting Jason out of her sight for fear that Shannon would be on him in a heartbeat; on the other, she didn't want to smother him, and at some point she just had to trust him.

"You mean Destroyer, of course. Or rather, the man inside the suit." John Stone rubbed his jaw thoughtfully with a sound like cinder blocks scraping together. "Young Harlan Washington did repair the Soldier after the first time they fought. It was part of the bargain we struck with him in return for a lighter sentence. He certainly would have had the chance to learn about the technology, and he had the skills to apply it."

Jack and Sally watched as the techs replaced the armor plating on the horse. "Why horses? And how did these losers get them?"

John Stone shrugged. "Horses are useful creatures and fairly simplistic compared to something like the Soldier. I imagine their central processors aren't very complex. If Washington actually built these, he might not yet have reinvented the technology required for the higher brain functions of the Soldier."

Switchboard walked into what the team members were already calling The Stable. "*Los Vaqueros—*" He referred to the robbers, whose name meant *The Cowboys* "—said they bought the horses online, if you can believe that. Apparently they robbed several Guatemalan and Mexican banks to obtain the funds for them." He held up a hand to forestall Jack's interruption. "We've already checked. The website is gone, and the only cache we've found is of a password-protected entry page. Homeland Security's got their computer division on it, but they're not optimistic about retrieving much more than that. The seller covered his tracks very well."

"All right," said Jack. "Let's make several assumptions here, and yes, I know exactly what that means. Suppose these idiots did manage to acquire these highly-advanced devices using stolen funds. And let's further suppose that they were in fact built by someone familiar with Steel Soldier technology. And just for kicks, let's suppose it was Destroyer. My question is why? The man builds top-of-the-line *battlesuits*, using technologies far advanced over anything else out there. Why mess around with goddamn *robotic horses*?"

"He needs money," said Sally with a sudden insight. "We destroyed his last battlesuit."

"Well, technically it was you who destroyed it," Jack reminded her. "Credit where credit is due."

"Ok, *I* destroyed it," continued Sally, "but if he didn't have a spare suit handy, he'd need to build himself a new one. That's going to cost him big bucks. Why not build something quick and dirty and sell it for a big profit?"

"Why don't you think he'd have a backup suit available? The man is the king of contingency planning."

"It's that contingency planning I'm thinking of," said Sally. "Would he have a backup suit that was more advanced than his current ride? I don't think so. Would he keep an old suit lying around when he could cannibalize it for the next model? Probably not."

"Good point," conceded Jack.

"And unless he's already developed his next generation technology, he's probably going to be spending a lot of time and money building the next suit."

"And when he does," John Stone grumbled. "Everybody better look out, because it'll be worse than anything we've seen yet. With the kind of mindset he has, you know he'll come gunning for Just Cause again. Especially you, Sally."

"I'll be careful, Mr. Stone," she smiled.

Jack burst out in laughter. "Slow and cautious, that's my girl."

She decided to give in to temptation and go check on Jason. Maybe he'd finished practicing and would be up for a little recreational exercise. She almost blushed at herself as she headed for the dorm. She let herself into the room.

Shannon straddled Jason's lap with her arms around his neck.

Sally's perceptions accelerated until the scene was a frozen tableau spread out before her. She could see every nuance of detail from the look of surprise on Jason's face to the raw desire on Shannon's. She stood helpless in the doorway with her mouth hanging open and her eyes wide in surprise for what felt like forever. A massive landslide of emotions crashed down onto her: fury, despair, jealousy, hatred, disgust.

She ran.

She needed space, distance, the feel of wind rushing past her. If she ran fast enough, perhaps she could outrun the pain.

She tore down the hallway and left a vortex of scrambled air and a very confused janitor in her wake. In just a few seconds, she reached the perimeter fence. She ran along the edge until she spotted a break large enough for her tiny frame. She squeezed through the hole in the fence, which tore her t-shirt and scratched her face, and ran down a road bordered by trees on one side and open fields on the other.

The sun had already dropped behind the mountains. She ran east at a hundred miles per hour and left civilization behind her. Dark fields whipped past as she kicked up a dust cloud in her wake. Burning pain wracked her feet suddenly and she tripped as one of her shoes came apart. She skidded off the side of a dirt road into an irrigation ditch. She'd run the soles right through on her off-the-rack cross-trainers.

As Sally sprawled in the damp reeds of the ditch, her feet blistered and aching, the image of Shannon and Jason arose fresh in her mind and nausea washed over her like a bucket of icy water. She tasted bile at the back of her throat and vomited. Her heart hammered as she wiped her mouth with the back of one shaky hand. Dry heaves racked her body again and she moaned as her stomach and throat muscles quivered. She dragged herself out of the ditch and sat on the bank and had a good long cry.

After what felt like hours, she ran out of emotional energy. Her tears stopped and she just sat, miserable and hurting. Her feet burned and she wondered how badly she'd damaged them in her incautious sprint. She felt weak and foolish, and she had no idea where she was except a dirt road in the middle of some fields. The stars came out one by one overhead until the sky was filled with a hundred times more than she ever saw in town.

Sally got to her feet and nearly fell as the world spun around her. She felt lightheaded and terribly thirsty. She hobbled along the road until she came to an intersection of a paved road. She turned south in the hope that she might find her way to the interstate. She could see distant lights that must have been farmhouses, and near the horizon a line of lights that might be a freeway on-ramp. As she walked closer, she saw the bright lights of an all-night diner attached to a truck stop. She limped the rest of the way there.

Sally staggered up to the door and pushed on it stupidly for a minute before realizing she had to pull to open it. She stepped inside into a world of dim light bulbs coated with ancient grease, neon signs featuring popular brands of beer, and a comforting smell of coffee and French fries. There were a few patrons inside, mostly truck driver types in t-shirts, tight jeans, and baseball caps. They all paused in their eating or conversation as she took a hesitant step forward.

"My God, are you all right?" cried a heavyset black woman with her graying hair coiled into a bun.

Sally nodded. "I'm okay," she mumbled. "I just need to sit down for a minute."

The waitress, whose name tag read *Hazel*, took her to a booth and sat her down with a glass of water. "You sure you're not hurt, hon? You need me to call somebody?"

Sally sank onto the bench. "I'm fine. I just went for a jog and . . . and I got lost and fell in a ditch."

"All right, sweetie. What can I get for you? How about a cup of hot chocolate?"

"Please," said Sally. "And some ice and a towel?"

"Sure thing, hon. I'll be right back with that. You let me know if you want something to eat or need anything else, all right? It's just me out front here tonight, so you just give me a wave or a yell if you need me."

Sally sat and stared at ancient water rings on the surface of the table in front of her. The scene of Jason and Shannon replayed in her mind over and over again, as if taunting her. She was so lost in her own thoughts that she jumped when Hazel set down a glass of ice and a steaming mug of hot chocolate topped with whipped cream.

"Take your time with that, hon. It's plenty hot," the waitress said.

Sally nodded without really hearing. She poured some ice into the towel and began to ice her feet. They were bruised and scratched, but she hadn't damaged them as much as she'd feared. Years of running, even with her special boots, had toughened the skin with thick calluses. She hated her feet and thought they were ugly, but had to take special care of them nevertheless. Even her ministrations couldn't distract her from her thoughts.

"Honey, that chocolate ain't so hot anymore and you haven't touched it," said Hazel. Sally started and looked up into the waitress' kind face. "You look like you got something heavy on your mind. Want to talk about it with a complete stranger?"

Sally smiled sadly. "That's okay," she said, taking a sip of her lukewarm chocolate. "You've got other customers and stuff. I'll just finish this and be on my way."

"Suit yourself, hon, but you're the only one left and all I got left to look forward to is doing dishes . . . and I've done enough of them in my life to know they ain't in any hurry to get done any sooner."

Sally looked around to see that sure enough, she and Hazel were alone in the diner.

"You mind if I sit down for a few minutes?" The older woman slid into the seat across from Sally without waiting for an invitation. "Lord, that feels good. I been runnin' all day and this is the first chance I get to sit. I recognize you from your picture in the paper. You're the one named after a song. What's it again?"

"*Mustang Sally.*"

"That's right. I always liked that song. Well, Miss Sally, what brings you all the way out here to the middle of nowhere? Let me guess . . . man troubles."

Sally lowered her eyes. "Is it that obvious?"

"Believe me, I've had enough of my own to know what they look like on someone else's face."

"I caught my boyfriend cheating on me." Sally's voice quivered a little as she admitted aloud what she'd seen.

"Hmmm . . ." she said. "Well he must be blind or stupid, because anyone could see you're a real peach."

For some reason, the term struck Sally as funny. "Got any words of wisdom for me, Hazel?"

"Honey, I could write a book with all my words of wisdom. Problem is, folks who really need them ain't bright enough to buy a book and I'd still be waiting tables here."

"Oh, I don't know," said Sally. "You've got a way with words."

"They ain't none of them that haven't been said a thousand times before." She smiled confidently. "For example . . . *if you love someone, set them free.* You heard that before, right?" Sally nodded. "And if he returns, he's yours forever. If he doesn't, he never was. That's plain and simple. Took me a couple of husbands before I took that one to heart."

"So I should just let him go? Let him get his jollies with someone else?"

"This boyfriend of yours . . . how old is he?"

"He's almost twenty."

"Then he's young enough he don't know what he wants yet. He probably won't know when he's twice that age. Boys that age ain't thinking with their brains, if you catch my meaning."

Sally smiled a little. "I can be guilty of that myself."

Hazel burst out laughing. "Oh, honey, we're all guilty of that! That's something the Lord gave us to remind us we ain't much better than the animals. But He gave us the ability to control it, and that's what makes us human."

"I guess so."

Hazel leaned forward. "Listen, hon. In any relationship, one person is always begging the other. You can be the one doing the begging, or you can be the one in control. Took me a couple more husbands to figure that one out."

"So you're saying I should make him beg?"

"What I'm saying is that if he truly loves you, you won't have to make him beg. He'll do it all on his own. You just have to give the boy some time to understand his own mind. Now do you want him back?"

She thought for a few seconds. "Yes," she decided. "Yes I do."

"Then you just give it a little time and see what happens. Let him go. He'll decide whether he wants to beg for you or not. And if he's got a smart bone in his body, he'll beg."

"Because I'm a peach." Sally chuckled. She didn't feel very much like one; to borrow one of Jack's favorite vulgarities, she felt more like ten pounds of shit in a five pound bag.

"Exactly."

She finished her chocolate, which was very good in spite of not being warm anymore. "Thanks, Hazel. I guess I did need someone to talk to."

"Well . . . we ladies got to stick together," said Hazel as she leaned back. "I was like you once, Miss Sally— young and in love. I even have a little power of my own."

"Yeah?" Sally perked up, interested.

"Oh, it ain't nothing so fabulous as yours." Hazel held up a finger, concentrated, and an ice cube leaped out of Sally's glass and skated across the table. "Not much good for anything, 'cept if I drop my pencil."

"It's still a parahuman power," said Sally. "More than most people will ever have. Didn't you ever try to do anything with it?"

"Lord, no. This is my life, hon. I never wanted more than what I have, and I'm perfectly happy with what I do have. I'm a waitress, and damn good at it. And at the end of the day when I go home, I know I've been the best waitress I can be. I can't even imagine myself as some kind of superhero like you, hon. Can you imagine me trying to squeeze these hips into a Spandex suit?"

Sally laughed, but then stopped for fear of offending Hazel, but the waitress smiled and chuckled at herself in a good-natured way.

She looked at her empty cup and her good cheer dissipated. "Well, I should get going. I've been gone for a long time and they're going to wonder what happened to me. What do I owe you for the chocolate?"

"On the house, hon."

"Are you sure?"

"Ain't no thing."

"Okay. Thank you very much, Hazel." Sally stood up and limped toward the door.

"You'd better not be leaving here on foot, young lady." Hazel took on the stern air of an authoritative mother.

Sally looked down at her filthy, bare feet and blushed. "I . . . I guess I kind of am." She looked out at the highway. "I'm not even sure where I am."

Hazel picked up her phone. "I'm calling you a ride back into town, honey. Don't you worry none, we all get lost from time to time. Sometimes we have to find our own path, but other times someone will be there to show us the way."

CHAPTER FIVE

"Heav'n has no rage like love to hatred turn'd
Nor Hell a fury, like a woman scorn'd."

-William Congreve
The Mourning Bride
1697

May, 2004
Denver, Colorado
Just Cause Headquarters

"I don't care! We're through!"

Sally's intention to keep a cool head with Jason had lasted almost two minutes into their conversation, but then her temper flared like a spark in dry brush. She'd cornered him in the rec room and stood before him like David confronting Goliath.

"Look, I said it was an accident," Jason growled.

"Oh, right. She just happened to fall into your lap."

"I told her I wasn't interested!"

"Was that before or after I walked in on the two of you? How far would it have gone, Jason?"

"I was pushing her away!"

"*How far would it have gone?*" Sally screamed at him.

He closed his eyes and took a deep breath. It was dangerous for him to lose his temper with his strength because things might get broken. Like walls or people. "Not that far," he said at last.

"Did you sleep with her?"

"No!"

"But you did before, right?"

"What has that got to do with anything? I didn't do anything this time!"

A new voice interrupted them. "Sally, Jason . . . what the hell is going on?" They turned to see Juice filling the doorway, with a thunderous expression darkening his face.

"Nothing," growled Sally through clenched teeth. "I was just leaving." She tried to push past the team leader, but he wouldn't let her.

"Not so fast. I could hear the two of you all the way down in the cafeteria. I won't have this kind of behavior on this team." Juice folded his arms.

Sally caught a glimpse of someone in the hallway behind him, who looked in with interest and a sardonic smile on her face. *Shannon.*

White-hot rage exploded through Sally as she slipped into fast-perceptions. Before Juice or anyone could move, she ducked past him and into the hall. Her fingers closed around Shannon's blouse and she shoved the taller girl up against the wall. "You . . . you fucking gutter slut!"

Shannon melted away into mist and drifted back through the wall out of Sally's reach.

A hand the size of an Easter ham closed around Sally's arm. Juice spun her around to face him. "You. Are. Out. Of. Control." He spoke in his courtroom voice. "You are confined to quarters." He looked around at Jack and Shannon. "I don't have time to deal with this right now, but I want all three of you in my office tomorrow morning. Nine o'clock. If you're not there, you're off the team. Period."

Sally stalked down the hall and into her room. She threw herself onto the bed and screamed into her pillow long and hard until her throat was ragged.

She must have dozed off then, because a tentative knock on the door woke her up. "Sally? It's Sondra. Can I come in?"

Sally unlocked her door and swung it open. The winged woman stepped in and looked around, a paper bag clutched in one hand. "Doesn't even look like your room," commented Sondra. "Maybe we could, you know, throw some clothes around or something . . . make it look a little more homey." Sondra's attempt at a joke didn't improve Sally's disposition in the least. For the past few months Sally had hardly been in her room, and it was unusually clean for her.

Sally flopped down on her couch, folded her legs up underneath her, and clasped her arms around her stomach as if it hurt. She made a noncommittal grunt.

"You know, Juice is pretty angry with you. You want to tell me what's going on?"

"Yes. No. I don't know. Maybe?"

"Well, maybe you'd rather talk to Ben and Jerry too?" Sondra pulled a pint of Super Fudge Chunk ice cream and two spoons out of her bag. "They're excellent listeners. And very sweet about it."

"Okay," Sally said. "Crack that open and pass it over."

For a few minutes the two women passed the pint back and forth in silence until the ice cream was gone.

Sally sighed as she dug out the last bite. "You don't have another one hiding in that bag, do you?"

Sondra chuckled. "Babe, we don't all have eighteen-year-old metabolisms. I'd still like to be able to squeeze into my costume."

"But you're gorgeous, Sondra. I don't know what you could possibly have to worry about." She looked with admiration at the Native American woman's flawless skin and shining black hair.

"You'll understand when you're older."

Sally rolled her eyes. "I've been hearing that my whole life."

"Me too." Sondra's laugh was musical, as if a songbird sang alto. "So what's going on? Juice said you were screaming at Jason and then jumped Shannon. That hardly sounds like you."

"I walked in on them."

"You didn't!"

"Yeah, I did."

"Were they fooling around?"

"No," said Sally. "They were just kissing."

"That conniving little bitch," said Sondra. "No wonder you came unglued."

Sally shrugged. "It was just as much Jason's fault as hers. He said he pushed her away, but at some point he let her get as far as she did." She looked at the empty ice cream carton in her hand, sighed, and threw it in the general direction of her kitchenette. It bounced along the floor to roll in a tight circle several feet away from the trash can. That was fine, it wasn't going anywhere, and nobody was coming over to give her cause to clean up. She'd put it into the trash later.

"Now that's the Sally I know." Sondra chuckled and put a friendly arm around Sally's shoulders. Her wings rose above them both like a feathery canopy. "So what are you going to do now?"

"I don't know," replied Sally. "I guess we're broken up now."

"Think you'll get back together?"

"I hope so, but he's going to beg first. Not me."

"I'm really sorry, kiddo," sighed Sondra. "If Jack actually got involved with any of his starlets, I'd be furious too."

Part of Jack's job as the team's public relation's officer was to escort various Hollywood starlets to parties and functions.

"But you've never had any doubts?"

Sondra sat on the couch and spread her wings slightly to avoid sitting on them. "I did once. I thought that just maybe Jack might have had designs on this one singer."

Sally's eyes widened. "You're kidding! Which one? What did you do?"

"Oh, just some blonde chippie one-hit wonder. I told Jack I'd cut off his nuts and feed them to a dog if he was screwing around." Sondra's eyes sparkled with humor.

"But he's invulnerable to everything," said Sally.

"He took me seriously. And I'd have figured out a way if I had to. Fortunately I didn't have to. She traded down for some no-name actor."

"I still think you guys ought to just get married." One of Sondra's feathers had fallen to the carpet. Sally picked it up and smoothed out the soft brown barbs.

"We talked about it just last week. I don't know, though. Maybe neither one of us is the marrying kind. Whatever that means."

"I'd like to get married someday." Sally realized what she'd said and her eyes teared up a little. A romantic concept like *marriage* was pretty painful in light of recent events.

"Well . . . you're still pretty young. You've got plenty of time before you even need to start worrying about such a thing."

"I guess you're right. I'll be right back." Sally walked into the bathroom to wash her face and put her hair up. As she twisted her long tresses back, her eyes fell on the horseshoes she'd left by the sink. She scooped them up and went back out to Sondra.

"Hey, take a look at these and tell me if you think they're identical."

Sondra examined them closely with her yellow-irised eyes. Like her namesake, she had exceptional vision. "I don't know, Sally. They look very similar, but I can't say for sure they're identical."

"Yeah, but if you look past the obvious signs of aging, they're the same right down to the chips out of the edges. You haven't spent as much time with them as I have. They *feel* the same."

"So what are you saying?"

"That body I found last week . . ." Sally swallowed a nervous lump in her throat. "What if it's *me?*"

"How could it be you?" Sondra fixed an intense gaze on Sally.

"I don't know. What if I go back in time?"

"Sally, have you ever heard of Occam's Razor?"

"No. What's that?"

"In essence, it says that given any number of possible causes for an event, the simplest is the most likely." Sondra preened one of her wings by using her fingers to groom each feather.

"Huh?" Sally looked blank.

"It's the *KISS* principle. Keep It Simple, Stupid. What's more likely? That at some point in your future you will mysteriously travel back in time, which is impossible as far as anybody knows, and be killed in the mid-1800s or that this is just a coincidence?"

Sally shrugged, unconvinced. "It sounds a lot more stupid when you say it like that."

"Sally," said Sondra as she smoothed down her wing and started on the other. "I know you're a science fiction buff, and that means there are always alternative explanations for events. But in this case, I think it's pretty unlikely."

Sally sighed. "You realize that you're probably jinxing me just by saying that, and I'll get sucked into a wormhole or something tomorrow."

The two women looked at each other in silence for a moment. Then Sondra started to giggle; so did Sally.

Sondra wiped tears of amusement from her eyes. "Okay, I do need to get going. Is there anything you need?" She touched Sally's arm.

Sally shook her head. "I'm stuck here. Maybe I'll just wander around the Internet or something."

Sondra grimaced. "Sounds horrid. I'll find you some entertaining links and you can surf to your heart's content."

"Sure, that'd be great." Sally hugged Sondra. "Thanks for coming by. If I ever needed a best friend, it's now."

"I'm here for you. whenever you need me."

The winged woman left and Sally decided she was too tired to do anything else and opted to lie back on her couch, put her feet up, and close her eyes.

She awakened from a terrible nightmare and jerked to her feet before she reached full consciousness. She practically vibrated with tension as she stared around in unfamiliar darkness. The slightest noise would have sent her running in panic. As her blood thundered in her head, she recognized the familiarity of her own suite.

She sank back onto the couch, fuzzy-headed and logy. Her hands still shook. "No more ice cream before bed," she said aloud to the silent darkness. The clock beside her monitor showed *4:24 AM* in glowing green numerals. She'd been asleep for almost twelve hours.

Her stomach growled.

She didn't bother to open her refrigerator. She didn't keep much in it except beverages; if it couldn't be heated in a microwave, Sally couldn't cook it. Admitting defeat and going to the cafeteria regularly was much safer than setting off her room's smoke detector or sprinklers by burning water on her little stove. She wondered if she was permitted to leave her quarters to eat. After more hunger pangs, she decided her house arrest probably didn't mean no meals. She'd slip into the cafeteria and grab a quick breakfast and be back in her quarters before anyone noticed. Her lack of cooking skills had yet to screw up cereal. *Pour into bowl, add milk* was about her speed when it came to the arts culinary.

She stepped into some sweats and her soft fur-lined moccasins and left her room. Headquarters was still on night-time lighting, which meant only every fourth overhead light was on. Long shadows filled the hallways as Sally padded to the cafeteria. The tantalizing scent of fresh coffee teased her as she entered the cafeteria. One corner was well-lit and some of the overnight crew members were taking a break there. The long buffet bar sat empty with clean stainless steel bins neatly stacked to one side.

At least the coffee bar was well-stocked. Coffee was the lifeblood that kept the team operating most days. Jack had paraphrased Sun Tzu when he told Sally that an army marched on its stomach, and so did Just Cause function on its coffee. She poured herself a cup and doctored it with lots of cream, sugar, and hazelnut syrup. She added two boxes of Raisin Bran and a small carton of milk, sat at the nearest table, and stared into her bowl without really seeing it.

"Is this seat taken?" asked a deep voice.

Sally looked up to see Juice, a stack of papers under one arm and a large coffee mug in his other hand. She looked back down at her tray again. "Go ahead."

He spread his papers out and sipped at his coffee. "Don't usually see you this time of morning, Sally. In fact, I don't recall *ever* seeing you up this early."

She made a noncommittal grunt.

"You know, I don't envy you, being the first third-generation hero. You've been in the spotlight your whole life, trained to be a superhero your whole life. You've never really had a chance to do anything else, to be a normal person."

Sally didn't reply, although Juice's words expressed some of the exact things she felt.

"I feel a certain responsibility for you," said Juice. "I've known your mother since before you were born, and your father was a good friend of mine. His death was very hard on all of us who knew him. I promised on his grave I'd do my best to look out for you. What

I'm trying to say is that if you need anything, come to me and I'll do what I can to help. I see within you almost limitless potential in the Just Cause organization. I know we're asking you to grow up awfully fast, but I've never questioned your place here on the team."

She nodded, unsure of what she should say. His smile gleamed white in his dark face before he busied himself his paperwork.

Sally finished her cereal and returned to her room. She spent the next few hours surfing around the internet with no pattern or plan.

Eventually the time came and she went to Juice's office. Sally couldn't look at Jason or Shannon.

In his office, Juice waved them to come inside. "Sit down," he ordered. "Listen carefully, because I'm only going to say this once and I don't like repeating myself. I don't ever want to see or hear a repeat of what happened yesterday. Whatever is going on in your personal lives needs to stay there. Do not let it affect this team."

Shannon opened her mouth to say something and Juice held up a hand.

"I will not tolerate teammates screaming at each other in anger or attacking each other. There is absolutely no excuse for that type of behavior. I'm writing up all three of you for conduct unbecoming to an official representative of the U.S. Government. This will go into your permanent personnel file."

Juice glared sternly at the three young heroes.

"And I'll guarantee that pissing me off is the fastest permanent way off this team. Any of you can be replaced at any time."

Juice's cell phone rang. He held up his hand to indicate that the others shouldn't leave just yet and touched the speaker button on the phone. "Juice. Go ahead." He started to pick up his cup of coffee but it never reached his lips. A strange expression crossed his face as he listened to the voice on the other end. "Say that again."

CHAPTER SIX

"The Boy Scouts' motto is 'be prepared.' I'd like to think that Just Cause's motto is 'pretend like you're prepared.'"

-Jack "Crackerjack" Raymond
The Tonight Show
July 7, 2002

May, 2004
Denver, Colorado
Just Cause Headquarters

"What do you mean, a *mountain?*" Juice set his coffee cup back onto his desk. There was a pause as the voice on the other end of the connection shouted at him. Jason, Sally, and Shannon all looked at each other with curiosity. "I see," said Juice. "We'll check it out right away, Will. Keep me informed." He hung up his phone, a troubled expression on his face.

"Who was that?" asked Sally.

"Your friend, Stratocaster from the Lucky Seven." Juice drained his coffee and absent-mindedly crushed the cup before anyone could point out that it was stainless steel. "Damn. I lose more cups that way. I should just stock up on paper ones instead." He deposited the mangled metal vessel into his desk-side wastebasket with a muffled *thunk*.

"What did Stratocaster say?" asked Jason.

Juice didn't answer. Instead, he tapped a button on his desk phone. "Command Center, who's running the show today?"

"Riley, sir," replied the cracking voice of a man who couldn't be much older than Sally was. "*Go ahead.*"

"Do we have any satellites that can give me current images of North Dakota?"

North Dakota? Shannon mouthed to Jason, who shrugged. Sally glared at her.

"Yes sir," said Riley. "Target?"

"Rugby, which is apparently a real place. Send the feed to my office." Juice typed a few commands on his keyboard and the large wall-mounted flatscreen monitor lit up.

The little hourglass icon on the screen performed its lazy, repeated upending as the Command Center established a link with the satellite cameras. Juice's fingers tapped on the mahogany of his desktop as he waited. In a moment, an image appeared in a window from the camera, updated every two seconds.

What they saw was impossible.

A large mountain had sprouted from the high plains of North Dakota. It had pushed aside buildings and roads in its sudden lunge for the heavens. Emergency vehicles clustered along the roads around the mountain. The unnatural peak had a flat top upon which rested something that looked very much like a castle.

"Son of a bitch," muttered Juice. "Command Center, can you tell me what exactly we're looking at here?"

"You're seeing the same thing as we are, sir," said Riley. "We're starting to receive reports. The mountain apparently just grew out of the ground, but GPS can't find it and neither can Minot Air Force Base radar. It's got a physical profile, but doesn't seem to be detectable by instruments. They're scrambling Air National Guard jets from Fargo for a flyby. Hold on, sir, we've got updated information coming in now."

"Hey . . ." Jason pointed at a blob on the screen that wasn't there a second ago. "What's that?" The camera reset and the blob had moved.

"There's another one." Shannon touched the screen in a different place.

"Sir?" Riley sounded aghast.

"Go ahead, Riley."

"We're getting reports of . . . some kind of flying creatures circling the mountain. Sir, local law enforcement is calling them dragons."

Juice stood up. "Dragons."

"Yes, sir. Your orders?"

The team commander took a deep breath and cocked his head first to one side then the other to loosen kinks in his neck. "Call out the troops, Riley. I want the *Bettie* on the pad and ready for departure in fifteen minutes. Briefing in ten minutes in the conference room."

A swirl of purple energy formed out of nothingness in the middle of Juice's office with a squalling sound of distortion and feedback. Sally recognized it from her past experience with the Lucky Seven. Stratocaster stepped out of the whirling vortex of energy. His guitar blazed with incandescence and sparks danced among the standing hairs of his purple mohawk. He looked around. "Nice office."

"Stratocaster," said Juice as calmly as if people materialized in his office all the time. "What do you know about this?"

Stratocaster looked at the monitor. "Shit," he said. "It's already bigger than I thought it would be."

Juice glanced at Sally, Jason, and Shannon, who stood and waited to hear Stratocaster's information. "Hadn't you three better be gearing up?"

"But—" began Shannon.

"No," Juice retorted.

"But—" added Sally.

"No to you too. It'll come out in the briefing. I promise. Now *move.*"

Grumbling, the three young heroes trudged out of Juice's office. The last thing they heard was Stratocaster say "we're in big trouble," before Juice shut the door.

Shannon became insubstantial and rose, ghostlike, through the ceiling to the dormitory on the second floor.

"I, uh, guess I better go change too," mumbled Jason.

"Yeah, I guess you better." Sally growled. "Try not to screw her before the meeting." She spun on her heel and flashed down the hall to the stairwell. Part of her felt gleeful at the cutting remark, but mostly she felt bad that she'd said something so terrible to him.

She wiped away an angry tear as she threw on her costume in a blur of motion. Then another tracked down her face. Then another. For several minutes she had to just lie on her bed, hug her pillow, and sob.

Her phone beeped. "*Sally? We're waiting on you. Is everything all right?*" asked Juice.

She wiped her eyes. "Sorry, I lost track of the time. I'll be right there." She rushed to the bathroom and scrubbed her face. She glared at her reflection; her puffy eyes wouldn't hide the fact that she'd been crying. She pulled her goggles down over them. Better. She left her room in a flash of red and yellow and was at the conference room a few seconds later.

For once, Sally was actually the last one to a meeting. Jason sat away from Shannon and wouldn't look at her. For that matter, he wouldn't look at Sally either. Fine, thought Sally. Two could play at that game. She flopped into an empty seat between Switchboard and Doublecharge and put an expression of rapt attention on her face, focusing all her attention on Juice and Stratocaster.

Juice nodded at her. "Most of you already know Stratocaster from the Lucky Seven. He's here to tell us what he knows about events currently unfolding near

Rugby, North Dakota. Approximately half an hour ago, a mountain grew out of the geographical center of North America. He believes he knows why. Will?"

Stratocaster nodded, his tall spiky mohawk bobbing. "There's a legend among mages that every thousand years an Archmage will rise, drawing all magic in the world into himself."

"And do what?" interrupted Jack. "Build mountains in North Dakota? Make everyone pay more for downtown parking?"

"It's a lot more serious than that." The muscles in Stratocaster's jaw stood out like cords. "The last Archmage enslaved much of Africa for almost a full generation. Were it not for her own children, mages in their own right, she might have eventually held sway over the entire world. Each millennium, the Archmage has been more powerful and more dangerous."

"Like how actual parahumans are evolving?" asked Doublecharge. "We're more powerful now than our predecessors."

"Yes, but imagine a single parahuman able to rule a continent the size of Africa. And now imagine one who has decided he is strong enough to take on North America. If he successfully conquers the United States, he'll be able to rule the entire world."

"*He.* You know who it is or are you just using the term generically?" Sondra flapped a wing the way someone else might have shrugged.

"His name is Wolfgang Frazier. I battled him in Tokyo last month. He's incredibly powerful. I barely escaped with my life." Stratocaster's hands shook for a moment. Sally realized the man was terrified.

"What did he want from you?" asked Switchboard.

"My magic. When a mage slays another mage, he absorbs all the magic contained in the victim. Eventually he will reach a critical mass and draw all magic in the world to himself. He's nearly there. Even now, I can feel myself drawn toward him. We have to stop him."

"He's built a castle on top of that mountain," added Juice. "And has what look like dragons patrolling the skies around it."

"Can't fault him for a lack of creativity," said Jack. "What's next? Armies of Urukhai? Nazguls?"

"Don't take magic lightly, Jack," said Sally. "Maybe it's not all super-scientific, but I've seen Strat in action. It's real. He can do things parahumans can't."

Jack shrugged. "Whatever."

"At the very least," said Juice in his courtroom voice, "this person has violated American soil and airspace, and we've been ordered to intervene by the Director. As always, we'll attempt a peaceful resolution first."

"Followed by aggressive negotiation." Jack grinned.

"The *Bettie* is on standby. We're leaving in five minutes," said Juice. "Will, can you join us? You're the only expert on magic that we have available."

"Actually, I'd prefer to cower in a dark corner, but you'll probably need me." Stratocaster strummed his guitar for emphasis and swirls of energy spilled off the strings and transformed into lavender-scented smoke.

"I still say there's no such thing as magic," Jack whispered to Sondra as they headed out of the conference room.

Sondra kept her wings close about her like a feathery cloak so nobody would trip over them. "Whatever you want to call it, lover, it's certainly something we should worry about. Growing a mountain takes a lot of power no matter where it comes from."

Outside, Just Cause's supersonic transport jet was already powered up. The *Bettie*'s turbofans were howling at a high idle. Sally was pleased to see Ace would be their pilot. Fairuza "Ace" Bruck was a veteran from the Israeli Air Force and flew the *Bettie* like an extension of her own body. Ace, her helmet on and visor down, looked out from behind the bulletproof cockpit glass and nodded professionally at them as they climbed on board.

"I hope it's not going to be like this all year," said Doublecharge, resplendent in her white, black, and yellow costume as she tightened her seatbelts.

"What do you mean?" asked Sally.

"Four emergency call-outs already and it's only June. Last year we only had two all year."

Ace announced they had clearance to lift.

"Go," said Juice.

The engines' howl increased to a scream as the *Bettie* lifted vertically off the pad. For the next couple of minutes, conversation was impossible over the shriek of the turbines. After climbing for most of a minute, Ace rotated the jet nozzles aft and the *Bettie* accelerated to the northeast.

"E.T.A. to Rugby, North Dakota, approximately forty-five minutes, sir," said Ace over the cabin speakers in her clipped, accented tones.

"Thank you, Ace. Give us a ten minute warning."

"Roger that."

"All right, Will. We've got some time. Can you give us all a crash course on magic theory in thirty minutes?" Not even Jack quipped at Juice's serious tone.

Stratocaster leaned back in his seat, crossed his Doc Martens, and clutched his guitar like it was a security blanket. "There's not that much to tell. A mage can do anything he can conceive of, so long as he can control the power."

"Anything?" asked Shannon. "You just think of it and it happens?"

He shrugged. "More or less." He ran a quick arpeggio across the frets and a spinning globe of yellow and blue sparks appeared in the air in front of him. It bounced across the cabin to encircle Jack's head.

"Hey, cut that out." Jack waved at the sparks to no effect. They shrank to pinpoints of light before vanishing altogether.

"Most mages work with spells. Those are evocations they've practiced over and over until they can control them easily. Some are more improvisational, which is how I tend to work."

"So what's the deal with the guitar? Is it magic too?" Jason, a guitarist himself, tapped his fingers on his knees. Sally could tell he was itching to take the snow-white electric into his own hands.

Stratocaster laughed. "I've never been entirely sure. I can't perform magic without it. If it's a psychological crutch, it carries a lot of weight with me."

"What kind of magic does this Archmage guy use?" asked Sally.

"I don't know," said Stratocaster. "My guess is spell-based, since he's so good at what he does. But he's accumulated so much magical power, he's not really limited by much of anything."

"How does he accumulate magic? Is that something we could block or interrupt?" asked Sondra.

"When a mage is killed, all that magical energy is released. If another mage is nearby, he will absorb it all, becoming that much more powerful." Stratocaster looked up, worried. "A great number of my colleagues have disappeared over the past year. I believe he's been hunting them. You can't block or interrupt his power. It's become a part of him."

"'*There can be only one*,'" quoted Jack from the *Highlander* movie.

"For all I know . . ." Stratocaster looked somberly at the rest of them. "I may be the only one left."

"So what you're telling us is we're going to be facing a man with an unbelievable amount of power, who can make things happen with a thought," said Juice.

"That's about the size of it."

"Fine," said Doublecharge. "How do we stop him?"

Stratocaster looked at her with sadness and panic evident in his eyes. "I have no idea. At this point, I think we'd have to kill him to stop him."

"I'm not particularly keen on killing," said Juice. "It leaves a bad taste in my mouth."

"What if he's unconscious or comatose?" asked Switchboard. "We've got Deep Six sleeper sets on board."

"Hmmm. A coma might work." Stratocaster rubbed his chin in thought. "But all he'd need was a flash of coherent thought to be free once again. The problem is getting to him and knocking him out in the first place."

"Leave that to us." Jack spoke with confidence.

"I hope it's that easy, for all our sakes. I'll do what I can to counteract his magic with my own, but honestly he's much more powerful than I am."

"Look," said Sally, "you said he's only limited by the power of his imagination. Well, he's imagining castles and dragons instead of missiles and tank divisions. He's got a thing for the fantastic. Maybe we can use that somehow."

"That's a good point," said Sondra. "If he tends to think along those lines, that's a limitation we can exploit. We play by his rules, lull him into a sense of complacency, and then we break those rules."

"Unless by then he's already beaten us," Shannon pointed out. "I say we sneak in, knock him on the head, and ship him off to Deep Six."

"Sir?" Ace interrupted them. "Ten minutes to target."

"Thank you, Ace." Juice leaned forward to address the others. "Okay, here's the plan. We'll have two teams: insurgence and reserve. Doublecharge will command the reserve team, of her, Sondra, and Switchboard. Since the three of you are the only fliers, you're in a better position to scope out the entire situation. The rest of us will attempt to enter the castle, then find and subdue this Archmage. Will, you're with us."

"What else am I going to do, sit here and wait to die?"

Juice rolled his eyes at that. "All right. For the insurgence team, primary mission is to locate and incapacitate Wolfgang Frazier. There is no secondary mission objective for the insurgents. The reserve team's primary mission is to patrol the area and to assist the insurgence team if required. Secondary mission objectives are to assist local authorities in any way requested. Are there any questions?"

For once, even Jack stayed silent despite being handed a straight line. Nobody else said anything either. Sally felt pre-combat butterflies in her stomach.

"Sir, I have hostiles approaching on intercept vectors. They don't show on radar. Only visual," said Ace from the cockpit.

Juice looked sharply at Stratocaster. "Could they be illusions? Could this whole thing be some huge illusion and that's why it's not registering on any instruments but cameras?"

Stratocaster shrugged. "No way to tell unless they interact with us."

"Sir, they're not very fast but they're angling to intercept." The clipped tone of Ace's voice made it plain she'd rather be talking with the *Bettie*'s guns.

"Hold your course, Ace. Do not fire unless fired upon. Remember that this is public airspace and there are civilians beneath us."

"Yes, sir."

"Give me a fly-by of the target. I want a good look at it before we deploy."

"Roger that. Three minutes to target." The *Fasten Seat Belts* indicators lit up.

Tension mounted among the heroes as they went through their various pre-combat rituals. Juice cracked his knuckles. Doublecharge made sparks jump between her hands. Sondra checked the safeties on her custom fifty-caliber handguns. Jack yawned.

Suddenly, Ace shouted "*Ben zona!*" She flipped the *Bettie* over and pointed her nose toward the ground in a spiraling dive. She cursed some more in Hebrew over the cabin speakers as a bright stream of energized plasma shot from the mouth of a dragon to clip the edge of the *Bettie*'s wing and melted one of the elevators. Heat washed through the cabin and Sally felt prickling like incipient sunburn on the right side of her face.

"Evasive maneuvers. Stand by," shouted Ace, late on the warning.

The plane shook as a passing dragon buffeted it with its tail. The cabin lighting shorted out and alarms shrieked. Sally got a very good look at the dragon as it passed over the plane's wing. It was enormous, with a body the size of a small helicopter and a wingspan to match the *Bettie's*. Thick scales like tank armor protected it and its face could have scared Godzilla.

"Permission to return fire, sir?"

"Granted!" Juice braced himself between the seat in front of him and one across the aisle. Sally could see his arm muscles quivering.

Chattering thunder filled the air as Ace opened up with the machine guns in the *Bettie*'s nose. She jinked the jet left and right to avoid plasma jets from the dragons. A tremendous explosion outside the plane starred two of the portside windows.

"Scratch one bogie, sir. They explode when hit."

"Nicely done, Ace. How many more?"

"Not sure, sir. They don't—son of a bitch!" With a bright flash from near the tail section, a fist-sized hole appeared in the hull. The edges glowed white-hot. The *Bettie* shuddered and Sally felt her stomach try to leap out of her throat. Wind whistled through the cabin with deafening volume.

"Ace?" called Juice over the noise.

"I'm a little busy here, sir." Ace vectored the jet nozzles forward to kill the *Bettie*'s momentum. Sally watched out a window as three dragons wheeled about and closed in on them.

A new voice came over the cabin speakers. "Attention, Just Cause. This is Lieutenant John Howard, Air National Guard. Mind if we join your party?"

"Plenty of room at the bar, Lieutenant. Don't be shy," said Ace.

"*Happy Hooligans* at your service. Let's go, 119th!" With a roar, three F-16 fighters raced past like steel counterparts of the attacking dragons. One of the dragons turned to face the new threat and took a missile right up its snout for its trouble. The dragon exploded in a colossal fireball that sprayed cooked dragon meat across the side of the *Bettie*.

Sally looked over at Jason. His face was white with terror. Her own nerves sang like taut violin strings and her accelerated perceptions had kicked in and forced her to experience every nuance of the danger they faced.

"Ace, can you get us to the ground?" Juice shouted.

"We're going to the ground no matter what, sir. I'm trying to get us there in one piece." The plane heeled over and began to tumble toward the ground. Overstressed metal shrieked and the airlock assembly ripped away. Jason's seat belt snapped and he was flung hard into a bulkhead with a yelp of pain. Ace tried to regain some kind of control, but the *Bettie* fell like a wounded bird.

"Everyone who can, get out now," shouted Juice. "We'll regroup on the ground. Charge me up," he added to Doublecharge.

Jack swung his bag over his shoulder, ran to the back of the jet, and leaped out into the swirling sky.

With a crackle of electricity, Doublecharge fed power into Juice to increase his strength and toughness. "Go!" said Juice, and she flew out after Jack.

Shannon faded into mist and then vanished. While insubstantial, she could drift safely to the ground unharmed by impact, dragon, or explosion. Switchboard levitated himself out of the gaping hole.

"Sally, with me," shouted Sondra. Sally shrank back into her seat, terrified of falling. Ever since she'd ridden Destroyer on what should have been a one-way trip toward the stratosphere, she'd been afraid of falling. She shook her head, not wanting to leave her seat, not wanting to leave Jason, knowing she had to do both. "Girlfriend, we don't have time for this!" Sondra wrapped her muscular brown arms around Sally and dragged her to the back of the plane.

"No, wait! What about Jason?" screamed Sally as she looked back at him. Their eyes locked and she saw in them his love for her. Not for Shannon; for *her*. Then Sondra leaped into the open air with her wings spread wide and her arms wrapped around Sally like they were tandem-skydiving.

"Stratocaster can get them out!" Sondra shouted over the noise of air combat. Sally screamed and thrashed. "Do you want me to drop you?" hissed Sondra in her ear.

"No!"

"Then hold still!"

Sally tried to be a good passenger as Sondra cupped the air in her wings, and turned their tumble into a spiraling descent.

The Air National Guard jets made another strike and one more dragon exploded into flames. Two dragons still wheeled in the air, but they were hard-pressed by the fighters as they provided cover for the descending heroes.

Sally watched as the engines on the *Bettie* gave out. Their once-proud transport was a broken shell of her former glory. Purple flashed from within the cabin and a glowing sphere emerged that held Juice, Jason, and Stratocaster inside it as Ace ejected from the cockpit.

Seconds later, the *Bettie* smashed into the ground. Her remaining munitions exploded from the impact and tore the wreckage apart in a brilliant fireball. Burning pieces of the jet flew up and out in all directions.

A dragon closed in on Sondra and Sally. Sally squealed in terror. She needed to run; it was the only way she knew to get to safety, but she was still too high up to drop from Sondra's grasp.

"Shit. Sally, I'm going to need my hands."

"I can't!" cried Sally in a panic.

"Sally, there is a very large dragon coming toward us and I can't reach my guns!"

"I can't!"

Lightning engulfed the dragon. Doublecharge rose up behind the dragon as raw electricity poured out of her. The dragon's wings collapsed and it plummeted toward the ground, its scales charred and smoking.

The Air National Guard jets took down the final dragon with another heat seeker missile. The pilots waggled their wings in tandem before they turned back east toward Fargo.

Sally clutched Sondra as the winged woman glided down toward the ground. "I'm sorry I lost my head."

"That's okay. Flying isn't for everyone. We're down now." Their feet touched the ground and Sally immediately crumpled to dig her fingers into the hard Dakota soil.

Sirens screamed as emergency vehicles and the rest of the team converged on their position.

"Don't worry, folks, Just Cause is here. Everything's under control now," said Sondra under her breath. Sally could tell that Sondra didn't believe it for a second.

Neither did she.

CHAPTER SEVEN

"A group of parahumans poses a far greater threat to us than an individual might. Just Cause is the best, the brightest, and the biggest hero organization in the world. No one person in their right mind would want to challenge that."

-Rick "Lionheart" Lyons
Time Magazine
December 3, 1976

May, 2004
Rugby, North Dakota

The magically-created mountain loomed in the background as Just Cause regrouped. The team clustered around Juice and awaited new orders. Jason was getting his left ankle taped up. The paramedics said it was sprained and maybe broken. Juice gave rapid-fire orders to a North Dakota State Trooper, who pushed his hat onto the back of his head to mop his brow.

"But they're mostly just engineering and water supply battalions out here," said the trooper. "We don't have combat battalions."

"They're still soldiers, aren't they?" asked Juice. "Get the Governor to mobilize whatever National Guard units he can."

"I don't think I have the authority . . ."

Juice changed to his courtroom voice. Greater men than the State Trooper had wilted under that voice. "I'm here as a direct representative of the Department of Homeland Security, and I'm giving you the authority to make that call, Trooper, because I don't have the goddamn time."

The trooper mumbled something apologetic, mopped his brow again, and turned away to speak into the radio clipped to his shoulder.

A Pierce County SUV pulled up to the group. Almost before the vehicle ground to a halt on the dirt road, the passenger door flew open and a furious Ace stomped out. She flung her helmet to the ground so hard it cracked. Her accent, normally almost undetectable, came out thick in her fury. "Sixteen years! Sixteen years in the Israeli Air Force and not once did I lose a jet!" she shouted at Juice. "And now you bring me to dragons and look at me. I'm a pilot without a plane. What am I supposed to do now?"

"Easy, Ace. You're alive and so are all of us, thanks to your flying," Sondra said as she tried to smooth things over. "Has anyone seen Jack?"

The young deputy who'd delivered Ace swelled with pride. "The guy who fell without a parachute? Jolson's bringing him. He landed a few miles away."

The trooper that Juice had ordered to call the Governor returned with a sheepish look on his face. "Mr., uh, Juice? The Governor wants to talk to you."

Juice caught Sally's attention, a plea in his eyes. *Coffee?* He mouthed silently at her. She nodded. "Yes, sir, this is Juice," he said into the cell phone the trooper offered him.

Sally turned to the young deputy. "Excuse me."

"Hmmm?"

"Coffee. Where can we get some?"

Right on cue, a catering truck pulled up, horn honking, and the front of a long procession of motor homes, pickup trucks, motorcycles, and one solitary news van. Doublecharge was aghast. "What the hell is this?"

Switchboard shrugged. "This is better than reality television. This is an event."

"This event is going to get civilians killed." Doublecharge grimaced. "Those dragons will incinerate anyone who gets too close."

Another sheriff's cruiser pulled up and a filthy-but-excited Jack tumbled out. "Would you believe I hit the only bog in fifty miles?" he said. "I've got mud stuck in places I didn't even know I had."

"All right, we're all here," said Juice. "Trooper?"

"Y-yes sir?"

"Set up a perimeter to keep these bystanders back. We've already seen dragons. I don't want to know what else this guy is going to bring out."

"Yes sir," said the trooper, relieved to be given something mundane to do like crowd control. He was obviously a little overwhelmed by the presence of so many parahumans.

"All right . . . around the circle, I want observations and thoughts. Make it fast, people," said Juice. "Jack, I assume you've been busy while being chauffeured all over the countryside. What have you got?"

"Radar and GPS can't find this mountain, but it's clearly there," said Jack. "The 119th fighters did a direct flyover before returning to base. They reported that all navigation systems went crazy on approach."

"I was just starting to notice that myself when I got distracted by the dragon trying to chew the wings off the *Bettie*," said Ace.

"Like space itself is being warped around the mountain," said Sally.

"Why here?" asked Juice. "No offense meant to the locals, but Rugby, North Dakota? It's not really the point I would choose to begin the conquest of North America."

"It's the center of the continent," said Stratocaster. "A lot of magical power is concentrated here. From here he can reach equally in all directions."

"To do what?" asked Sondra. "Take over the country? He's hundreds of miles from anything of strategic significance."

Stratocaster fixed her with a serious gaze. "I don't know, but I'm sure it's bad, whatever it is. He's got enough power to do all this." He motioned to the mountain with its aerial guardians flapping around it. "He's a devious bastard. Whatever he's planning, this is a big part of it."

"I can't see any other way to get inside his castle except by direct approach." Juice studied the mountain through binoculars borrowed from the State Trooper.

"That's got to be playing right into his hands," said Doublecharge. "Let the three of us give you some airborne support and reconnaissance." She gestured to herself, Sondra, and Switchboard

Shannon looked up toward the summit of the mountain. "If he's got a fantasy thing going and we start playing outside those rules right away, he might start thinking outside them too. I happen to think Juice is right."

Brown nose, thought Sally, although she herself had to agree.

"My original plan stands," said Juice. "The three of you will be backup for the rest of us. With one change." He looked at Jason. "Sorry, Jason, but I can't let you come along."

Jason grimaced at his ankle. "I know. I'd just be a liability. Not any good to anyone."

"One other change," said Ace. They turned to look at her. She had requisitioned one of Jack's machine pistols and cocked it with a decisive slap. "I'm going in too."

"Absolutely not," said Doublecharge.

"Oh?" Ace's face twisted into a snarl. "I have more combat experience than all of you put together. I may not be a trained commando, but I'm not afraid of a firefight either." The diminutive woman stalked over to glare up at Juice. She barely came to his shoulder; in fact, she was only a couple of inches taller than Sally.

"Nobody is doubting your abilities or your willingness," said Juice.

"It's because I have no powers, is that it?"

"We don't know what to expect inside."

"Then you don't know if you'll need me or not. Better to have me along. Somebody needs to think like a normal person."

"She's got a point there, Juice." Jack smiled as he made sure the rest of his weapons were loaded. "We do tend to have parahuman blinders a lot of the time. Might do us some good to have a more mundane perspective."

Sally didn't say anything, but she hoped Juice would agree to let the spunky pilot come along; her dedication and professionalism was inspiring.

Juice sighed. "All right."

They set up Jason as the liaison to local authorities, and arranged to have him relay information to and from the assault party as needed. The six heroes—Juice, Jack, Sally, Shannon, Ace, and Stratocaster—rode toward the mountain in the two sheriffs' SUVs. Overhead, Doublecharge, Switchboard, and Sondra flew high point.

The unnatural mountain loomed in front of them. "Are we going to just walk up the side of it?" Sally asked.

"Maybe," said Juice. "Satellite imaging showed what looked like a path."

"A path?" Jack rolled his eyes. "Maybe he's got a nice convenient platter for us to lay our heads upon before he cuts them off. Well, your heads, anyway."

"Didn't you ever play role-playing games?" asked Sally. "We did in the dorms all the time. There's always a path, loaded with traps and ambushes and stuff."

"Sally, why don't you pretend for a moment that we're stuffy, uncool adults and explain to us how this all works?" said Juice.

"Speak for yourself, boss," said Jack. "I'll only admit to not knowing about the conventions of the genre."

"Think of it like a series of challenges," said Sally. "Designed to soften us up, to make us use our powers, to weaken ourselves. Maybe one or two of us don't make it. It's his way of showing that he's powerful enough to toy with us. He's watching it all for entertainment."

"Go on," said Juice.

"And once we get to him, he'll imprison us, gloat, tell us all his plans, and then conveniently forget something important. Then we free ourselves and defeat him."

Jack burst out laughing. "I had no idea it was so easy. Maybe we should save ourselves the trouble and just order him to give up now. *Surrender, Dorothy!*"

The deputies pulled up to the base of the mountain. Sally couldn't hear any ambient background sounds. Even the droning of the trucks' engines seemed stifled in the still air. A rough-hewn path wound its way up the side of the mountain. Juice dismissed the deputies and the team prepared for their ascent.

The mountain's steep sides loomed over the heroes and made Sally feel even smaller than normal. The narrow pathway could only accommodate two people side by side if they were extremely friendly with one another and one was only Sally's size.

"I think we'd better hurry," said Stratocaster in a strangled voice. "He's doing something. Something bad. I can feel the draw on my power."

"All right then," said Juice. "Sally, take the point. I'll follow behind you, then Jack and Ace. Will and Shannon on rear guard."

"We'll cover you as you climb," said Doublecharge. "Sondra will take high watch while Switchboard and I stay nearby."

Jack grinned. "And me without my ten-foot pole."

"I thought you didn't know anything about gaming," said Sally.

He shrugged. "I'm pretty sure everyone knows about the ten-foot pole."

They began to climb. The path wasn't too steep, and was forgiving and mostly free of loose rock and slippery spots.

"Cave entrance up ahead," said Switchboard.

Sally rounded a bend and faced a dark cave in a rock wall. Jack passed a pair of flashlights up to the front. Sally and Juice shined them into the blackness. With a strange rushing sound, a great stream of bats flooded outward. Switchboard and Doublecharge barely had a chance to dive out of the way as the flying rodents spread out into a cloud. Ignoring the group on the ground, the bats swarmed around the flying heroes. Jack and Ace raised their guns, but Juice ordered them to stand down. None of the assault party, except for Stratocaster, could have easily fought against a swarm of creatures. Overhead, electricity crackled as Doublecharge charged the air around her. Crisped bats rained down like tiny meteors.

"You three, stay here at the cave mouth," said Juice. "Make sure nobody comes up behind us."

"We got it," said Sondra, swatting at a bat that tried to bite her.

The others advanced into the cave. "Is this part of separating us? Softening us up?" asked Juice.

"Yeah," said Sally as she shined her light onto a stairway carved out of the rock. "*Hey, where do these stairs go?*" she fed the *Ghostbusters* line to Jack.

"*They go up,*" he said right away. "And so do we, apparently."

The stench of bat guano filled their nostrils as they made their way up the stairs. A hundred feet in, Sally stepped onto a stair that gave way. Her lightning-quick reflexes allowed her to leap backward as several more steps cracked and tumbled into a deep pit. The others crowded in to shine their lights into the pit. Rusty iron spikes lined its floor some forty feet below. Jack whistled. "All the comforts of home."

They crossed the gap in the stairs without any problems and continued up. A few minutes later a large, heavy blade scythed across the stairwell and cut empty air between Sally and Juice. "That was close," muttered the big man as he swung a foot hard at the flat of the blade and snapped it off cleanly.

"Not much imagination," said Ace.

"Well let's not give the man any new ideas." Jack seemed less concerned than the others. Sally figured he must have believed his invulnerability should handle anything the Archmage could dish out.

An odd wave of energy passed through the ground, walls, and air around them, like the shockwave from an explosion, the sudden change in air pressure making Sally's ears pop. "What was that?" Juice asked.

Stratocaster's face fell. "I think we're in trouble. That was a summoning spell."

"How can you tell?" Sally looked up the stairs with apprehension creeping up her spine.

"And summoning what?" added Shannon

"I don't know on both accounts," said Stratocaster. "Somehow I just recognize the way the magic was used. It might be because of something I learned from some friends in Japan. Whatever it was, I think we should hurry. There's something else building up. He's working on something big."

"Right. Double time then," said Juice. "Stay sharp."

They rounded the last bend in the stairs to enter a great hall filled with skeletons sporting swords and shields. A great stone rumbled down behind them to seal off the stairwell. Likewise around the room, Sally saw other doorways slam shut, leaving the six heroes to face several dozen opponents.

"Take them," said Juice without hesitation, and Just Cause went to battle.

Juice and Jack waded into the walking bones fearlessly, Juice with his fists and Jack with a sword that he yanked from a skeleton's bony grip. In spite of their armor, the skeletons seemed fragile. With no sinew or muscle to connect the bones to each other, only magic held them together. A good strong blow was enough to break the spell and shatter them into pieces which dissipated into smoke. Shannon entered the fray and used her powerful spin kicks to send skulls clattering off the walls and fading into nothingness when the skeletal warriors came close to her. Stratocaster fired off chord after chord from his guitar; each one sent a skeleton flying into pieces. Ace fired off a few rounds from her pistol and blew apart some skulls.

Sally realized everyone was doing something but her. An idea surfaced; she knew Jack had a reel of light, strong cord in his pack. She ran to his discarded bag, found the reel and ran to one of the columns holding up the castle roof. She looped the cord around it and tugged. It held fast. She ran crisscross through the hall with the cord trailing behind her. She dipped between and around skeletons. When the cord got difficult to pull on from all the twists, she brought the reel over to Juice.

"Hey, boss . . . pull on this," she said and pressed the cord into his hand. He wrapped a few lengths around his hand and gave a mighty yank. The cord stretched taut and snapped through a dozen skeletons like a garrote.

He grinned. "Do that again."

Sally felt better about herself than she had in days as she made another circuit around the room. Within a few minutes, all the skeletons had been defeated to leave the Just Cause heroes alone once more.

"Is anybody hurt?" asked Juice.

Nobody had worse than scratches and bruises.

"This is getting ridiculous," said Shannon. "Are we facing a villain or a twelve-year-old geek?"

"Destroyer was only thirteen when he first fought Just Cause," said Sally. "Age has nothing to do with it."

Ace brushed sweat-soaked bangs off her forehead. "What's next?"

Eerie laughter echoed throughout the hall, a low chuckle of eminent pleasure. The heroes clustered together and glanced around for the source of the sounds. "What, indeed?" asked the voice.

"Show yourself, Frazier." Stratocaster adjusted the knobs on his guitar.

"William. How nice of you to deliver yourself to me."

Jack nodded above them toward the shadows. "There. He's up there. I'm sure of it," he whispered.

"Tell me, William," said the voice. "How did it feel to take the power from the Saitos? Was it everything you ever imagined? Don't you wish you could feel that again?"

"Who are the Saitos?" asked Juice.

"Long story. I'll tell you later if we're not dead." Stratocaster frowned at the shadows Jack had pointed to. "You can't hide forever, Frazier."

The voice turned ugly. "Neither can you. And now that I've found you, you won't escape me again." A figure descended from the shadows on an icy breeze, dressed in burgundy-trimmed black robes over his pale skin.

Jack stepped forward, pistol raised. "Hold it right there, sucker."

Frazier smiled coolly. "Simpleton." He made the smallest of gestures with one hand. *Something* passed through the air between him and Jack.

"What the hell?" Jack looked perplexed as whatever-it-was lifted him from the ground and suspended him in a swirling cloud of nothingness.

"Magic, fool," said Frazier. Jack was hurled against a wall with enough force to crack the stones behind where his body impacted. He crumpled to the ground and lay still.

"Jack!" Sally tried to step forward, but found she couldn't move. From the angry grunts of her teammates she figured that they were likewise paralyzed.

"Now, William. We can't have your little friends interfering. You and I have unfinished business." Tiny sparks rose up from the floor as the Archmage's heels touched the ground.

"Let them go, Frazier. This is between you and me. They're innocent bystanders in this."

Frazier threw back his head and laughed. "Ah, William. Don't you know by now that nobody is innocent?" With a gesture of his hand, Stratocaster's guitar flew from his grasp. The brilliant white instrument spun through the air and bounced across the floor. Each impact looked like it caused physical pain to Stratocaster.

"What . . . do . . . you . . . want?" hissed Juice through lips and teeth that were mostly paralyzed.

"I'm impressed," said Frazier. "Speaking through my magic paralysis has got to be very painful. Perhaps I will indulge you. After all, I am going to kill you."

Another cliché, thought Sally. *He's monologuing.*

A new voice interrupted. "Perhaps that's not such a good idea, my lord." An older man wearing blue jeans and a cotton work shirt stepped out of the shadows. His silvery hair fell around his face and shoulders and he would have looked more natural on the back of a horse than in a magic castle.

Frazier lifted a languid arm and Sally felt herself rise into the air. "Why?" Frazier asked, full of petulance.

"Suppose they got free? Then they would know about your plans."

Sally wondered if she could somehow shake herself loose using her super-speed.

"But it's a brilliant plan, Seth, and it's all going exactly as I figured it would. Did you see the way that plane went down? Magnificent!"

"Of course, my lord. But just the same . . . it might be better to merely kill them and be done with it. You have more important tasks than to waste time on these would-be heroes."

Frazier rubbed his chin in thought. "Yes, perhaps you're right. It's time I began the spell in earnest."

Sally's paralysis had slight play, enough to allow her to breathe. She twitched herself back and forth against it by shifting her weight as fast as possible. Each time she moved against it, it gave a fraction of an inch, as if the spell were weakening. If she got free, she only needed a second to close with him and hit him hard on the head. Mage or not, a 600-mile-per-hour punch would knock him into next week.

"Of course, my lord. I'll begin making prep—" a muffled pop interrupted the man and a bright green feathery growth appeared in the center of his throat. A look of confusion crossed his face before he fell to the ground.

"What? Seth?" Frazier ran over to the other man and stared down at him in horror. Sally felt the paralysis give a little more. *One second. Come on.*

"He's done for the day, and you're next unless you release my friends right now!" Jack's voice echoed throughout the large chamber. Sally managed to turn her eyes enough to see him leveling a small pistol at Frazier. His clothes were torn, and he was covered with rock dust from where he'd smashed into the castle wall. He'd retrieved Stratocaster's guitar and hung it over his shoulder by its strap. "That was a tranquilizer dart. This next one's a bullet. Your move, Frazier."

Sally was never so happy to see Jack alive and in one piece. She renewed her efforts to free herself and wiggled herself back and forth until the room blurred.

"You shall pay for that!" Frazier rose into the air, his face blotchy and red. Flames limned his hands. Jack fired as Frazier cast a jet of incandescent flame at Jack and enveloped him in a burning cloud. The bullet flared briefly in midair and disappeared into acrid vapor.

Jack stepped closer toward Frazier, his grin plain through the firestorm around him even as his clothing flashed into ashes. "Can't hurt me that way. Now knock it off . . . there are ladies present." His pistol melted under the onslaught and he dropped the glowing lump of metal.

Frazier's eyes narrowed. "Breaking you will be a pleasure. I shall have you lead my armies. An indestructible general." He halted his fiery attack.

Jack turned to the only thing he had left: Stratocaster's guitar, somehow incredibly unscathed by the recent abuse it had sustained. Jack swung it around in front of him. "All right, I really didn't want to have to resort to this. Give up, Frazier. I've got a guitar and it's loaded."

Frazier's eyes narrowed. "You're no mage."

Jack lowered his right hand to the strings, ready to strum. "You want to find out the hard way?"

Sally struggled at the magical bonds which held her in place, but to no avail; they wouldn't weaken any more than they already had.

Frazier raised his arms over his head, a gesture not of surrender but of aggression. "You have no power!" he screamed. His palms glowed with a violet aura.

Jack brought his hand down across the strings and released a discordant shriek from the white guitar. Sally and the others were dumped to the ground as Frazier's magical bonds dissolved.

A glowing, swirling storm of energy the size of a baseball appeared in the air between Frazier and Jack.

"Jack, give me the guitar," hissed Stratocaster.

"You fool! What have you done?" Frazier backed away as the glowing sphere grew to the size of a bowling ball. Sally felt a breeze move past her face toward the energy ball.

An evil grin crossed Jack's face. "I don't know. But if you don't surrender, I'll do it again."

"Jack, give me the guitar right now!" Stratocaster's voice was urgent and tinged with fear. The sphere grew to the size of a beach ball and now Sally could feel it pull at her.

"Sally, return Will's instrument to him." Juice picked himself up off the ground.

Sally ran to Jack's side. He handed her the guitar without looking; his eyes never left the Archmage. Frazier's attention was transfixed only on the glowing energy, which continued to swell.

"Ace? You got him?" Jack called.

"Dead to rights, sir," she replied, her pistol clutched in both hands and leveled at Frazier.

As Sally handed the guitar over to Stratocaster, Frazier waved a hand and circles of crackling blue lightning enveloped him, his assistant, and Jack. The three men vanished.

"Jack!" screamed Sally.

The sphere in the center of the room grew to the size of a small car. Sally felt her feet skid across the floor toward it.

"Will, can't you stop it?" called Juice.

"I'm trying." Stratocaster played hard and fast. His fingers flew across the fretboard. Sparks danced around him like he was an Independence Day attraction. Everyone looked for anchor points as the pull of the sphere increased.

Ace lost her footing and slid toward it. Her gun spilled from her fingers and whirled into the vortex to vanish with a crackle like an overloaded capacitor. Sally leaped forward and locked her hands around Ace's wrists to help brace her and keep her from sliding into the glowing ball. She felt hands on her ankles and glanced back to see Shannon hanging onto her, her face contorted with grim determination. A moment later,

Juice added his own considerable weight to try to anchor them all.

There was a flash of lightning and a powerful smell of ozone filled the air. The thunder nearly deafened them all. A crack appeared on the front of Stratocaster's guitar. "Shit, I'm losing it!"

Sally gasped as Ace left the floor, pulled straight toward the heart of the swirling vortex. Her own body lifted as well as the sphere's pull exceeded even the Earth's gravity. Blood pooled in her head and made her vision go red. Sally felt like her arms might rip right from their sockets. Ace looked into her eyes with resigned hopelessness and released her hold on Sally's wrists.

"No!" growled Sally through clenched teeth. "I won't let you go." She owed Ace her life after the pilot had rescued her from a twenty-thousand foot fall over Guatemala in a daring maneuver that could have splattered both of them as well as the *Bettie* across a dozen square miles of jungle.

Lightning flared again and one of Stratocaster's strings broke with a twang. Then another snapped, and in a quick chain reaction the remaining four strings separated. Whatever magic he'd been working failed and his guitar shattered into pieces. He succumbed to the pull of the vortex. Juice lunged out with one hand to snag his ankle as he flew past.

This is another *fine mess you've gotten us into, Stanley*, thought Sally. If Jack was still there, and she'd had any breath to spare, she'd have said it and he would have laughed.

The energy sphere grew again. Ace's flailing feet contacted it with a flare of dark red energy. The pull increased a thousand fold, and they all disappeared into the whirling storm of energy.

CHAPTER EIGHT

"Numerical superiority is of no consequence. In battle, victory will go to the best tactician."

-General George Armstrong Custer

Location Unknown

The first thing Sally felt was strong heat on her face; she was sweating underneath her breath mask and goggles. Through her closed eyelids, she could see great light as it poured down upon her. She became gradually aware of sounds as they filtered in through the fog in her brain: wind, birds, insects. She wondered if she might be able to move one arm. Pins and needles jabbed through her as her nerves awoke, but she still reached up to pull her goggles and breather mask off. A breeze played across her sweaty, hot face. She rolled onto her side and opened her eyes.

She lay on dry prairie grass on the side of a hill. The bright sky held few clouds. A wave of vertigo and nausea swept over her and she fell back to a prone position, and threw an arm over her face to shield it from the merciless sun. She felt terribly thirsty and her head pounded like a drum solo from Jason's band. She told herself this was no time to be sick, and made herself look around.

Juice was sprawled face down on the grass, one arm outstretched in Sally's general direction. Shannon, Stratocaster, and Ace likewise laid in the grass nearby. Juice was closest to her and she thought she could cover that short distance without fainting. She reached him, but only barely. The entire world spun around her for a few moments and threatened to send her careening off into oblivion once more.

She stripped off her gloves and checked for a pulse on Juice's neck. She sighed in relief when she found a strong one fluttering under her fingertips. "Juice?" she croaked with a mouth almost as dry as the surrounding land.

He stirred and groaned. "What the hell happened?"

Sally licked her lips. "I don't know, sir. But we're all here. I mean, all of us who fell into the . . . the whatever it was."

Juice rolled up into a sitting position and hung his head forward between his knees. "I haven't felt this bad since my bachelor party. Let's make sure nobody's hurt and then figure out where we are."

They got the other three awakened in short order. Everyone complained of dizziness and nausea, but other than that nobody was injured.

"Just Cause, this is Juice, come in," said Juice into his radio. There was no reply. He changed channels. "Doublecharge, Juice. Please respond."

Sally's eyes met Ace's. She found no comfort there.

Juice made one more adjustment to his radio and switched it to the emergency channel. "Breaker nine, breaker nine, anyone receiving this message please reply. This is Juice from Just Cause requesting any agency to respond."

Only gentle, unbroken static issued from the radio.

"Why do they not answer?" Ace scanned the horizon.

"Where are we, anyway?" asked Shannon.

"Any ideas, Will?" asked Juice.

The mage shrugged. "We could be anywhere."

Sally checked her phone. "No signal at all. I thought these were satellite phones."

Juice looked skyward, as if he might be able to spot a satellite. Something about the sky struck Sally as odd, but it was Ace who identified it. "No contrails," she said. "I haven't seen a sky this empty since 9/11."

"Feel up to a little run, Sally?" asked Juice.

She nodded. "Yes, sir. How far?"

"Two miles out, circle our position, and report back. And be careful until we find out where we are."

Sally lit out at an easy lope of sixty miles per hour. She wanted to feel the wind on her face as a reminder she was still alive. Gentle rolling hills filled the landscape, covered with wild grasses and weeds, with a few stands of trees here and there. It was actually very beautiful country, wherever it was.

She topped a rise and skidded to a stop. Her mind reeled from what she saw and she dropped to the ground in a flash and hoped she hadn't been seen. In a shallow valley below her sat a sprawling encampment. She saw horses and wagons and tents, and men dressed in blue military uniforms. Hats. Brass buttons. Rifles. *Swords.* A United States flag flew proudly in the breeze, but it looked odd. After a moment, she realized what was wrong with it: not enough stars. She counted them, and then counted them again to be sure.

Thirty-seven.

Sally ran back to where Juice and the others awaited her, much quicker than when she'd left.

"That was fast," said Shannon.

Sally's hands shook like leaves in a gale. "I . . . I think we might have traveled back in time." The words came out in a rush, almost too fast for anyone to understand. She was terrified; it seemed more and more likely to her that the bones and horseshoe she'd found were her own.

"What leads you to that conclusion?" asked Juice.

"I saw a military camp with horses, old uniforms, and a flag with thirty-seven stars."

"Hmmm." Juice rubbed his jaw. "Sounds like a re-enactment. Don't they try to do a lot of those in the summer? Did you see any spectators?"

Sally stamped her foot. "I'm not being silly. I know what I saw. No cars, no fat tourists with cameras. If it's a re-enactment, it's only for the benefit of the participants."

"How far away? Maybe we should all take a look. At the very least we need some water and a working radio or phone," said Shannon.

Sally estimated the distance in her head. "Maybe three miles."

"Move out," said Juice. "Don't leave anything behind."

They collected their scattered gear, such as it was, and began to walk in the direction Sally had found the camp. The hot sun began to take its toll and sweat dampened their costumes. Juice pulled off his shirt and tied it around his shaved head in a makeshift turban. Shannon pushed up the sleeves and rolled up the legs of her unitard and carried her cloak instead of wearing it. Ace unzipped the top half of her flight suit and tied it around her waist to reveal an olive-colored tank top.

Stratocaster sighed as he gazed up toward the sun. "Damn all you dark-skinned types. I'm already burning." Sally nodded; she too could feel the tingling on her face of sunburn to come.

"Strat, if we are back in time," said Sally in a low voice. "Can you do anything to get us back?"

He shrugged. "Without my guitar I'm pretty well useless. I couldn't do a card trick, much less perform any real magic."

They spotted columns of smoke from campfires in the distance. Sally scouted ahead to make sure she was guiding them to a safe vantage point. They reached a hill and she told them they'd be able to see the camp from its crest. Juice nodded and ordered everyone to stay low.

"I thought you said it's a re-enactment," said Sally.

Juice smiled, his teeth white in the growing dusk. "Let's just say I'm being cautious."

They crawled to the top of the hill and stared down into the valley campsite. It was bustling with activity. Men cared for horses, cleaned their weapons, and gathered around campfires to eat, converse, and laugh. A few had struck up an inspired little band of harmonica, fiddle, washboard, guitar. Some men cavorted merrily around and kicked up their heels in a jig.

"I wish we had some binoculars," whispered Will.

"I wish we had another plane," said Ace. "I feel naked without a cockpit around me."

Sally heard a rustle of grass and the unmistakable click of a firearm being cocked.

"Don't move," said Juice before any of the others could react.

"Heh. You're quick, nigger," said a voice. "I was going to say that."

Sally looked in the direction of the voice and saw a man in the same blue uniform that the others in the valley wore. Instead of boots, he wore buckskin moccasins and had feathers stuck into his cap. His skin was the color of the earth and his face was proud. He had a long rifle leveled at them. "Heh. You must be spies, hey?"

"No, we're . . ." began Juice, but Will interrupted him.

"We're a traveling circus," said the mage.

The Indian's eyes narrowed under his cap. "Circus? What are you doing here spying on the regiment, hey?"

Juice opened his mouth, but Will surreptitiously kicked him. "We're not spying. We saw the smoke from your fires and were hoping to seek shelter. We were, uh, waylaid by Indians. They stole all our wagons and stuff."

"Heh. I think you better come back to see the boss." He pursed his lips and issued a peculiar whistle. A moment later two more men, similarly dressed in uniforms with feathered caps and moccasins, rose up from behind cover to flank the heroes. "Get moving."

The scouts escorted Sally and the others down toward the encampment. She wasn't so concerned about the rifles; she could run away at any time, but she grew uncomfortable as they marched down into the camp proper. Men gaped at her and the others open-mouthed. She realized that if they had indeed traveled back in time, these soldiers might not have seen women in a long time. Sally's costume, and those of the others, was equivalent to lingerie.

The stench in the camp was horrible. Horse urine competed with unwashed bodies and dirty clothing, and mixed with a dash of campfire smoke, food, and coffee odors to make a foul miasma. The scouts brought them right to a large tent guarded by a fat man with a thick beard. "What in the Sam Hill?" said the man as he regarded the five heroes.

"Heh. I found these lost foals in the hills to the south. I thought the General would like to see them, hey?"

"Like to see what, Curley?" said a voice inside the tent. A man in his mid-thirties pushed aside the flap and stepped out. His cavalry shirt was unbuttoned and Sally saw a trace of lather on his cheeks. A thick mustache all but obscured his mouth and his eyes sparkled with bright intensity. He looked the bedraggled heroes up and down. "Well. Aren't you a sorry-looking lot? Joe, see if you can round up some decent attire for our guests so the men will stop finding reasons to walk past my tent over and over." He directed this last to the fat man, who saluted and ran off.

"Now then . . . I'm General George Custer, 7th Cavalry, U.S. Army. Whom do I have the pleasure of addressing?"

Will glanced at Juice, who returned only a stony gaze. "We're, uh, circus performers."

"Circus performers," repeated Custer. "Go on."

"We got lost in the hills, and, our, uh, wagons were stolen by Indians."

"I see," said Custer. "From back East, are you?"

Will smiled. "Yeah. Chicago."

"Tenderfeet." Custer smiled back "I'm from Ohio myself. Now, I'd find our conversation much easier if I had your names."

"Oh . . ." Will's gaze locked with Sally's. *Do something!* she implored him silently. "This . . . this is Sally Swift, the, uh, fastest hands in the West."

"What?" she said faintly.

"And this is the Great, uh, Shandini of the Orient, who can escape from any lock with ease." He waved to Shannon, whose jaw dropped.

The rock star in Will's personality took over as he warmed to his subject. "All the way from Deepest Africa, I present to you Jimbo, The World's Strongest Man." He pointed to Juice. "And finally, from the golden sands of Persia, uh . . ."

"Asa," said the diminutive pilot. "Dancer."

"Charmed, I'm sure," said Custer. "And you, sir? Who are you?"

"Oh, me? I'm, uh, Mohawk William Kramer. I'm the what-do-you-call-it, the ringmaster."

"Can't say that I can really imagine what kind of show the five of you would put on," admitted Custer. "But I'm not really well-versed in circus life. Now what did you say you were doing out here in Dakota Territory?"

"We got lost, then robbed, as I said," replied Will. "In fact, we've been wandering for so long, I'm not even sure what the date is."

"June twenty-fourth."

"1876?" said Juice suddenly.

"Of course," smiled Custer. "Now then . . . we're going to be performing a major maneuver tomorrow, and I can't have civilians wandering around where they might get killed. I'm going to do you a great service and keep you here until after we've completed our engagement. Then perhaps before we let you go on your way you could provide some entertainment for the troops. Ah, Joe . . ." The bearded man returned with an armful of clothing.

"Couldn't find nothin' big enough to fit the nigger," said the man. "But leastaways I got some shirts and trousers for the ladies. Ain't nothin' else suitable." He blushed behind his beard as he stared at them.

"Well, it can't be helped. Joe, will you please make sure our guests have food and drink? I'm afraid we weren't really expecting company and don't have much to offer beyond bedrolls and tents."

"That's very considerate of you, General," said Will.

"I will, of course, post a guard to make sure you're safe." Custer's tone was friendly, but still implied he didn't trust them.

"You're too kind." Will bowed.

Joe took them to a stuffy tent and arranged for bedrolls. Soon the five heroes sat down to a meal of bread, baked beans, and salted pork. There was coffee, but it bore more resemblance to the sludge that Sondra drank than anything that came out of a carafe at Starbucks. They stuck to water, drinking from tin cups.

Shannon sniffed at the blanket on her bedroll. "I think there are lice in this."

"That's the least of our problems," said Will.

"Still think it's a re-enactment?" Sally asked Juice.

"No. It certainly seems like we've somehow traveled through time. And Will is right. We've got a much more immediate problem than lice in our beds."

"Like what?" Shannon brushed her hands across the coarse shirt she'd buttoned over her costume top.

"June 24th, 1876. Dakota Territory. I thought things had started to sound familiar. A very big, famous battle is going to happen tomorrow, and most of these men are going to be killed."

The others looked at him blankly.

"Don't any of you know any history? Little Bighorn. Custer's Last Stand."

"So what do we do?" asked Ace.

"We can't do anything. We need to get out of here as soon as possible," said Will.

"Yeah," said Sally. "We can't risk altering the future. Assuming we haven't already, that is."

"How do you know we are? You're our resident sci-fi buff. What do you know about time travel, Sally?" Juice kept his voice low.

"Nothing. There are all kinds of theories. But that's all they are, theories."

"We can't avoid everyone forever," said Juice. "Even from a practical standpoint. We're already here. I think we need to do everything we can to get back to our own time. We have to assume that our presence is not changing the future."

"How can you assume that?" asked Shannon.

"Because otherwise there's no point in us even trying to get back. Who knows what kind of things might have changed." Juice folded his arms. "For all we know, our present was constructed from our existence in this time. Maybe it even depends on it."

Sally flopped backward onto her bedroll and threw her arm over her eyes. "Time travel gives me a headache."

Ace leaned back on her own blanket. "I'll ask again, because somebody needs to keep their perspective grounded. Funny that it's me who has to do it. What do we do?"

"Short term, we need to get away from here as quickly as possible. We can't get caught up in the battle tomorrow. It will be a massacre. Long term, we need to get back to our time. Will, we were brought here by magic. Can you magic us back home?"

Will shook his head. "Not a chance in hell. Not without my guitar."

"Does it have to be your guitar? Could you play any guitar?" Shannon asked.

"I doubt it. I've tried to use other instruments and it never seemed to work. I just wasn't attuned to them. Besides, I wouldn't even know how to get us back even if I had a functional guitar."

Juice finished his beans and pointed his spoon at Will. "Who does, then?"

"What do you mean?"

"There must be mages during this time period. Don't you know any?"

"God, I don't know." Will screwed his fists into his eyes. "I can't think . . . I'm so tired."

Juice sighed. "We're all tired. Four hours of sleep, starting now. That's an order. That takes us to . . ." He consulted the clock on his phone, which he'd secreted deep in a pocket. "One-thirty. That should be after a change in the watch. We'll make our escape then."

"I wish I had your confidence, sir," grumbled Ace. "You make it sound simple."

"Hey, we're Just Cause," said Sally. "Making the impossible sound simple is our stock in trade."

Chuckles resounded throughout the tent. Shannon turned down the lamp after struggling with the unfamiliar arrangement of knobs for a minute.

For some time it was quiet inside the tent. Outside, soldiers went about their late night business and kept quiet so their comrades could rest before battle.

"Tesla," whispered Will in the darkness. "Nikola Tesla. He can help us if nobody else can."

"He was a mage?" asked Juice.

Sally hadn't been able to sleep a wink either. She listened but stayed quiet.

"Damn good one. Nobody but the other mages knew. He mixed technology and magic in ways nobody else ever had, or ever has since. He's our best bet."

"Where is he now?"

"I'm not sure," admitted Will. "Somewhere in Europe? Maybe Austria? He'd be young right now. Probably still in school."

"Maybe he could build you a new guitar," piped up Shannon from across the tent.

"A better guitar," added Sally.

"Are any of you asleep?" asked Juice, who sounded like he was smiling.

"I was," grumbled Ace. "Until you all started yapping."

"Leave the lamp off," said Juice.

"Fine," said Shannon. "I'm not sure how to restart it anyway. I don't have any matches."

"Let's plan our escape, then." Juice sat up in the darkness, a big shadow against the light tent wall.

"I wish Jack was here," said Sally. "He's good at stuff like this. I hope he's okay."

"He won't be born for another ninety years," said Juice. "And for what it's worth, I wish he was here too."

"Speak for yourself, sir. I wish we were back in our own time," said Ace.

"Good point. Thank you, Ace. Let's make sure we stay on task. Oh, and Ace, you can knock off the sir while we're here."

"Yes sir."

After much whispered discussion, they had what they thought was a workable plan. Shannon would find five horses for them and make sure they were stocked with provisions, especially a map and compass if she could find one. Then she and Sally would incapacitate whatever guards they needed to so that they could make a clean, quick getaway. Once clear of the camp, they would head south and try to find a railroad or a fort so they could make their way to the East Coast and, eventually, across the ocean. They'd use the traveling circus story as cover and as a way to make money along the way.

"Heh. Sounds like a good plan," said a voice and the scout Curley stepped into the tent. He held a hooded lantern which released only a minimal amount of light. "Problem is, you got about ten thousand Sioux between here and your railroad. I think you gonna have trouble there, hey?"

Everyone froze as they realized their cover had been blown. Sally glanced at Juice, ready to act at his order.

Juice didn't move, and Sally could see his attorney's mind gearing up to go to work. "You're absolutely right, Curley. Very perceptive of you. How long have you been listening outside the tent?"

"Heh. Pretty long time now. Heard some pretty interesting tales. Not the usual white man's lies, hey?"

"So what do you want to do about it? You've got something in mind or you wouldn't have come to us at all."

"Big battle coming tomorrow. You called it Custer's Last Stand. He's gonna die, hey?"

"I can't answer that, Curley."

"Well, maybe I'll scout the rear to be safe. I have no plans to die for him."

"We can't stop you," said Juice. "And it's really none of our business what you do, anyway. We're not even supposed to be here, now."

"Heard that too. I believe in fair trade. You give me good value. I always thought Custer was a stupid white man, now I know for sure. Hopefully I will live through tomorrow's battle. In return I will help you to get away from here. Good idea, hey?"

"That's very honorable of you," said Juice.

"Heh. I think so too. You better get ready to leave. Scouts coming back already from Little Bighorn valley. We fight tomorrow or Monday at the latest."

"What's your proposition?" Juice clasped his hands behind his back.

"I already said, I give good value for your trade. You said what happens in the battle. You give me half an hour, I put together your supplies and horses. Meet me up at the hill where I found you, and I'll show you the best way to go." Curley smiled at them in the flickering light of his lantern.

"And that's it? No tricks?" Ace looked doubtful.

"No tricks, pretty lady. You saving my life, perhaps. Only fair that I save yours, hey?"

Ace's mouth dropped open in surprise, as if being called *pretty lady* was the last thing she'd ever expected to hear.

"How do we get up to the hill without being seen?" asked Will.

"Heh. Do I have to think of everything, white man? Half an hour. Don't be late." Curley grinned at them and left the tent.

Juice looked toward Shannon and motioned for her to follow. She nodded and vanished into nothingness.

"How are we going to get there?" asked Will again.

"It's late, it's dark, and we're superheroes. We'll manage," said Juice.

"You know what we really need is a diversion," whispered Sally.

A shout from outside the tent echoed through the campsite. "*Injuns! In the supplies!*"

The alarm raised, soldiers ran from their tents. Some were yanking on their trousers over their union suits, others just grabbed their rifles and ran.

"You think they caught Curley?" asked Ace as they watched the ruckus.

"I hope not," said Juice. "He seems pretty sharp. Whatever happened, this is our chance." He ordered everyone to remove anything clearly from the future and to put them on a blanket. They dropped phones, watches, and Ace's semi-automatic pistol into the pile. Juice rolled up the blanket, tied it around his waist, and nodded. "Let's go. Sally, watch our flanks."

They exited the tent and hurried for the darkness beyond the edge of the camp. With the general alarm raised, soldiers were looking for Indians, not a small group dressed in castaway cavalry uniforms. Shannon rejoined them as they reached the darkness and led them to where Curley awaited them with five packed and saddled horses.

"Did you get caught?" Sally asked Curley.

"No way. It was some Sioux or maybe Cheyenne from the village in the valley. So much for the element of surprise, hey? We'll be fighting them tomorrow for sure."

"Thank you, Curley. I'm glad we could trust you." Juice looked uneasily at the horses. "Are they trained and everything? What I don't know about riding could fill a couple of books."

"Heh. Cavalry horses will treat you right if you treat them right. Now you listen good. You head East for four days' ride. Maybe five if your asses get too sore. After you cross the third river, turn south. Seven or eight days, you'll find one of these forts if you don't get lost."

"This is making me feel real confident," grunted Ace.

"From there, you follow Oregon Trail back east," said Curley. "You got enough food and water for three days. After that, you better find more. I got you two rifles and two pistols; all I could sneak away. And bullets. Guns not much good without them, hey?"

"Curley . . . you're a lifesaver," said Will. "How can we ever repay you for this?"

"Heh. If I live tomorrow, that's payment enough for me." Curley screwed his face up into a smile.

"Curley, can I ask you something before we go?" Juice walked over to clasp hands with the scout. The Indian man grunted noncommittally, so Juice pressed ahead. "Why is it you're with the U.S. Army? Wouldn't it make more sense for you to be fighting to protect land that's yours?"

The scout shrugged. "It's not hard to see who will win this war. Indian tribes fight amongst themselves instead of against common foe. Maybe not tomorrow, but someday white men will rule this land. I'm just siding with the winner, hey?"

"Very astute," said Will. "May you live to enjoy it."

"Heh. I plan to. Now go before anyone notices his horse is gone." Curley saluted them all in the darkness. Then he trotted off over the hill back toward the camp.

There was a long pause.

"Which way is east?" asked Will.

CHAPTER NINE

30 miles to water, 20 miles to wood,
10 miles to hell and I gone there for good.

-Found carved on a deserted shack near Chadron,
Nebraska

August, 1876
Ogallala, Nebraska

A more adventurous traveler than Sally might have
described the journey from Little Bighorn to Fort Laramie
as *interesting*, but she found it more of an exhausting
daily chore than anything to be relished. She scouted
often to find safe routes through the hills. As the only
one with any riding experience at all, Shannon spent a lot
of her time teaching the others to ride and care for their
horses. They all spent a lot of time bemoaning the loss of
modern conveniences. Sally missed bottled water,
sunscreen, and potato chips. Will missed roads, his iPod,
and pizza. Ace hated being stuck on the ground, or even
worse, on a horse, and wished that Civil War-era firearms
weren't so temperamental. Shannon spoke volumes about
diet soda, and the joys of insect repellent. Juice said all he
wanted was a toothbrush.

And they all missed plumbing.

They stopped at each river and did their best to
bathe and wash out their clothes while watering the

horses and refilling their canteens. None of them had much in the way of survival skills, so they had rationed their food the best they could. The food, a term they used with reservations, consisted of hard tack biscuits, jerky, and dried fruit.

Eventually they'd been forced to hunt. Sally used her speed to bag a couple of rabbits and Ace managed to bring down a wild turkey. They had a nice little barbecue that night under the stars. It was good enough that for a little while they all felt more like they were camping than merely surviving.

The group stayed away from native American tribes as best they could to avoid any potential hostilities. Although Juice was loathe to do so, he allowed Shannon to raid some camps for a few supplies and trinkets which they could possibly trade.

By the time they made it to Fort Laramie, they were all a few pounds lighter but in good spirits. They'd had two weeks to prepare their acts and it was there that Mohawk William Kramer's Traveling Circus and Revue made their first performance.

They'd modified their costumes to give them a more festive appearance. Will wore the least-tattered of the cavalry uniforms and a Sioux headdress that Shannon had stolen from a tepee. Juice wore a loincloth over his uniform pants, Indian-style, and no shirt, to show off his powerful physique. Shannon wore her bodysuit without the cloak or hood and some silver jewelry she'd also taken. They'd altered Shannon's cloak and hood into a fairly scandalous outfit for Ace. Sally wore the smallest of the cavalry uniforms, albeit without the jacket.

They kept Will's spur-of-the-moment identities. Juice, as Jimbo, the World's Strongest Man, would amaze people with feats of strength. Shannon, Shandini the Great, would use her power to become insubstantial to escape from any bonds in which she was placed. Sally would perform sleight-of-hand tricks as Sally

Swift, Fastest Hands in the West. Ace would belly-dance to draw a lot of attention from the largely-male audience with her taut body and exotic looks. Will would work the crowd with his practiced stage-banter. And should he find a guitar, perhaps he'd strike up a tune or two.

Their performance went over pretty well. They'd had little time to practice or put together any semblance of professionalism, but their audience consisted largely of traders who'd been out in the wilds a long time. The men hooted and howled at the women, cheered and whistled every time Juice lifted something massive, and heckled Will enthusiastically.

In the end, they made enough money to purchase new supplies for their travels, as well as some period-suitable clothing. They also purchased three additional pistols and bullets. Juice wanted everyone to be armed. People in this time period understood guns, and respected them, he explained. There would be fewer questions to answer if they could defuse any troublesome situations by pointing a gun rather than blatantly using any parahuman abilities. Sally asked for and received the smallest two-shot derringer in the general store. It looked like a toy, but the proprietor assured them it was lethal at ranges up to fifteen feet. Will selected a regular six-shooter, like the ones Curley had given to Juice and Shannon. Ace was happy with the Winchester rifle from the cavalry camp, but Juice ordered her to also take a holdout pistol for herself. Besides his pistol, Juice carried the other rifle.

When they rode out from Laramie, heading south along the trail to Cheyenne and the Union Pacific Railroad, they felt quite pleased with themselves. Clean clothes, fresh food, and Will plucking away at a cheap guitar he'd found in a dusty corner of the general store had done wonders for their morale.

The first night out from Laramie, Sally woke suddenly from a particularly vibrant dream about Jason and sat up with a start.

"You all right?" Shannon asked. She was on late watch, and whittled away at a stick to pass the time.

"Yeah," sighed Sally. She found her canteen and took a few sips. Then she sat down, wrapping her blanket around herself, and stared into the embers of the fire.

"For what it's worth," said Shannon. "I'm sorry about what happened."

Sally looked at her in surprise. The apology was both unsolicited and unexpected. "What exactly did happen?"

Shannon shrugged. "I made a mistake. And you and Jason are the ones paying for it. I've felt really bad about it, but I didn't know how to tell you."

"Did you sleep with him?" Sally's tone was frosty.

"No. Well, not since the Academy, but you knew about that, right?"

Sally felt her cheeks growing hot. "He never said, but I thought as much. What were you doing in his room?"

"I was going to seduce him. I'm not going to lie to you about that. I guess you always have a special place in your heart for your first lover. I wanted to see if it was a fluke."

"A fluke? You were just going to . . . to use him?" Sally struggled to keep her voice quiet so as to not wake the others.

Shannon's face fell. "I suppose that's as good a word as any. But he said no."

"Was that before or after I walked in?"

"Before. He said you two were a couple."

"So what were you doing in his lap?" Sally hugged her knees.

Now it was Shannon's turn to sigh. "Trying to convince him anyway. I didn't . . . I don't want him for a boyfriend. I don't need that particular complication in my life with my work for Homeland Security. I just wanted to get laid. By him." She set down her knife and piece of wood. "I guess I'm a pretty shallow person. Anyway, I'm sorry."

"Can I ask you something?"

"Sure."

"What did he say about us . . . I mean, him and me?" Sally couldn't look toward Shannon.

"He just said that you were his girlfriend and he cared about you a lot and didn't want to screw that up," said Shannon.

Sally smiled. "That sounds just like him."

"He's a good guy, you know. You should really get back together with him."

"That might be a problem. He won't be born for another hundred and ten years."

Shannon grinned. "Kind of gives a whole new meaning to the term long distance relationship."

After their nighttime conversation, Sally found it a lot easier to talk to Shannon, and in the process discovered a new friend in the Irish-Japanese girl.

Cheyenne was a bustling little town. They decided to see if they could avoid having to do any more performances and sold the horses for rail fare. "Now that we're in a more populous region," said Juice, "I want us to keep absolutely as low a profile as possible." They bought train fare as far as Chicago. Juice and Will had conferred and decided that Boston was probably the best bet for an end destination in America. From there they should be able to board a ship headed for Europe and make their way to Austria.

"What happens when we get to Chicago and need money?" asked Sally.

"I'm sure some opportunity will present itself," replied Juice.

They boarded the train and found it a welcome switch from traveling through the wilderness. The seats were comfortable, the breeze blowing through the cars was pleasant, and the rhythmic sound of the engine chugging away lulled Sally to sleep.

That all ended when the engine broke down five miles out of Ogallala, Nebraska. The train ground to a halt in the middle of the prairie and Sally sat up and looked around. She wondered if they were taking on water or passengers or something, but there seemed to be nothing and nobody around for miles. Will asked the conductor what happened and was informed the engine had thrown a rod and wouldn't be going any further. It would be a few days' wait while the railroad brought a heavy engine in from Cheyenne to tow the broken locomotive onto a siding so a new engine could complete the trip.

After riding for more than a hundred miles on horseback, a five-mile stroll seemed simple and relaxing to the time-displaced heroes, even burdened by their valises. Some of the passengers opted to wait with the broken train while others decided to walk to town. Halfway to town, a pair of wagon teams met them and brought them the rest of the way.

Ogallala was right in the middle of its busy season. Being a cow-town in the middle of summer, there were some twenty thousand head of cattle to the south and all the trail hands were staying in town. With the law of supply and demand in full effect, the Just Cause members acquired only one room in the second floor of Tuck's Saloon, at an exorbitant rate with meals not included. The Saloon was filled with cattlemen, who gambled, drank, and fought all night long. It wasn't exactly a restful place.

"We're going to run out of money," said Will after a foray to the general store for some basic foodstuffs the next day. "They're selling stuff at three, four times more than normal."

Juice counted the remaining cash they had left. "You're right, Will. This won't last us more than a couple of days and the train might not get here by then."

"You think we should break out the traveling circus again?" asked Sally. She hadn't been very excited about it that much in the first place.

"Actually, I've got a better idea if you all want to hear it," offered Shannon.

"By all means," said Juice.

"Everybody's playing cards downstairs. Why not gamble to increase our funds?"

"Well, for one thing we could lose. That's why it's called gambling," retorted Will.

"Not if we cheat," pointed out Shannon.

"Didn't they shoot people for cheating at cards?" asked Ace.

"No, wait . . . she's right," said Sally. "With Shannon in ghost mode, we have the perfect ace in the hole. We'll know when to hold 'em, and when to fold 'em."

"And when to walk away and when to run," said Ace. "I know that song."

"And so on," said Sally. "It's a good advantage and we won't get caught."

"Won't they get suspicious? Some of these guys do nothing but play cards." Will sounded doubtful.

Shannon shrugged. "As long as we pick hands to lose, it'll seem like we're good, but not cheating."

"We can't all play. It has to be only one of us. Who's going to do it?" asked Ace.

"Uh . . ." they all turned to look at Juice, who had an embarrassed smile on his face. "I—that is, my wife and I, we play a little poker up in the mountain casinos."

Sally's jaw dropped. "You?"

Juice shrugged. "Everybody needs a hobby. Mine happens to be playing cards."

"Are you any good?" asked Will.

Now Juice looked really embarrassed. If his skin tone had been lighter, he would have been blushing all the way to his scalp. "I netted about fourteen grand last year."

"Sounds like we have our man," chuckled Shannon. "Let's work out a system of communication and go make some money."

Half an hour later, Juice and the others went down to the main floor of the tavern. Shannon was already invisible and insubstantial, as it wouldn't do for anyone to see her snooping around the tables. Juice had made it clear that he didn't want the whole group kibitzing around him, so he suggested Will and Ace go find out if there was any news on when to expect a train. He smiled at Sally, told her to clean up as best she could so she could be his "lady luck," which made her blush to the roots of her hair.

Juice surveyed the room and looked at the various card games in progress and which tables had empty seats. "That one." He nodded toward a group of three that sat in a back corner. Sally slipped her tiny hand into his huge one and let him guide her across the crowded floor. He was easily the largest man in the room and people seemed eager to melt out of his way.

"Howdy," he said to the three mustachioed men at the table. They looked up at him. "Mind if I join you fellas?"

One man leaned back, sucked on a thin black cigar, and glared at him. "I ain't playin' cards with no nigger."

Sally felt Juice's hand clench and winced, but he made no other outward show of emotion.

"Relax, Hank," said the man in the middle. "His money's good as anyone else's, and if he's willin' to lose to us, I'm willin' to take it. You got money?"

Juice flashed some bills that he'd tucked into a pocket of his vest.

"Fair enough," said the man. "Grab some wood, stranger. This is Hank, and that's Joe. I'm Sam. Sam Bass. You heard of me?"

"I'm Jim, and no I haven't." Juice sat down gingerly in the chair, which creaked under his weight.

Sam smiled a predator's smile at him. "You will."

"Jesus wept, but you're the biggest damn cowboy I've ever seen," said Joe as he shuffled. "Whereabouts you from, Jim?"

"Boston." Juice tossed his ante onto the table.

"Five card draw fine with you?" asked Joe.

"'Cause if it ain't, you can always take your black ass elsewhere," grumbled Hank under his breath.

"Hank," said Juice with a smile. "I'm going to enjoy taking your money."

Sally sat next to Juice, held his arm and pretended to watch him play. Mostly she surreptitiously glanced around the tavern to watch for potential trouble. Occasionally she felt a brush of cool mist across her face as Shannon's ghostly form touched Juice with the code they'd worked out. Juice lost the first few hands, which made Sally nervous as she kept a mental tally on what cash they had left. Hank started upping bets, hoping to push him out of the game. When Juice took a large pot which almost tripled their starting wealth. Sally squeezed his arms gleefully.

The game continued for a couple of hours. Juice made a point of losing some large pots, which put the others more at ease when he won them back a few hands later. Soon the cheerful chatter waned as the pile of cash in front of Juice grew. Sally figured they had somewhere close to fifteen hundred dollars. Hank's face was dark red as he toyed with his cards; a lot of the money in Juice's pile had come from him.

"Well I'm hung if I can see how you're doing it," he said after losing another five hundred.

"Doing what, Hank?" asked Juice.

"Cheatin'."

Conversation in the immediate vicinity ceased as the loaded word hung in the air. People looked toward them with interest.

"Are you accusing me, or can't you stand that a *nigger* is kicking your sorry ass at cards?" Juice said softly.

"He's awful big, Hank," said Sam. "I hope you know what you're doin'. We all lost money to him. I ain't seen no cheatin'. He's just a damn good card player."

Sally was afraid things were about to get out of hand and tensed up, but Juice laid a calming hand on her shoulder. "Not that this hasn't been fun, but I think I'll call it a day. Joe, Sam, it's been a pleasure." Juice stood up from the table and turned his back on Hank to show the others he wasn't afraid of the man. "I think perhaps I'll see what other entertainment this town has to offer." He collected his cash and stuffed it into the pocket of his vest.

Juice and Sally walked out of the quiet tavern. Sally could feel every eye in the place focused on them. She kept glancing back toward Hank and the others, expecting to see pistols come out, but they managed to get out without any incidents. "Find Will and Ace," ordered Juice. "I'll bet we haven't seen the last of those guys. What'd we take off them?"

"About, uh, thirty-five hundred dollars." said Sally. "I kind of lost count."

Juice let out a low whistle. "No wonder they're pissed. Shannon, you here?"

She faded into existence next to him. "Nice playing, boss. I bet you'd have won without any help from me."

Juice shrugged. "Maybe. Certainly not so quickly, though. Sally, go."

Sally trotted off, careful to keep her speed down. She found Will and Ace at the train station. "I've got good news and bad news. What do you want first?"

Will smiled. "I've got nothing but good news. The train's on its way. It should be here within a half hour. What's your good news?"

"We've got enough money to go all the way to Austria and then some," announced Sally. "Juice had a really good run at the table."

"What's the bad news?" Ace's eyes narrowed.

"The guys he won it from are pissed. I think they might come after him."

Will shrugged. "So? He's bulletproof, isn't he?"

"No, she's right," said Ace. "We'll totally blow our cover if he gets into a gunfight. We'd better go find him. Maybe they won't feel so excited taking on a group."

They hurried back to meet Juice. He was talking in low tones to Shannon out front of the general store when they walked up.

"Train's a half hour away," said Will. "We going to have trouble before then?"

"I don't know," admitted Juice. "I really don't want to get into a fight, but damn, that guy made me mad. Calling me names I haven't heard for a very long time."

"Like what?" asked Ace.

"Hey, nigger!" shouted a voice from the direction of the tavern. They all looked to see Hank, Sam, and Joe standing in front of it.

"Like that," growled Juice.

"We done talked it over with Hank," called Sam, "and we reckon maybe he's right after all. Nobody wins that much that quick."

"We want our money back!" Hank had the flap of his holster undone. His hand hovered in its general vicinity, fingers quivering.

Juice put a stern expression on his face. "You boys lost to me fair and square. Looks to me like you're just sore losers." His courtroom voice boomed across the street. "Besides, there's five of us and only three of you. Hardly fair to you."

"You oughtta learn to count better, nigger," retorted Hank. "There's only four of you, and two of 'em are women. I ain't scared of them, nohow."

"Four?" Juice glanced around. "Where's Shannon?"

"Gone," said Sally, mystified.

"Better give it back, boy," said Sam. "Or there's gonna be trouble."

"You sure this is how you want to play it?" said Juice. "You don't know anything about us. We might all be crack shots."

Sam Bass smiled. "Well, I guess we're about to find out, huh? Maybe if you live, I'll let you join my gang. Fella of your size and smarts would go pretty far in that line of work. Better than driving stinking cattle."

Along the street, people ducked into doorways, behind barrels, and peered out windows. Sam and his two men stepped out into the middle of the street, standing in a line, clearly getting ready to draw on the group.

"You want me to disarm them?" whispered Sally.

"No. Do not do anything . . . unusual. In fact, step off, Sally. That little derringer isn't going to scare anybody." Juice didn't take his eyes from the three challengers.

"But . . ."

"Now, Sally." Juice undid the flap on his own holster. Will did likewise, a terrified expression frozen on his face. Ace calmly swung around her rifle and held it low across her body.

Sally stepped into the doorway of the store and wondered how she could possibly help if she wasn't allowed to use her speed powers. *Damn it all*, she thought to herself. *I'll use them anyway if I have to.*

In the silence, a shrill whistle from the approaching train sounded.

"We aim to leave on that train, Bass," called Juice.

"Oh, you'll leave on it all right. In a pine box!" shouted Hank.

With a thundering of hooves, a team of four horses pulling a wagon raced around the corner of the Ogallala House saloon, driven by Shannon and bearing down straight on Sam's gang. They dove out of the way as the team hurtled past.

Shannon didn't even slow down. As it drew alongside, she reached a hand down to Ace. Will and Juice leaped onto the running boards. Sally ignored

Juice's order about parahuman powers and flew out the door of the general store like a shot to climb onto the back of the wagon. Bass and his men ran to the front of Tuck's Saloon and untied their own horses to pursue. Cheers and catcalls resounded along the street as the cowboys reveled in the free entertainment.

Sally climbed up to the driver's box where Shannon held the reins with white-knuckled hands. "Where'd you get the wagon?"

"From a boy at the edge of town."

"With what? Juice has all the money."

"I, uh, made a deal."

"What kind of deal?" shouted Juice over the din of the horses and the clatter of the wagon.

Shannon blushed. "I showed him my boobs."

There was a brief pause, followed by a snort of amusement from Ace. The others quickly followed suit and soon chuckles and guffaws competed against the noise of the team. "Well, he was cute." Shannon giggled.

A bullet cracked into the tailgate of the wagon, followed immediately by the sound of the gunshot, which quelled their humor.

"Everybody get down," said Juice.

"They're going to catch us," said Will as he flung himself to the floorboards. Another bullet whistled over their heads.

"Then let's give them something to think about. Ace, if you please?"

"About goddamn time." She raised her rifle to her shoulder and sighted down the barrel.

"Try not to kill anybody," said Juice. He lifted his own pistol in as steady a grip as he could given the bouncing of the wagon.

"Hey," called Sally. "The train's behind us!"

"It'll catch up with us eventually," said Shannon. She shrieked as the wagon bounced over a small hillock like a speed bump and nearly threw everyone out of it.

Juice and Ace fired at the approaching Bass gang. They hit nothing but made the horsemen duck down along the backs of their mounts as they returned fire. One bullet splintered a sideboard; the others missed.

Ace snarled something in Hebrew as her rifle jammed. She dropped it and crouched down next to Will. He passed her his pistol. "Here," he said. "You'll get more use out of it than I will."

"Ow, dammit!" Juice yelped as a bullet ricocheted off his wrist. His pistol went flying off into the dust of their wake. "We're running out of guns!"

"Sally, get my pistol," called Shannon over the thundering of the horses' hooves.

Sally reached into her friend's belt, withdrew the pistol, and pointed it uncertainly towards the Bass gang. She slipped into accelerated perceptions, sort of aimed, closed her eyes, and pulled the trigger. The kick of the gun wasn't as bad as she expected but she still almost lost hold of it. As she opened her eyes, she saw Hank flying backwards off his horse, a look of surprise on his face and a hole in his shirt by the shoulder.

"Nice shot." Ace sounded impressed.

Sam and Joe slowed up their horses, evidently deciding that the pursuit of their lost thirty-five hundred dollars wasn't quite worth their lives; their quarry wasn't quite as helpless as they'd thought.

Shannon kept the team going at a good clip for awhile longer to put some respectable distance between themselves and the Bass gang. Eventually they saw the plume of coal smoke approaching from the west as the train drew near. Sally wasn't sure if it was going to stop as they waved it down, but the engineer tipped his hat to them and they heard the squeaking of brakes from the coaches.

As the train ground to a halt, a boy in his early teens, barefoot, and wearing a straw hat over a goofy grin jumped off one of the cars.

"Oh, Jesus." Shannon looked like she wanted to sink right through the wagon and hide in the ground. "This is his wagon."

Juice smiled. "Then it's only right we give it back to him. Plus some extra for the damage to it."

"So pay him already!" pleaded Shannon.

"We'll probably need all our cash money. You might need to use your other currency."

Shannon blushed as the others burst out laughing.

CHAPTER TEN

"Ere many generations pass, our machinery will be driven by a power obtainable at any point in the universe. This idea is not novel . . .We find it in the delightful myth of Antheus, who derives power from the earth; we find it among the subtle speculations of one of your splendid mathematicians . . .Throughout space there is energy. Is this energy static or kinetic? If static our hopes are in vain; if kinetic – and this we know it is, for certain – then it is a mere question of time when men will succeed in attaching their machinery to the very wheelwork of nature."

-Nikola Tesla
American Institute of Electrical Engineers
1891

September, 1876
Graz, Austria

Once the displaced heroes reached Chicago, it felt more like a vacation than survival, despite the stockyard stench that carried for miles outside of the town. While the train was on a maintenance layover, they bought luggage, new clothes, real food, and hot baths all around. Juice and Will sprung for shaves. If Will had retained his purple mohawk, it might have garnered them a lot of curious and unwelcome attention, but he'd taken a knife to it shortly after they left Laramie. Sally, Shannon, and Ace spent a lot of time fussing with the ridiculous women's fashions of the day: corsets, bustles, and petticoats. Sally was convinced that all the layers represented a form of medieval torture. Juice and Will were only slightly less uncomfortable in their stiffly-starched collars and layered vests and jackets, although Juice found himself a bowler hat that he said he really liked.

From Chicago, they took a train to Boston, where they booked passage on a steamship to Marseilles. Sally was terribly seasick for the first two days on board. The others were as sympathetic as they could be and brought her tea and crackers to settle her stomach. By the third day, she felt well enough to actually leave her berth and get up on the deck. As long as she didn't look down at the waves lapping against the side of the ship, the sea air did wonders for her demeanor and she was able to keep a couple meals down.

"Ugh," she said one night as she looked at her ribs in the mirror. "I've really lost weight."

"You know, there are women who'd kill to be able to say that," said Shannon as she idly turned pages in a catalog of the latest French fashions. "I don't think I've looked this *svelte* since my sophomore year."

"*Svelte*?" Sally laughed. "I can't even claim to be svelte. I'm too damn skinny. It's my metabolism. I eat like a horse and I can't gain anything. Between camp food and being seasick I bet I've lost ten pounds since we got here. And I didn't have that much to spare in the first place."

"Yeah, you look like you could use a milkshake or two. Or six."

The girls giggled at that.

"Don't worry. French food is all cream and butter and bread. You'll gain some weight back. I'm counting on you."

"Counting on me? For what?"

Shannon winked. "To eat my leftovers. I don't *want* to gain any weight back."

The rest of the seagoing voyage passed pleasantly. Sally spent as much time on the deck as she could, and wished she could get away with wearing much less clothing than current decorum permitted. She and Shannon grew practically inseparable. They made a special effort to include the standoffish Ace in their various Girls' Night functions. Unfortunately for their efforts, the Israeli woman didn't have much of a knack for social graces and seemed content to talk quietly with Juice and Will. Especially Will. Shannon suggested there might be some romantic sparks developing there.

Marseilles was as cosmopolitan a city as they'd seen. Will spent some time in the telegraph office to try to track down their objective. He found Tesla at the Austria Polytechnic institute, and so the team booked rail passage to the hamlet of Graz. The journey took them through Switzerland and the scenic Alps and as the leaves were turning, they arrived at their final destination. It took them less than a day to find Tesla and after his final class of the day had completed, he met with them.

Nikola Tesla, only a year or two older than Sally and Shannon, was a slender, intense man with dark hair and a narrow mustache. He spoke English, to their great relief. He listened intently as Will spoke to him about magic, identified himself as a fellow mage, and didn't bat an eye at the outlandish tale of time travel.

"Of course it would be possible. You're here, are you not?" he said. "We are all time travelers, of course, but most of us only move through it at a constant rate in a single direction."

"What we really need is a way to get back to our own time." Juice spun his bowler around a finger, a habit he'd developed since Boston.

"I see," said Tesla. "I'd suspect you all were perhaps insane, except for this man clearly knows about the mystical arts." He nodded his head toward Will, who bowed in respect. "But I'm only a dabbler. My knowledge of magic is far less than my understanding of electricity. And of that, I am still but a student. I'm not sure why you've chosen to come to me for help."

"It's because of how you integrate magic and technology," explained Will. "With your skills, you could possibly help me reproduce the instrument I need to work my own magic."

"Integrate magic and technology?" Tesla's eyebrows raised and he chewed on a pencil in thought. "What a fascinating idea. I've never considered it but now that you mention it, it seems so logical."

"Did we just change the future?" asked Shannon.

Sally shrugged. "How do we know we weren't the ones to give him the idea in the first place?"

"And you believe that you have the skill to effect a transport through time, once you've built your . . . instrument?" asked Tesla.

Will shrugged. "I hope so. Time travel is pretty new to me. I'm not sure how it works."

"I suspect you'd need some sort of anchor. Something that exists now and in your future."

"Like a building?" asked Shannon.

"Perhaps. Or an object. It should be a place or object with which you are very familiar. Magic is not an exact science, but I believe it would be fatal for you to materialize within solid matter."

Sally felt her heart start to race as an unpleasant idea popped into her head.

"That would tend to leave out most locations," said Juice. "How could we be certain we wouldn't appear in the same space as innocents?"

"Ideally," said Tesla, smoothing down his tightly--trimmed mustache, "you'd want to appear in a place devoid of people. You would also have to correct for the motion of the Earth through space as well. Certainly it will not be in this precise location in your future. But as you say, certainty is a problem. That's always been a problem with magic. It's one of the reasons I enjoy the study of electricity."

"What . . ." Sally's mouth had grown bone dry. "What if there was something that we knew passed through time from now until our own future? Something I knew where it was?"

"Huh?" Will's eyes widened as he tried to make sense of her statement.

Sally closed her eyes and spoke quickly. "Last month when I found those bones there was a horseshoe with them, and it looks exactly like one of mine right down to the chips and scars."

There was a long pause as everyone stared at her. "You, uh, want to run that past us one more time?" said Juice. "At a speed a little more . . . human?"

"Yeah," said Will. "You sounded like Alvin and the Chipmunks."

Sally explained herself once more, and all her fears came out as she talked. She felt terrified that she'd found her own bones and that she was going to die here in the past. The others listened intently.

"No wonder you've seemed out of sorts recently," said Juice. "Sally, I promise you we're not going to let you die here in the past. But it sounds like this horseshoe might be the very key we need. You say you left it in your suite?"

"Yes." Sally sniffled. She was nearly convinced that she wouldn't be making the return journey. But if it meant the others would return safely, well, that's what heroes were supposed to do: sacrifice for the greater good.

"And you know your suite very well. It's very unlikely that someone else would be in it. That's as safe an entry point as any I can think of," said Juice.

"I agree," said Will. "Now it's just a matter of getting there. Mr. Tesla?"

"Please. Call me Nikola," said the young man.

"Nikola, then. We're going to need the help of a luthier, some tools, and all your electrical knowledge. We're going to build me a new electric guitar."

"Fascinating. How does one electrify a guitar?"

"To amplify the sound," said Will. "I'm no scientist, but I know the basics of how to put one together. I'll leave the specific details up to you." He grabbed for some paper and fumbled with an inkwell and quill. "Um . . ." He looked at the others. "This is going to take awhile. You guys might want to find us a place to stay or something."

In fact, it took just under two weeks to complete the guitar. Tesla still had coursework to maintain and Will wasn't the best engineer, but with the help of the guitar maker, who didn't even *pretend* to understand what they were trying to accomplish, a solid hardwood body was shaped, with a neck, bridge, fretboard, tuners, and thin-gauge strings installed. Once the body was completed, Will did his best to explain the nature of electronic amplification to Tesla.

The young electrical engineer spent two sleepless nights mumbling to himself and drawing sketch after sketch of designs for the pickups which would detect and amplify the vibrations of the steel strings, which they'd had to have specially manufactured as the luthier normally strung his instruments with animal intestines and silk. Eventually, he decided upon one that he felt would function the best. He and Will built the devices and attached them to the guitar. Instead of trying to build an on board amplifier, Tesla dug deep into his magical tomes and came up with an enchantment that achieved an auditory effect which Will claimed in amazement was a close approximation of something called a *Marshall stack*.

While Will and Tesla worked feverishly to build the guitar and load it up with as much magic as they could, the others rested and explored the small hamlet of Graz. Juice stayed in the flat they rented; a black man in Austria was a curiosity and he didn't want to draw attention to himself or the others. Ace likewise stayed nearby, but her motives were more selfish. She spent a lot of time around Will when he wasn't working. Shannon claimed to have seen them kissing once and Sally told her with a smile to mind her own business. The two younger girls wandered through the streets of Graz together, looked at shops, and drank tea at cafes. More than once, they were forced to politely fend off the attentions of students at the Polytechnic Institute. Between Shannon's half-Asian looks and Sally's petite charm, as well as the mystique of being Americans in Austria, they found the earnest young men were very curious about them.

At the end of the second week, Will and Tesla had nearly completed the guitar. The last thing they did was to install a series of magical tone controls to modify the sound like an entire bank of effects pedals would have. Will acted like a kid in a toy store; the guitar that he and Tesla built was a far superior instrument to that he had carried previously. Its sound was thunderous, and as a magical conduit it was unparalleled. It had a very odd appearance, combining Victorian grace with modern design elements and Tesla's unique electrical architecture. Sally pronounced it an honest-to-God *steampunk* creation, and rolled her eyes when the others gave her blank looks. "They're called books," she said. "You all ought to look at them once in awhile. Science fiction? Ever hear of it?"

That afternoon, Sally and Shannon sat outside the small bistro which had become their favorite hang-out. They drank cups of strong spiced tea and nibbled on scones while bundled up against the chill of the Fall.

"You know, I could really get to like Austria," said Shannon. "I'll have to visit it when we get back home. You know, see how it's changed and all."

"Maybe it won't have changed all that much. Modern conveniences, maybe . . . but it might still be just as charming." Sally sipped her tea, careful not to burn her lips.

"I hope so." Shannon selected a chocolate-dipped scone from the tray provided by the cheerful hostess. "Say, look at that." She nodded her head toward a young man and woman arguing across the street.

The young man was angry, insistent, and gesticulated wildly. The girl, not much older than Sally and Shannon by her looks, hissed back at him in rapid-fire German. The man reached out and grabbed her arm. Her other hand looped around and caught him across the cheek in a lightning-quick open-handed slap. Sally was impressed. "She's fast. I mean, really fast."

"Should we intervene?" Shannon pushed back her chair. "Looks like trouble."

Matching red splotches colored both of the man's cheeks as his temper rose to the boiling point. He raised a fist up over his head. Sally checked to see if anyone was watching. "Be right back." She zipped across the street and closed her hand around the man's wrist.

"*Was auf—*" began the man.

Sally felt a little silly, confronting him in her fashionable-but-very un-super clothing instead of a costume. She raised her purse in threat. "Let her go, handsome, or you get the business."

The young woman looked shocked. The man glared at Sally and released his hold on the woman. Sally, her reactions amped up from her dash across the street, saw his jaw muscles clench as he started to swing at her with his free hand. She brought the purse up and around in a quick overhand loop. With a metallic *thunk,* it connected solidly with the top of his head. He dropped to the ground, knocked unconscious.

"*D-danke,*" said the young woman. "I . . . speak . . . small English."

"You're welcome." Sally beamed. "No reason to let him go on like that. He'll wake up with one hell of a headache and maybe think twice about picking on someone half his size in the future."

The woman looked confused as she tried to follow Sally's speech. Shannon hurried up to them. "What's going on? Everything happened so fast."

"It's all good," said Sally. "I was just explaining to . . . uh . . ." She shrugged at the young woman.

"Zala," said the woman.

"Zala," repeated Sally. "Huh. I was just explaining to Zala that hopefully this guy won't bug her anymore after this."

"I should say so," said Shannon. "What did you hit him with? I heard that from across the street."

Sally laughed and withdrew her horseshoes from her purse. "Never leave home without 'em."

Zala's eyes widened as she looked at the steel horsehoes.

"Great anti-mugging device. Maintenance-free. My grandma always said a lady should always have a horseshoe handy for mashers. Although . . ." Sally scrunched up her face. "I was never quite sure what a *masher* was."

Zala smiled. She had pretty, straight teeth. "Ya, ya. *Das Hufeisen.* How you say?" She pointed to the implements Sally held.

"Horseshoe," said Sally.

"Horse . . . shoe," repeated Zala. "Yah. *Wie der Blitz. Danke wieder.* Uh . . . thank you again."

"You're welcome."

"Zala looked helplessly at them. "You . . . names?"

"Oh. Silly me," laughed Sally. "I'm Sally. This is Shannon. We're just visiting here from America."

Zala nodded solemnly. "Yah. Cowboys."

Shannon burst out in laughter. "Such an impression we leave around the world."

The man Sally had hit groaned and stirred.

"Oh! Klaus!" said Zala.

"You better get going," said Sally.

"And so had we," added Shannon.

They headed in their separate directions. Sally and Shannon walked back toward the flat in which they were staying with the others. "You see her slap that guy? I wonder if she's a parahuman," said Shannon.

Sally shrugged. "She was pretty quick. I suppose there are parahumans here in the past. They can't have been very powerful, though." She reached for the doorknob and stopped with her hand on it.

"What's wrong?" asked Shannon. "You look like you just saw a ghost."

"I think maybe I have. My grandma said she got the horseshoe tradition from *her* grandmother. That's why she carried them as *Colt* back in World War II."

"Are you saying you think Zala is your . . . what, great . . . great . . . grandmother?" Shannon counted off generations on her fingers.

Sally shrugged. "I don't know. Speedy reflexes. Horseshoes. I'll have to ask Grandma Judy."

The next day they all trekked several miles out of the town and Will cut loose with some amazing magic, making sounds that none of them had ever heard come from a guitar before. When he used it to destroy, trees, boulders, and one small hill flew apart into splinters. But his power could also be used to repair, and the shattered earth swirled around to smooth itself out at the touch of his notes. Grass and trees sprang forth from the earth like a time-lapse film until there was no evidence they had ever been destroyed. Will's eyes shone and his body crackled with power as he absorbed ambient magical energy from the region, using the guitar as a conduit.

Tesla was very pleased. He'd learned a lot from Will's explanations, and felt that there were a lot of directions he could explore further. He was enchanted by Sally's description of Colorado and promised he'd visit it someday. He promised that he'd keep their secrets and wished them the best of luck in returning to their own time.

They booked rail passage back to the coast. Although they'd been frugal with their money, Juice was still worried that they wouldn't have enough to get passage all the way back to Colorado. Will solved that problem by conjuring up a bar of gold.

"Is it real?" Sally touched the cold metal in fascination.

"Yep," said Will with pride. "Good thing I'm not a greedy type."

"Hmmm." Juice frowned. "Did you actually create this out of nothing? You created matter?"

"Yeah. Why, is that a problem?"

"I thought I read somewhere that matter and energy can't be created, only changed."

Will laughed. "This is *magic*, dude! Physical laws don't apply." He strummed the strings once and a shower of rose petals fell from the roof of their car.

"Are you okay, Will? You don't seem like yourself," said Shannon.

"He's fine." Ace put a protective arm around his shoulders. "He's loaded with magic. That would make anyone a little weird."

"That's it. That's it exactly," said Will. He chuckled and the floral pattern on the seats of their cabin changed to a checkerboard.

"All right," said Juice doubtfully. "I just don't want it to turn into a problem."

"No problems. I promise. Not for us anyway. That bastard Frazier, though . . . He's going to have some serious problems." Will's joyful demeanor turned solemn. "I'll make sure of that."

CHAPTER ELEVEN

"What is life? It is the flash of a firefly in the night. It is the breath of a buffalo in the wintertime. It is the little shadow which runs across the grass and loses itself in the sunset."

-Crowfoot
Blackfoot warrior and orator

October, 1876
Denver, Colorado

The journey back to Colorado was eventful. A series of storms crossed paths with the heroes' America-bound steamship. In the mornings, they found the crew busy chipping ice off the decks. The choppy seas gave Sally another difficult bout of seasickness. She fell horribly ill for the duration and lost what weight she'd gained back during their stay in Austria.

By the time the liner dropped its gangplank in Boston harbor, Sally swore her feet would never again touch the deck of a boat. They spent a chilly night in Boston and gave Sally a chance to rest and recuperate from her massive illness. In the month that they'd been away, temperatures had grown cold and they all bought heavy coats for the rail journey.

As they waited for the train on the platform in Boston, a young black man came up to them, very excited, calling out, "John! John Henry! I thought you was dead in the War, down in Ala-bammy!" He ran up and pumped a surprised Juice's hand in excitement.

"I'm sorry, I think you have me confused with someone else," said Juice.

The man looked closely at Juice's face. "Well I'll be," he said. "You a relation of his? You could be his brother. I swear you look jus' like him."

"I'm afraid not. I was born here in Boston," said Juice.

"My name's Willie. Willie Washington. Named after the President," said the man with pride. "I work for the C & O. I'm up here with Mister Robbins, negotiatin' for steel prices. So you ain't got any family down South?"

"Uh, no. I sure don't. Listen, uh, Willie . . ." A shrill whistle sounded as a steam engine chugged alongside of the platform. Juice gave him a weak smile. "I'd love to stay and chat with you, but this is my ride here."

"Oh," said the man. "I didn't get your name, Mister."

"James." Juice hefted his valise and headed for the nearest car as the others watched him, entertained by his discomfort. "Nice to have met you, Willie."

"Same here, James." The man doffed his cap and walked away from the train toward the freight offices.

"John Henry?" asked Shannon. "Wasn't he that guy? That railroad guy?"

"Hey, yeah." Will started to unsnap the latches on the guitar case he and Tesla had built just before they left. "I remember that song from the Disney cartoon."

"Please," Juice sounded pained. "Spare us."

Will shrugged. "Suit yourself."

"Hey, maybe you're related to him. I mean, John Henry." Sally grinned at Juice. "I think I met my great-great-great grandmother in Austria."

"John Henry might not even have been a real person," said Juice. "A legend."

"You're pretty legendary yourself," said Ace. "It's not a bad thought that he might have been one of your ancestors if he existed, is it?"

Sally grinned at him. "I bet it's true. I'm going to tell your girls when we get back." She'd met his two daughters numerous times; neither of the teenagers exhibited the slightest bit of interest in anything involving their father.

"I'm sure they won't care in the least." Juice's eyes went far away for a moment, and Sally saw in him a father missing his children.

Temperatures dropped as they went further west, and by the time they passed through Kansas, snow blew through the air, accumulating along the dry grasses of the prairie. The train whistle woke Sally from a light doze. The cabin was cold and ice had formed on the windows. She ran a hand across the glass at high speed, melting the ice quickly with the friction. The sky was overcast and the countryside was completely covered with snow. Then she saw the reason the engineer sounded the whistle. A herd of bison trudged through the snow, their large furry heads coated with snow as they tried to uncover the prairie grasses.

Shannon leaned against the compartment wall, hunched under a blanket and snored gently. Sally leaned over and tapped her on the shoulder. "Huh?" Shannon opened her eyes and looked around blearily. "What's up?"

Sally pointed out the window. "Check it out."

Shannon looked at the herd in the snow. The train had slowed to a crawl. "I wonder if they're on the tracks or something?" She pressed her cheek against the cold glass to try to see toward the front of the train.

Over the clanking of the cars and squeaks of the suspension, three gunshots rang out. Two buffalo staggered and dropped into the snow. The sounds of masculine laughter, jeering, and catcalls could be heard from elsewhere on the train. Shannon and Sally looked at each other in horror. Another burst of shooting dropped more of the stately animals.

Shannon leaped to her feet, her face dark red. "This stops now," she muttered to Sally, and vanished through a wall to leave behind only a thin trail of mist.

Sally went out into the passage to look for the group of shooters. An icy breeze came from the open door at the end of the coach where a cluster of men had rifles out and laughed as they shot. Suddenly, the ghostly form of Shannon rose up in their midst. She dragged her fingers across her face, distorting it into a frightful mask, and screamed at them.

The men screamed likewise, and leaped from the train in fear, tumbling into the deep snowdrifts alongside the tracks. They made no effort to get back on the train as it pushed resolutely on past the slow-moving herd. Shannon solidified and looked very pleased with herself. "Did you see their faces?"

Sally frowned. "They could die out here, you know."

Shannon shrugged nonchalantly. "Seems a fair trade to me. Assholes."

"It's not right!"

Shannon's eyes narrowed. "Everyone has to die sometime, Sally. Not one person we've seen this entire trip is alive in our time."

"Yeah, but leaving them in the snow is pretty cruel."

"Not as cruel as shooting buffalo for sport. It's not like they were hunting for meat or something. Don't you know the buffalo were almost hunted to extinction during this time period?"

"Sure, but they came back. There are lots of them in our time."

"So that makes it okay that these guys were just shooting them?"

"Of course it doesn't. But it isn't any better for those guys to freeze to death."

Shannon paused, looking over Sally's shoulder at the horizon. "I don't think that's going to be an issue," she said quietly. Sally turned to look.

Four horsemen sat atop a ridge. It was hard to make out details at this distance, but their long dark hair, buckskin outfits, and unsaddled horses left little to the imagination. They began to ride downward toward the men in the snow.

"No wonder they hated white men so much," whispered Shannon.

"Shouldn't we do something?" Sally couldn't help but feel sorry for the men as they floundered around in the snow and tried to run after the train in spite of their scare.

"Look, what's done is done. If they're meant to survive, they'll tell their grandkids about the ghost they saw on a train once. If they're not meant to, what business is it of ours to interfere?"

"We already interfered. Or rather, you did."

"What's going on, girls?" asked Juice as he stepped up behind them.

"Nothing, sir," said Shannon.

Juice raised an eyebrow at Sally.

"Nothing." She felt her friendship with Shannon was starting to grow a little strained.

"Well, then let's get this nothing back inside where it's a bit warmer," said Juice as he guided the two of them back into the car.

The remainder of the trip to Denver was uneventful, if snowy. Sally and Shannon avoided speaking to one another about Shannon's actions on the train. When they'd stepped off the train into a chill wind carrying minuscule ice crystals, Will and Ace went to see about renting or buying a wagon and team and outfitting it for travel across the snowy plains. Juice, Shannon, and Sally pored over maps of the region as they tried to figure out exactly where the team's headquarters would be a hundred and thirty years later. They would have to place Sally's horseshoe where she would find it in the future. Once they did that, Will and Tesla had agreed that it would be the best possible chance for them to return to their own time.

Nobody talked about Sally's fear that she was destined to die. It was constantly in the back of her mind though, yammering to be let loose like a prisoner in chains.

Will returned without Ace, carrying his guitar case as if it were an extension of his own body. "Congratulations, we are now the proud owners of a Benchley and Rowe covered wagon with a pair Clydesdales." He winked. "Same as the beer company."

"Where is it, uh, parked?" asked Juice.

"There's a shop just up the street. Ace is supervising while the owner finishes outfitting it for us."

"How much money is left?"

Will extended his hand and dumped a handful of coins into Juice's upturned palm. "Enough for souvenirs. Not much beyond that, I'm afraid."

"*This magnificent feast represents the last of the petty cash,*" quoted Sally, turning to Jack's favorite standby movie *Ghostbusters*. She missed him terribly, as well as Sondra and Jason and everybody else. Now that they were so close to reaching the end of their journey, she really felt the rift of time between her and her dearest friends.

"Let's go have a look at this wagon," said Shannon.

They hurried up the road, keeping well away from the deep, ruts lined with frozen mud and horse dung. They passed several shops and a couple taverns on the way, all cheerfully lit with hanging lamps and the smoke pouring from chimneys promising warmth and comfort within. Sally shivered, wondering if she'd ever be warm again.

Benchley and Rowe was a large building with a tall façade and a lot fenced with split rails. Numerous horse-drawn contrivances were parked within it from basic haulers all the way up to fancy coaches. The proprietor was a fat man with a fringe of oily black hair, a gleaming bald pate, and cheeks reddened from exertion. A deeper, more pronounced redness around his nose spoke of much strong drink.

"Ah, good day t' ye, friends!" The man had a rich Irish brogue that immediately made them feel at ease. "Yer lovely companion said ye'd be arrivin' momentarily. Ay've just been takin' care o' last-minute adjustments. If ye're sure ye'll be travellin' in such weather as this, ye'll need the best that Patrick Benchley can provide. Sure an' that's me name . . ." He rushed behind the counter and emerged with an armful of leather tack and hurried into the back of the store.

Shannon grinned. "He sounds *exactly* like my grandmother."

"His assistant is fetching the horses from the stables. Aren't Clydesdales the really big horses?" asked Ace.

"Yep," answered Shannon. "They're the SUVs of horses. We should get where we're going with them doing the hard work."

Benchley stuck his head through the door. "Young Thomas just arrived wi' yer horses. We'll have ye ready in two shakes o' the lamb's tail." He vanished again.

"He's certainly eager to help," commented Sally.

"I kind of get the impression that this is his slow time of year," said Will. "I think we've spent more money here than anyone in months. Now all we have to do is find the right spot."

"Not much in the way of landmarks or GPS to help us, unfortunately," grumbled Juice. "We'll just have to get there by dead reckoning. Ace, I'm going to count on you to figure the distance and direction. You're probably the most experienced that way."

The diminutive Israeli woman nodded.

"Shannon, you're driving the team. I'll ride up front with you and keep watch. Sally, stay under the tarp and keep that horseshoe safe. Will . . ." Will's face broke into a cheerful, slightly zany grin. "Will, do whatever it is you need to do to prepare. I'd like to have a hot shower and sleep in a bed tonight."

"Amen to *that*," said Shannon.

Benchley came bustling back into the front room of the shop. "All ri', gentles . . . yer wagon's all loaded an' the team is hitched. Ay'm certain ye'll find it all in order. If ye'll follow me? Bundle up, though . . . it's ri' cold out back, and the snow's pickin' up." His bald head shone with a fine sheen of sweat from his hustling. He wrapped a thick wool scarf around his neck and jammed a beaverskin cap down over his ears. Thus accoutered, he led them through the cluttered back of the shop into the yard beyond.

The snow was really starting to fall and the wind likewise had picked up. Benchley beamed like a kid at Christmas as he cuffed the boy who fiddled with the horses' harnesses. "Well? What d'ye think?"

Painted in a fine, glossy black, the wagon seemed to glow in the darkness of the day amid the snow. Fine filigree in gold leaf decorated the panels in between the vertical supports holding up the large canvas cover. The wheels had small steel rivets nailed into them for increased traction in the snow.

The wagon would have seemed overly large if not for the gigantic horses harnessed to it. "Look at the size of those things," whispered Sally to Juice. "I bet they weigh a ton each." She stepped up to one of them hesitantly. She barely came up to its shoulder. It lowered its head and blew out a lungful of steamy breath which smelled sweet, like hay in the summer.

"Go on, miss . . . 'e won't 'urt ye!" The boy grinned.

"Uh, what do I do?" Sally looked up at the massive beast that regarded her with some sort of equine interest.

"Give 'im a lump o' sugar, or an apple."

"Oh . . . I don't have one. I'm sorry." Sally felt crestfallen as she looked into the mournful eyes of the horse. The boy stepped over to her and pressed an apple into her hands. He nodded as she held it up gingerly. The behemoth stretched his neck down and took the apple gently from her hand. Sally looked at the others and grinned. "What are their names?"

"Whatever ye want, miss," said Benchley.

"But I calls 'em Sampson and Delilah," said the boy. "Sam and Delly for short." He ducked a poorly-aimed blow from Benchley.

"Well, everything seems to be in order," said Will. "I suppose we'll be on our way then. Thanks for doing such a bang-up job on short notice, Mr. Benchley." He handed the last of their cash to the proprietor, who made it disappear.

"My pleasure, sir. I hope ye have a safe trip. The weather's not much good for travelin' now."

"We'll be fine, Mr. Benchley, thanks." said Juice.

Shannon swung up onto the driver's bench. Juice joined her. The others climbed up the short ladder in the back of the wagon and under the canvas cover.

The boy ran to pull open the barn doors while Benchley shouted some last-minute suggestions at them. "Light the lamps; they'll give ye a bit o' heat for those inside. There's blankets and furs aplenty for ye too."

Sally waved at the boy as the two horses pulled the wagon out of the barn into the lazily swirling snow. He waved back. She drew the flap at the back of the wagon shut. Will lit the oil lamps hanging from the overhead frame with a single strum on his guitar. Ace grabbed one of the blankets from the floor and wrapped herself in it as tightly as she could, then pushed out through the front to stand behind Shannon and Juice, squinting into the wind.

"That way," she said in a moment, pointing to the right. "I saw bridges across the Platte as we came into town. Once we cross one of them I'll have a better sense of where we are. What I wouldn't give for a decent modern landmark."

"Yeah, we'll have to complain about that if this doesn't work," chuckled Will as he lounged back against the sideboard and ran his fingers quietly across the guitar frets.

"Don't even joke about this not working," admonished Sally. "We've got to get back."

"Don't worry, Sally. All we have to do is get that horseshoe to the right location and then it's *sayonara, 1876*." Will smiled.

The Clydesdales were sure-footed despite the accumulation of snow and had no problem pulling the wagon, although they didn't move fast enough to please anyone. Sally, especially, felt impatient and Juice banished her to the back of the wagon after the fourth time she'd popped out of the front flap to check on their progress.

"Are we there yet?" she grumbled to herself.

A couple of hours passed and the sky darkened as the sun dropped behind the mountains. Soon it was dark enough that Juice called a halt for the night. "Without landmarks and the sky clouded over, we've got no way of knowing where we are for certain. It would be foolish to flounder around in the darkness out here. We'll camp here and find our departure spot in the morning."

"Early morning, I hope," muttered Sally. "I'm ready to shave my hair off. I'd kill for a bottle of conditioner."

Shannon laughed from the driver's seat.

Suddenly Sally's perceptions accelerated until the world seemed to be frozen in place. She didn't understand why; something had happened that she'd missed, at least on a conscious level. She looked around the wagon; nothing out of place. Will's eyes were half closed and he was locked in a loving embrace with his guitar. Ace was rummaging around in the bag of food. Juice had pushed aside the flap and was moving into the back of the wagon. Shannon was standing on the driver's seat, an odd expression on her face.

A slender feathered shaft protruded from her chest.

Sally screamed and pushed past Juice in a blur of motion. Shannon was already starting to topple off the wagon as Sally reached her. She slapped two more arrows out of the air before they could strike her friend. Another arrow splintered in slow motion against Juice's tough skin.

Ululating yells echoed around the wagon as several horsemen rode in on them. Sally dragged Shannon into the comparative safety of the wagon, and ducked under another hail of arrows. She forced herself to slow down enough to make herself understood. "Help her!" she hissed at Will, who looked stunned at the sudden turn of events.

Frustrated at her inability to move in the thick layers of clothing, Sally shrugged out of them until she only wore her corset, shift, and pantaloons. When she and Shannon had shopped for clothes, she'd made a special effort to find a corset compatible with physical activity. She took the extra half second to lace her boots back up, because she was going to need protection for her feet. She figured that she could act fast enough not to freeze to death for the seconds she'd be in the snow. To the others it would have seemed as if Sally's clothing simply exploded off her as she jumped through the flap and off the wagon.

She tucked and rolled as she hit the snow and kicked up a big cloud from the speed of her impact. She took a moment to look around and mark the opposition: seven men on horseback, all with long dark hair and various feathers, beads, and baubles decorating their garments. Three of them carried long rifles and the others were armed with spears and bows.

She scooped up a handful of snow; it was good, wet stuff, the kind that sent kids off building forts and snowmen. She ducked underneath the wagon, compacted it, and hurled it at 300 miles-per-hour at one of the riders bearing rifles. The snowball caught him high on the chest and sent him flying backward off his horse. She picked off the second in quick succession but missed the third as the snowball disintegrated in midair. He snarled and raised the rifle in apparent slow motion. Flame belched lazily forth from the rifle's muzzle. Sally easily stepped aside as the bullet smacked into the side of the wagon.

A wallop of sound burst the seams of the canvas wagon covering as Will unlimbered his guitar in preparation for some kind of magic. The Native Americans stopped short from the sound. One of them, braver than the others, loosed an arrow at her. Instead of slapping it aside, she grabbed it out of midair and flung it back at him. It whipped across the intervening air to pierce his forearm as if it were a bug to be put in a display case. He yelled in surprise and pain.

The wagon shivered as Juice leaped off it. Electricity crackled all around his body. Will must have generated a powerful charge to boost Juice's strength to Herculean levels. One of the riders yelled something incomprehensible and charged on his mount. Juice widened his stance and opened his arms. The young man leaned hard to one side and reached out as if to touch Juice. Ignoring him for the moment, Juice sidestepped right into the horse's path and dug in his heels, leaning forward, pushing his chest against the horse. The great animal's muscles quivered as Juice brought its momentum to a halt. The Indian flew up and over the horse's head to land in an undignified heap in the snow.

"Go away!" Sally reached for another snowball.

A blast of music tore the wagon's canvas into shreds.

It was enough to convince the Indians that they were out of their league. The injured ones hobbled back to their mounts and swung their legs over their horses' backs, and they rode away to disappear into the blowing snow.

"Shannon?" Sally asked Juice.

He shook his bowed head.

"No!" She climbed back into the wagon where Will and Ace knelt over Shannon. Her form seemed translucent and Sally realized she could see the wagon's floorboards through her friend's body. The arrow still protruded from her chest. "What are you doing?" she screamed at Will. "Why aren't you fixing her?"

He looked at her, sadness in his eyes. "I can't. I've been trying. Nothing I'm doing is working."

"No pulse," said Ace.

Juice poked his head through a tear in the canvas. "I don't know how long those bastards will stay away from us. I'm sure to them we look like easy pickings."

"Wait . . ." cried Sally, barely able to see through the tears coursing down her face. "Can't we do something? We're *superheroes!*"

Will frowned. "I'm no doctor, and I don't even think a doctor could bring her back. The arrow went in between her ribs. I think it hit something really important."

"Maybe we can use the snow to keep her cold, while I go find a doctor in town!" Sally said in a rush. "People come back from death all the time!"

"Sally . . ." Juice put a massive hand on her shoulder.

"No! She can't be dead! *It was supposed to be me!*" Sally collapsed onto the floorboards. "It was supposed to be *me!*" she whispered.

Juice didn't see any need to travel further. He found a shovel in the wagon and dug a grave in the frozen earth beneath the snow.

Sally laid her horseshoe on her friend's chest, knowing that in a hundred and thirty years, a few months ago, she would find it again. "I forgive you," she whispered. "I'm sorry." She couldn't watch as clumps of frozen dirt began covering Shannon.

They cut loose the horses from the wagon. Juice figured they'd have enough sense to find their way back to civilization and shelter. They watched the large animals trot off in the general direction of Denver. "All right then," said Juice. "Let's go home."

"Sally, concentrate on your horseshoe," said Will. "You know it well enough to picture it in your mind. Every notch, every place it's been rubbed smooth by your hands. Everyone else, concentrate on Sally. Better, put your hand on her. When she *goes*, the rest of us should be pulled along with her."

"Are you sure this will work?" asked Juice.

"Nope, but it's got to be better than the alternative." Energies swirled around Will in the snow as he played and his music warped the very fabric of reality.

CHAPTER TWELVE

"Parahuman problems generally require parahuman solutions, and it is because of that need that we come before you today. The laws as they stand now do nothing to prevent parahuman criminals from perpetrating their crimes against individuals and society at large. But those same laws make it illegal for those parahumans who would protect us to do so. The time has come for those laws to change, and this esteemed body has the power to effect that change."

-Adrian Crowley
U.S. House of Representatives
August 14, 1969

July, 2004
Denver, Colorado
Just Cause Headquarters

It was a much gentler magic that transported them than the storm which deposited them in 1876, thought Sally. She felt a sense of motion that had to be her body's response to traveling through the dimension of time at an unaccustomed speed. Despite being blind, deaf, dumb, and unable to breathe or move, she felt no sense of panic. She could tell the others traveled near her as they drifted through the fields of magic.

Gradually, her senses began to come back online, as if she'd been a computer going through a reboot. She no longer stood in snow, but on carpet. The freezing wind which had blown around them had been replaced by quiet warmth. A strange yet familiar smell permeated the air. It took her a moment to place it. It was hair spray. *Her* hair spray.

The room was pitch black except for the Happy Puppies screensaver on her computer. "Juice? Ace? Will?" she whispered.

"We're here, Sally," came Juice's deep voice. "Can you turn on some lights in here?"

"Yes, sir." She tripped over the edge of the couch and sprawled on the carpet. She picked herself up and got to the light switch by the door. A moment later the room was bathed in light.

Suddenly Sally realized just how incongruous they all looked in their Old West garb, as they stood in the middle of her suite. She longed to run to the bathroom and leap into a steaming hot shower, to use real soap and shampoo, and to wrap herself up in the thickest, softest towel she could find.

"Check your computer." Juice scratched at his scraggly beard, shot through with gray that he normally hid by shaving his whole scalp. "Let's find out when we are."

Sally slipped into the chair and wiggled her mouse. She entered her password at the prompt but the computer rejected it. She frowned and typed it in again but to no avail. She took a deep breath and typed very carefully, making sure the CAPS LOCK key was off and concentrating on hitting each and every key correctly.

Nothing.

She turned to Juice. "My password isn't working."

The door to the suite banged open. Three soldiers in full combat gear rushed in, P-90 assault rifles raised. "Freeze!" they shouted.

Juice raised his hands. "Easy there, son, we're not here to cause any trouble. Who's in charge?"

More soldiers took up positions in the doorway and the hall beyond. Sally felt very nervous with so many guns being pointed at her.

One of the soldiers spoke into his helmet microphone. "Command Center, you might want to page Ms. Goodwin."

"I'm already here, Sergeant," said a feminine voice beyond the door. A woman in her mid-forties dressed in a severe business suit stepped around the corner. Her shoulder-length dark hair was pulled back and she looked at them curiously over rectangular glasses.

"Be careful, ma'am," advised the soldier.

"Always, Sergeant. Well . . ." She gazed with intense curiosity at Juice and the others. "This is unusual. I'm Christine Goodwin, Homeland Security."

"James Forsythe. Juice. What is today's date?"

Goodwin raised an eyebrow. "July 20th."

"2004?"

"Yes. You've been missing for seven weeks, Juice."

"What's going on? Where's Doublecharge?"

"She'll be joining us shortly. Now, if you'll please divest yourselves of those interesting antiques you're carrying, we'll remove you to a more secure location." Goodwin crossed her arms in a no-nonsense way.

"I don't understand," said Sally. "Why are you treating us like we're the bad guys?"

Goodwin glanced at her. "Until we can verify your identities and that you haven't been turned by the enemy, we have to consider you prisoners. I hope you understand that this is for safety's sake. Now, if you'll drop those pistols and that instrument and come with us."

Will shrugged and laid his guitar on Sally's couch. "I can't promise it'll stay there on its own."

The others laid down their weapons. Their pistols and rifles which had appeared so shiny and new in 1876 seemed dull and fragile compared to the high-tech assault weapons the soldiers brandished.

"Keep your hands in plain sight at all times," said the sergeant. "Move. Single file. No talking."

They were escorted to the largest of the holding cells that Just Cause used to keep prisoners until they could be claimed either by local law enforcement or Deep Six. The troops stationed two guards at the door and more outside. Sally and the others were ordered to sit quietly and remain silent.

The locks on the vault-grade door slid open and hydraulics moved the heavy round door aside to reveal Dr. Grace Devereaux. Sally suddenly felt that everything was going to be okay. Dr. Grace, as Sally had grown up calling her, was the daughter of Lane Devereaux, who founded Just Cause back in the '50s. She'd cared for Sally's mother all during her pregnancy and had been the family doctor for most parahumans in Just Cause for twenty years. She was in her mid-fifties, but looked much younger; living in Paris agreed with the woman. She ran the International Parahuman Research Institute and was the world's foremost authority on parahumans and their powers.

Juice smiled warmly at her. "Grace, what a pleasant surprise to see you."

"Likewise," said the doctor. "They said you were probably dead. Or captured. I'm here to determine for sure that you're you."

"And then we'll be let go and someone will tell us what's going on?" asked Sally.

Dr. Grace's brow furrowed. "That remains to be seen." She opened her bag and removed some electronic devices and a palm computer. "Now then, you've all done this before," she said as she removed a plastic tube from a wrapper and inserted it into a device. "I have all of your genetic imprints on file." She held the device up to Juice, tube extended. "Blow."

Juice blew into the tube until the device beeped. Dr. Grace ejected the tube and sprayed something resembling an asthma inhaler into the hole before inserting a new tube. Sally and Ace each took a turn on the genetic breathalyzer.

"What about Will?" Juice asked. "His imprint won't be in the Just Cause computers."

"You're right, it's not." Dr. Grace popped a fresh tube into the device before she handed it to Will. "But it is in my own files." She looked around. "Where is Shannon Tokugawa?"

Juice's jaw tightened. "Killed in action. I'll give further details at debriefing."

Sally sniffled as fresh tears welled up in her eyes.

After Will finished his test, the doctor pulled a data card from her device and inserted it into a port on her palm computer. A moment later she looked up and smiled at them encouragingly. "They're our people," she said, her voice cheerful. "Confirmed to eight decimal places."

"Satisfied?" Juice asked Goodwin.

She glared back at him. "Not yet. It's one thing to confirm you are who we believe you to be. It's another to know that you haven't been tampered with."

"What exactly is it that you're so worried about?" asked Sally. "You think we're criminals or something?"

"Not criminals. Enemy agents."

"Enemy agents?" Ace leaped to her feet. "How dare you accuse us of that?"

Goodwin remained impassive. "We are at war. The Archmage's forces have gained a strong foothold around that damned magical mountain. Your teammate Crackerjack is currently leading those forces. You've all been missing for seven weeks. For all we know, the Archmage has been preparing you to infiltrate right into the heart of our defenses, here."

"Jack's leading his armies?" Juice's mouth dropped open in shock.

The door to the holding cell opened and in walked Switchboard, followed by the Lucky Seven's Juliet and a boy Sally didn't recognize. "Hell of a thing, isn't it?" Switchboard smiled.

"Juliet, what are you doing here?" asked Will.

"They pulled us off the front lines," she said in her soft, reedy voice. "They said there was a situation back here."

"Who's the kid?" asked Ace.

"Name's Michael Copeland," said Switchboard. "Top of the class in this year's Academy graduates."

"Copeland . . . Copeland . . ." murmured Juice. "That name is familiar."

"My father was Mento," said Michael. "He, uh, was sort of a bad guy. Went up against Just Cause in the '70s."

"That's right. Whatever happened to him?"

Michael blushed. "He, uh, went straight after that. Found Jesus. Married a nice mid-Western girl, and they had me."

"And you decided to go into the hero business instead? Good for you."

Goodwin cleared her throat. "This is hardly the time or place to interview potential candidates for your team, Juice. They're here for a reason. A gestalt."

Juice looked blank. "What's that? I'm not sure I know the word."

"It's something psi users can do when we get together," said Switchboard. "We can amp up each others' abilities. The whole is greater than the sum of its parts."

"We're going to cross-examine your minds," added Juliet. "Between the three of us, we should be able to find any sign that they've been altered in some way."

"Will it hurt?" asked Ace.

"Not at all," said Switchboard. "You won't even know we're there. It should only take a couple of minutes each. We work fast."

Juice cracked his knuckles. "Well let's get on with it then. I'm ready for a real shower, a change of clothes, and a debriefing."

There was no ceremony, no joining of hands or anything like that. Sally was a little disappointed in the lack of spectacle. Juliet closed her eyes, but Switchboard seemed to just unfocus his and Michael just looked around and grinned nervously.

"They're untouched, as far as we can tell," said Switchboard after several tense minutes.

"So are we cleared, Ms. Goodwin? May I assume command of my team once again?" asked Juice

A muscle twitched in the older woman's jaw. "Very well, Juice. Welcome home."

"It's about time," muttered Ace.

"All right, who on the team is here right now?" Juice asked Switchboard.

"Just us plus the other Hero Academy graduates. Doublecharge, Desert Eagle, and Mastiff are flying in on the *Marilyn*. They're expected within an hour."

"Fine," said Juice. "I want everyone available in the conference room in one hour for debriefing. That gives us some time to clean up." He paused, considering. "Have the kitchen throw together some trays or something. I haven't eaten in a hundred and thirty years, and I could get outside of a sandwich like you wouldn't believe."

"A hundred and . . ." Michael looked confused.

"One hour," reiterated Juice. "Sally, Ace, Will . . . hit the showers."

"Yes sir!" they chorused.

Five minutes later, Sally sat under the steaming hot spray of her shower and cried for the loss of her friend. Shannon's death weighed heavily on her. A hundred and thirty years meant nothing when they'd been talking mere hours ago. She hadn't gotten to say goodbye. Sally promised herself she wouldn't ever take a relationship for granted again. Life was too short, and too many parahuman heroes had the misfortune to die with their boots on, *killed in action*, as Juice had said.

Once she wound down her grief, Sally settled about the business of really getting clean for the first time in months. She worked half a bottle of shampoo through her hair followed by most of her favorite coconut-scented conditioner. She scrubbed her skin pink with her loofah and did her face mask twice. Once out of the shower, she took the extra time to blow dry her hair and brushed it until it snapped with static electricity, and then decided to leave it down without braids.

She knew she'd be expected to dress in costume for debriefing, but decided to wait until the last possible minute; she'd been stuck in stuffy Victorian fashions for almost three months of subjective time and was enjoying the freedom of being unclothed.

She called her mom back in Arizona to let her know she was back and all right. Her mother changed emotions so rapidly that even Sally had a hard time keeping up; one second she was relieved her daughter wasn't dead, the next she was furious that Sally had gone and disappeared for seven weeks. Sally looked up at her wall clock and saw that she only had five minutes to finish getting ready. She promised to visit just as soon as the whole mess with the Archmage was taken care of, and said goodbye.

Four and a half minutes later, dressed in full costume, Sally entered the conference room. Doublecharge, Sondra, Jason, and Switchboard were all there, along with Juliet from the Lucky Seven, Icebreaker from Just Cause's Second Team, the young psi Michael, and several other youngsters she didn't recognize. She squeezed Sondra and buried her face in the scent of her friend's feathered wings. They smelled like baby powder, like home. "I missed you," she whispered.

"I missed you too . . . but not as much as someone else," said Sondra. Sally nodded as her eyes fell on Jason.

He looked awful. His face was haggard, and even more stubbly than normal. He looked like he'd lost some weight and his eyes were shadowed by terrible dark circles, as if he'd hardly slept in days. He had a long cut on one cheekbone that was healing. Sally frowned and thought it looked bad enough it might scar. She looked around the table and realized he wasn't the only one in the room recovering from an injury. Doublecharge had a cast around her left forearm. Icebreaker had four parallel scratches on the side of her neck that looked uncomfortably like fingernail marks. Even Sondra had a bandage around one of her legs.

Sally slipped into the empty seat beside Jason. He smiled tentatively at her. She took his hand under the table and gave it a squeeze to let him know all was forgiven, and she didn't let it go.

"All right, let's get down to business," said Juice. "I know you've all got questions about where we've been and what happened and I'm going to do my best to answer them. Let me get introductions all around, and then I'll begin. After that I want a full report on the situation with the Archmage."

Doublecharge introduced the five new faces at the table. They were the just-graduated class from the Hero Academy. Michael, whom they'd met earlier, was introduced as Ment. He dressed all in black and looked like a junior extra from the *Matrix* movies. Next to him was a girl wearing a dark red cloak and a highly polished Romanesque helmet with a visor covering her eyes. A sword was slung on the back of her chair. She was Minerva, the granddaughter of the Just Cause founder Lady Athena. Another girl, a genetic dwarf, sat on the table beside Minerva, dressed in a white outfit with puffy tufts at her wrists, ankles, waist, and throat. Sally's first thought was that she looked like a poodle in her getup, but quickly squashed such rude thoughts. The girl was Snowball, a powerful ice blaster, on a par with the old Just Cause villain Winternight. Carver was a thin boy in a red and purple outfit who never sat still.

He could slice through solid matter with his hands, arms, or entire body if he chose. Doublecharge introduced the boy called Octane who wore no costume but whose body seemed to be made from shiny black goo. His body was made of a liquid polymer that he could reshape into any form.

The five Hero Academy graduates had been brought in as emergency backup when the majority of Just Cause disappeared. Doublecharge had her hands full with five new, untested members, and had assigned them to base duty.

Juice proceeded to recap events from the time they entered the Archmage's castle up to the time when Stratocaster brought them back from the past.

"Any questions?" Juice asked, forty-five minutes later.

"I've got one," began Sondra. "Why did you reappear seven weeks after you disappeared? I'd think that if you were traveling through time, you could have come back a lot closer to when you left."

Juice turned to look at Will. "I've been wondering that myself, Will."

Will looked perplexed. "I was trying for the day after we left. I thought that would be a safe time to return. But it seems that there is some kind of . . . well, I guess you could call it a buffer zone. The large expenditures of magic, from growing Mount Rugby to the broken spell that sent us back in time, kept me from bringing us back any sooner than now."

"I see," said Juice. "Sort of like magnets repelling each other?"

"Yeah, I guess," said Will. "But that's not all. There's going to be another huge magical expenditure. It hasn't happened yet. We only had a very narrow window of time in which we could have arrived and we only just made it."

"A magical expenditure," said Doublecharge from across the table. "Can you be more specific?"

"No I can't. But it's going to be very big. Bigger than anything I've ever imagined." Will's face looked drawn as he contemplated what it would take for that much magic to be used at one time.

"You think we're going to fail. You think he's going to win," Sally said. "Well, he's not. We won't let him."

"I couldn't have put it better myself, Sally." Juice smiled. "Although I'd probably have used a lot more words to do it. It's the lawyer in me." He leaned back. "Now, I'd like to know just what's happened during the time we've been gone."

Doublecharge and Christine Goodwin took turns detailing the events which passed since Juice and the others disappeared. The Archmage made his threat a reality, and Jack was leading the man's armies. Frazier had drawn a legion of the dead from the very bones of the earth, and his troops had gained a foothold and were slowly but inexorably pushing the edges of his territory further and further out.

The governors of North and South Dakota, Michigan, and Montana had mobilized their National Guard troops to try and hold the front. Unfortunately, the majority of combat units were deployed in Iraq and those left behind were undermanned and under-equipped. Redeploying troops back to defend American soil had begun, but it was a logistical nightmare and happening much slower than required. The President had ordered Just Cause and the Second Team to the battle lines, and called upon the other teams around the country to come and provide what support they could. The Lucky Seven and Divine Right responded right away to the call to arms. Within two weeks, they were joined by the New Guard and the Young Guns, as well as a handful of independent heroes.

Jack was either brainwashed or being magically controlled to fight for the Archmage, and he had become a fearsome opponent. The Archmage directed his efforts from behind the walls of his impregnable castle. He had outfitted Jack in a great suit of armor, with a sword of black steel. Their indestructible friend rode into battle on an enormous black charger that breathed flame and struck sparks from its unshod hooves upon the ground. Instead of slaughtering the National Guard troops they faced, the Archmage's armies captured and dragged them back to the castle as prisoners. Once there, Frazier used the same magic upon them as he had upon Jack, and so he supplemented his armies of the dead with civilians, soldiers, and seven parahumans that had fallen. Every day his armies grew and the defenders had to fall back. Units were being brought in from around the nation, but it wasn't happening nearly fast enough. The President didn't want to give the appearance to the rest of the world they'd lost control of part of the country, even if it was in rural North Dakota. Homeland Security was endeavoring to keep a lid on the severity of the crisis, because America's enemies wouldn't hesitate to capitalize on the situation if they understood how bad it had become.

Goodwin brought up a Powerpoint presentation, showing a map of the Dakotas and the Archmage's territory. Different-colored icons represented the various super-teams and military units. A sidebar, which showed unit strengths decreasing over time, painted an all-too-clear picture of a losing battle. She highlighted the salient points and then turned to look at Juice.

"We're running out of options and running out of time. If Stratocaster can't use his so-called magic guitar to stop the Archmage, the use of WMD has not been ruled out."

"Weapons of Mass Destruction?" Juice leaped to his feet. "These are American citizens we're talking about here! These are the people we're sworn to protect!"

The now-familiar tic appeared in Goodwin's cheek. "The fact is we are losing this fight. This man has invaded American soil and has attacked our people."

"Nuclear weapons can't be the final solution! That's like removing an ingrown toenail by cutting off your foot!" Juice's expression was thunderous.

"James," said Doublecharge quietly. "You haven't been there. You haven't seen what he's doing. Nothing we've tried stops him. Special Forces teams have disappeared and resurfaced later leading his own units. His damn dragons and . . . what the hell are those other things again?"

"Gryphons," said Sondra.

"Gryphons," continued Doublecharge, "are taking down fighter jets, helicopters, and missiles. He has anticipated our every move and countered it."

"You're taking her side in this?" Juice's mouth dropped open in disbelief.

"No." She glared at Goodwin. "I want to make that very clear. I've had to brief the President twice personally. I do not and will not recommend we escalate this conflict to higher levels. There has to be a way to stop him conventionally. All I'm saying is that we haven't found that solution yet."

Goodwin frowned at her. "He is the single greatest threat to National Security in the history of our country. He. Must. Be. Stopped." Each word was like a rifle shot.

"He will be, Ms. Goodwin. We've got something he can't have predicted. It's not much of a hope, but it's the best we've got." Juice turned to look at Will. "What do you need?"

"A good night's sleep, for a start," admitted the guitarist with a yawn.

"We could all certainly use that," agreed Juice. "Twenty-four hours' leave for everyone except for duty requirements. Starting now."

For the first time, Goodwin's face showed some real emotion. She was scandalized. "I don't believe I'm hearing this!" she cried.

"Ms. Goodwin," said Juice. "My people have been on high alert for seven weeks. Those of us who were lost in the past for even longer. We are all exhausted. I'm taking a single day to rest and recuperate before tackling this problem head-on. Is one day going to lose us the war?"

"No, I suppose not," said Goodwin grudgingly. "His progress hasn't been rapid, just steady."

"My wife and children have not seen me for seven weeks. It's been even longer for me. I'm going to go see my family before heading out to fight in this war. Any soldier deserves that much." Juice's eyes grew bright.

"Very well," Goodwin growled. "Twenty-four hours."

"Meeting adjourned," said Juice. "Everyone get the hell out of here and don't come back until tomorrow night."

CHAPTER THIRTEEN

Growing up is never easy. You hold on to things that were. You wonder what's to come. But that night, I think we knew it was time to let go of what had been, and look ahead to what would be. Other days. New days. Days to come. The thing is, we didn't have to hate each other for getting older. We just had to forgive ourselves . . . for growing up.

-The Wonder Years television series

July, 2004
Denver, Colorado
Just Cause Headquarters

Sally sat on the bank of the Platte River, several miles away from Just Cause Headquarters, and watched the water flow past. She'd spent the better part of a lonely, sleepless night tossing and turning, wishing Jason had been free instead of tied up with monitor duty. By five A.M., she'd given up the pretense of sleep and went for a walk.

She'd had no destination in mind when she set out. A cool front had crossed the region in the night and fog rolled across the area. She hadn't worn her costume and didn't use even the slightest bit of super-speed. She wandered north for awhile, then west, and eventually found herself on a bridge overlooking the river, near where she and Jason had parked on their first date and been interrupted in a make-out session by a patrolling cop. The sound of the water as it lapped against the banks soothed her and she decided to follow it for awhile.

After finding a place isolated enough she could no longer see or hear any traffic, she sat down on a rock and let herself stop for the first time in month. Tears spilled down her face, partly from grief and partly from the temporary removal of stress. She knew Shannon's death hadn't been her fault, and that it had somehow been preordained by the course of time, but that didn't make the hurt of losing a friend any less. The Archmage seemed only a distant threat for the moment, and she felt like she could take a deep breath and blow away some of her accumulated tensions.

Eventually, the sky brightened in the east and the fog began to lift. As it did, Sally's tears stopped and she felt empty yet somehow relieved. Soon she stopped sniffing, her cheeks puffy and tight from crying, and just watched the water pass.

"Goodbye, Shannon. Thank you for being my friend," she whispered aloud.

Her phone buzzed her a text message from Jason. *Where R U?*

River by our lake, she texted back.

Can I C U?

Please.

She felt her eyelids grow heavy and thought perhaps she ought to get up and sit on one of the benches by the lake so Jason could find her. Instead, she slid forward off the rock to sit on the rich earth at the river's edge with the rock at her back. Maybe she'd just close her eyes for a few minutes. It was so peaceful there with the constant, gentle rush of the water. *Just for a few minutes*, she told herself as sternly as she could. *This is no place to zonk out.*

Footsteps through the tall reeds brought Sally sharply awake. For a moment she didn't know where she was, and then her eyes found him.

Jason.

He was dressed down in baggy cargo shorts, a black muscle t-shirt, and blue Converse high tops. His hair flopped down into his face as usual and a few days' of blond stubble dotted his chin and along the bandage on his cheek.

"There you are," he said, and stopped several feet away from her. "I've been looking for you."

"I fell asleep."

"Are you okay?"

She smiled. "Yeah. Yeah I am. Come here, sit with me."

He stepped over a fallen tree and flopped down next to her on the earthen bank. "I'm glad to see you, Sally. I missed you a lot."

"I missed you too, Jase."

"Look, uh . . ." He blushed. "I'm really sorry about that whole thing with Shannon. It was really stupid of me, and . . ."

Sally touched her hand gently to his lips. "Shhhh," she said. "I know. We talked."

"Oh."

"It's okay. I forgive you, Jase. I love you, you big dummy." She punched him on the shoulder.

"I love you too. I wasn't really sure until you weren't there but now I know."

She crawled into his lap to embrace him and luxuriate in the feel of his strong arms around her. Her perceptions accelerated to maximum, something which happened often when she was with him. It was a reaction she couldn't always control; it was her subconscious way of making the moments last much longer. The only problem was that it was hard to interact with him. She had to concentrate to relax herself.

Her lips found his and she felt electric shivers course down her back. Her body ached with desire for him. She took his head in her hands, careful not to dislodge the bandage, and proceeded to kiss him with the raw, naked hunger of someone starving. Minutes passed and they remained locked together. Each heartbeat echoed throughout Sally's head like a thumping subwoofer.

"I want you," she whispered into his ear. She nibbled on his earlobe. He struggled to get away, and she squealed in delight because she knew it was one of his hot buttons. His muscles that could bend steel bars were no match for her quick reflexes. Jason lost his balance and fell backward onto the soft earth and Sally straddled him. His cheeks were red and she could feel him harden for her. She panted with exertion and lust.

"Right here?" he gasped. "Right now?"

"Yes." Sally swung her legs up onto his chest and yanked her shorts off her slender hips. "Right here. Right now." Mad with desire, she didn't care if the entire world saw her loving him. "There are so many things that could happen to us." She felt her eyes brim with tears. "We could die tomorrow. We could die today! I want you to love me, Jason, like I want to love you. Because . . ." She could hardly breathe because her chest was so tight. "Because right now we have each other, and that's the most important thing in the whole universe." She pulled her sweatshirt over her head to leave herself only in a skimpy tank top.

Jason's eyes were wide. "Okay."

The river continued its slow journey, the rhythm of its passage lending itself to their lovemaking. Sally slid back and forth across Jason's hips. The thin cotton of her top tugged at her nipples as she gyrated. She came almost immediately and moaned as she ground her pelvis against his. His eyelids fluttered as she dug her fingers into his thick chest. The muscles stood out in her forearms like ropes.

A flock of geese flew overhead; their casual cries offered a counterpoint to Sally's sighs. Jason felt like a molten steel ingot inside her. His hands found hers and she could feel them clench as he fought to last as long as possible, to prolong the inevitable. Finally, his back arched and she had to squeeze him hard with her thighs to keep from being bucked off as he finished; finished for *her*, because he loved *her*. The sensation of Jason's juices flowing into her after months of nothing brought her full-force to another orgasm, even more intense than the first. She cried out with it, primal and throaty, and then flung herself forward, her head on his chest so she could listen to the pounding of his heart.

Eventually, Sally climbed off him and found her clothes. "God, I'm a mess," she grumbled in a good-natured way. "No mysteries about what we've been doing today."

Jason smiled. "It didn't seem like you were all that concerned about appearances."

Sally smiled back. "I wasn't, Jase. That was wonderful. Best sex I've had in a hundred and thirty years." She pulled her sweat-matted hair into a rough braid. "I'm ready for a shower."

"Want company?"

"Yes, please, but can we sit here for a bit first? I need to be held."

Jason swung himself around to lean against the rock on which she'd sat earlier. Sally arranged herself into his arms. "What's on your mind?" he asked.

"I came out here because . . ." She took a deep, shuddering breath. "I guess I needed to say goodbye to Shannon. Everything happened so fast, even from my perspective," said Sally.

"So you two wound up as pretty good friends by the end?" Jason nuzzled her neck.

"Yeah. We talked one night. She said how sorry she was she'd put the moves on you. I forgave her. I guess we just kind of found each other because there wasn't anyone else we could really connect with."

After awhile, he asked, "Are you still mad at me?"

"No. I made peace with it in my own mind. I know that you had no intention of hurting me and that you pushed her away. I forgive you, silly boy." She twisted around in his arms and dug her fingers into his side, where she'd long ago learned he was extremely ticklish despite his innate toughness.

He yelped and flailed as he tried to worm away from her questing fingers. They wrestled until he achieved a superior position on her by straddling her legs and holding her arms out away from her sides. "So, you thought your *Drunken Baboon* style could defeat my *Iron Butterfly* style? I laugh at your insolence." He threw his head back and gave his best bad-Asian-martial-arts- -movie-villain cackle. "Now I shall apply to you the ancient technique of Japanese ear-nibbling."

"Don't you dare!" squealed Sally as she struggled against his powerful arms and legs.

"Ha! Foolish wench, you shall pay."

Sally shrieked with glee and flailed her head from side to side to keep her highly sensitive ears away from Jason's questing lips, teeth, and tongue. "No fair using super strength on me!"

Jason moved one hand to hold her head still and used his body to keep her free arm from doing much more than slapping ineffectually at his back. He went to work on her ear, teasing the lobe and nibbling at it. She moaned as shocks of pleasure shot through her. He'd been delighted the night he'd discovered that he could drive her wild just by giving her ears a little attention.

He moved a little bit too far to one side and she saw her opening. She lifted her head and nipped him right on the thick muscle where his shoulder ran into his neck. It was a playful, puppy bite that caught him by surprise. He lost his concentration and Sally slipped her hands free, wrapping them around his neck and pulling him down to her. She covered his face with kisses.

"Again," she whispered in his ear. "I need you, Jason. I love you."

"I need you too. I love you."

After their second bout of loving, they decided that as nice as it was sitting by the side of the river, the day was growing far too hot and the mosquitoes far too numerous. Jason offered Sally a lift back to headquarters.

"Not just yet," she said. "I'm hungry. Want to get something to eat?"

Jason grinned. "You just said one of my favorite words. Pie at Lazzarino's?"

"That sounds wonderful," she said, although she'd have gone anywhere he suggested just to be with him.

They went and had pie at the same little restaurant they'd been to on their very first date. Sally had a slice of lemon pie with a precariously-swaying tower of meringue that was like eating sugary clouds, while Jason demolished most of a Georgia peach pie. Afterward, for the next hour, his native Southern accent was much more pronounced, making Sally feel like a belle out with her gentleman. They returned back to headquarters and fell asleep together on Jason's couch in front of a DVD.

After spending the rest of day with Jason, Sally felt so happy she thought her heart might just burst. They ate dinner together in the cafeteria and talked about movies and music and similar things of little consequence. Then they took a long walk together, hand in hand, just enjoying each others' company. Afterward, they retired to Jason's suite, and Sally curled up in his arms like a gleeful puppy and they slept beside each other.

The next morning, the team reconvened in the conference room.

"I trust everyone enjoyed their furlough?" asked Juice as he sipped from a steaming cup of coffee with undisguised relish.

Murmured assents echoed around the table.

"All right, then," said Juice. "I've been reviewing the current situation in the Dakotas in depth, and I'm not going to beat around the bush with this. I think we need to rescue Jack away from the enemy."

"What?" Christine Goodwin was so shocked she leaped to her feet. "How can you think of one man when so many are at risk?"

"The Archmage has invested a lot of time, effort, and magical energy to make Jack into his General," said Juice. "From the reports I read last night, Jack has been at the forefront of every major offensive maneuver since being captured and turned. In spite of his great power, the Archmage has shown little in the way of imagination or true strategic thinking. He's banking all of his efforts on Jack leading his armies. I believe that if we take away his General, it will set his plans back significantly. It will create chaos and disorder in his organization. And into that chaos and disorder, we will be able to insert a covert team to take him down for good and end this war."

Goodwin opened her mouth to argue, but then apparently thought better of it and sat down again. "Well," she said at last. "I can't fault your logic, at any rate. I won't deny that your friend Jack has been a real thorn in our side since his conversion. But what's to stop the Archmage from just converting someone else to lead his armies? What if the next general is you, Juice? Or her?" she pointed at Sally. "Or anyone in this room or elsewhere?" Her jaw tightened, bones standing out in sharp relief beneath her fair skin. "Show me how your proposal will hurt him as much as you anticipate."

"I can't do that, and you know it." Juice's voice stayed even, but Sally saw a vein throb in his temple and realized he was furious. "But all the evidence I've reviewed points to him thinking in a very linear fashion, instead of having numerous contingency plans. If something doesn't go as he predicts, he panics and loses control of himself."

"Yes, and Juice was right about another thing . . . there is a lot of the Archmage's magical energy tied up in Jack," said Will. "That's energy he will lose temporarily if we can recapture Jack and break the hold on him. He'll regain that energy eventually, of course, but it'll take time. And during that time, he will be weaker."

"It's the thermal exhaust port in his Death Star," murmured Sally.

Everyone stared at her.

"Sorry," she said, trying to remember that not everyone on the team had her geeky sci-fi fan tendencies. "Every great fortress has its weakness; that's why every great fortress eventually falls."

"Sun Tzu?" asked Switchboard.

Sally shrugged. "I don't think so. It's something Lady Athena said to me once." She smiled at Minerva. The slight young girl raised the corners of her mouth slightly from under the shadow of her helmet. Sally had liked Lady Athena the few times she'd met the stately older woman who'd been one of the founding heroes of Just Cause along with her grandmother. She resolved to make some time to get to know Minerva better. For that matter, she thought, she really ought to get to know all the new members. They seemed so young to her, more from the lack of experience than an actual age difference. Someday soon, she would be fighting shoulder to shoulder with these young strangers, and she wanted very much for them to be her friends. She would never again let selfish feelings prevent her from forming friendships with her teammates.

"Sally, you're absolutely right, and Will, I can't argue with your logic either. I'm committed to rescuing Jack. I believe that will be the key to our success in this conflict," Juice said.

"Not that I believe for the slightest moment this is a democratic organization, but I believe I'd like to put this matter to a vote." Goodwin frowned.

"Of course." Juice folded his arms. "All those in favor of rescuing Jack?"

In unison, every person in the conference room except Goodwin raised their hands. "I see how it's going to be. However . . . Don't forget for a moment that you are all representatives of the United States Government and as such you are beholden to follow the chain of command."

"Believe me, Ms. Goodwin, I haven't forgotten that. In fact, I took the liberty of phoning the President earlier this morning to discuss our strategy, as I certainly didn't want to go against the chain of command."

"You didn't!" Goodwin was aghast.

Juice allowed himself a smug smile. "He's quite a pleasant man. Great sense of humor. And he has granted me full authority in resolving his parahuman problem. In fact, he seemed quite pleased that I was willing to accept the full responsibility for solving it. I'm certain you'll receive a memo from Homeland Security shortly." His smile faded as quickly as it had come. "Your services are no longer required here."

"This isn't the end! You haven't heard the last of me!"

Sally and several others burst into muffled giggles at the grade-Z movie villain language.

Juice glared at them all sternly. "I don't appreciate your Gestapo tactics among my own people, Ms. Goodwin, and I think even less of your willingness to resort to mass-destruction weaponry to solve this problem. You'll want to take care that never comes out publicly if you want a future in civil service."

"Just what are you saying, Forsythe? You'd leak that to the press?"

"It doesn't have to be me. There is a room full of people here and every one of us heard your statement. Trust me, it would be best for you to go back to your home office and play with your threat scenario simulations and terror assessments and let me do my job." Juice folded his arms to indicate he was finished with the discussion.

Goodwin's face was nearly purple, and throbbing veins stood out on her neck and forehead. She looked like she was going to speak once more, but instead just grabbed her briefcase, snapped the latches shut, and marched out of the room.

Applause broke out around the room. Juice tried to look angry at it but eventually he gave in and grinned at the adulation.

"*You haven't heard the last of me!*" said Stratocaster. Laughter erupted.

"In all seriousness, though," said Doublecharge, "she could really come back to bite us in the ass. She's got the Director's ear, and she's pretty influential. You've taken a huge risk making yourself responsible for this situation, old friend."

Juice ran a hand over his freshly-shaved scalp. "I'm not blind about how I've set myself up here, Stacey. But in doing so, I'm insulating the rest of you if we fail. I get to be the sacrificial lamb and the rest of you can continue with whatever Plan B you come up with. If we succeed, it only makes Just Cause appear that much better in the eyes of the public. Success is credited to the organization, failure is blamed on the individual." He finished his coffee with gusto.

"Boss, I don't know how you sleep at night," said Sondra, shaking her head.

Juice smiled back at her. "Usually because I'm exhausted. Now, let's see if we can't get a workable plan to recapture Jack. Will, you've been researching that. What's it going to take?"

Stratocaster stood up and paced around the room, making random colorful motes of energy float away from his guitar as he noodled on the strings while he walked. "As I see it, there are going to be five major obstacles to overcome in recovering him. First is his own natural invulnerability. We can't hurt him, or even knock him out conventionally."

"What about non-conventional means? Knockout gas, or psionics, or even more magic?" asked Switchboard.

"I expect that brings me right to the second obstacle, which would be his armor. I'm sure that Frazier has anticipated Jack's few weaknesses. The armor he wears likely protects him from such things as mental powers or inhalants. To be able to affect him at all, we'd have to somehow get him out of it."

Octane's body shifted into a fair approximation of a man-sized can opener. An oily, chemical scent exuded from him, like hot plastic. "All you need for that is the right tool."

"I hope it's that easy," said Stratocaster, "but I seriously doubt it will be."

"Go on, Will," said Juice. "Let's get everything else laid out on the table before we open the gallery to comments."

Stratocaster nodded and continued. "Third is Jack's sword, which is a magical weapon that has so far been able to cut anything put in front of him. It's a highly dangerous device, and I'm not sure I can contain it. As long as he's swinging it, it's a lethal threat to any of us. Somehow we have to get it away from him.

"Fourth is his horse. This infernal beast has powers all its own, from striking up flames with its hooves to causing fear and loss of morale to those looking upon it. He hasn't ever been unseated from it. I believe that it has the capability to carry him to safety as long as it can reach him. All pursuit of this horse has failed. We have to get him away from this horse and keep him away from it, or it away from him as the case may be." Will reached for the water pitcher in the center of the table.

"What's the last thing?" asked Sondra.

Will sighed, looking for all the world like a lost little boy. "The biggest problem of all is that Jack appears to have some innate magical ability."

"What?" cried Sondra in shock.

"I'm afraid it's true," said Juice. "Those of us who went back in time did so because of a spell which Jack cast, whether it was intentional or not."

"Well, you learn something new every day," grumbled Doublecharge. "So how does this change things?"

Will fingered a trill high on the guitar's neck, conjuring a miniature thunderstorm that wandered across the conference room tabletop, leaving behind a trail of fine mist that evaporated within a few seconds. "Being slightly magical himself makes Jack an excellent conduit for the Archmage's power. You could think of Jack like a solar battery. Frazier charges him up with magic and then turns him loose. Without Jack's innate power, Frazier would have to keep a steady stream of magical energy flowing toward him in order for his armor, horse, and sword to function as they do. He may still have to keep the charge going when Jack is out and about, but certainly at a diminished capacity."

"Assuming you're right, and I know that's a big assumption on our part," asked Juice, "Can we interrupt this flow, and what happens if we do?"

"No reason we couldn't. Jack could probably still function for quite awhile with the magic he's absorbed, but eventually that power would drain away and we could deal with him."

"The problem has been that we couldn't ever stop or hold him long enough," said Sondra. "It must be because of this magical transmission."

Will fixed all of them with a steady gaze. "I can block the transmission, but not for very long. When I do, it will be like a flash of lightning on a dark night. The Archmage will know exactly where I am and will make every attempt to capture me so he can absorb my magic, and as near as I can tell, I'm the only other mage left in the world. He takes me out, he'll have absolute power, and I don't think you can stop him."

Juice toyed with a pen in his thick fingers. "Then we'll have to work quickly, and in two groups. One will be charged with protecting you from whatever the Archmage can throw at you and the other will deal with Jack. Icebreaker, I think the Second Team would be best-suited for defending Will. You have the heavy hitters and the experience to fight against overwhelming odds."

"Thanks, I think," said the second-in-command of Just Cause's east coast team as her blue-tinged skin radiated waves of cold across the room.

"The interns will remain here on standby. We have a lot of resources pooled in the Dakotas, and I wouldn't put it past some of our old foes to try something while we're so distracted. Juliet, do you suppose The Spark would consent to return here as a temporary commander?"

The slight woman nodded. "I'm sure he would. With the Seven down to four these days, we're spread pretty thin. I'll ask him." She closed her eyes to contact the Lucky Seven's leader telepathically. A moment later she smiled. "He'll be on his way shortly. He suggests that the rest of the Seven be part of the team defending Will."

"I concur," said Juice. "We should keep those who know each other the best together. And Will is unquestionably the lynch pin for our success. If we lose him, we lose this war. The more help we have protecting him, the better off we'll be."

"That leaves us." Sondra gestured to the core Just Cause team. "We're on Jack detail?"

"He's our teammate," said Juice.

"Good point," said Doublecharge. "We should review our various training sessions to determine how best to overcome Jack."

For the next two hours, the team went over the various tactics that had been used against Jack, both successful and unsuccessful, in Bunker training. Everyone brought up theories on how to exploit various weaknesses of his. Many of these were dismissed by Juice as impractical or impossible to implement given Jack's current magical powers.

Eventually, they began to develop what they believed was a workable plan. After checking his watch, Juice ordered everyone to take an hour for dinner and mental health break. Everyone moved to the cafeteria and the discussion ended up continuing over huge platters of burgers, salad, and home-baked cookies.

After Jason had eaten his fill of six burgers with all the trimmings and a dozen peanut butter and chocolate chip cookies, he and Sally went for a walk around the compound in order to get some fresh air after being cooped up in the conference room for four hours. They'd only been out for a few minutes before they happened upon Will and Ace, who were doing a lot less walking and a lot more kissing on a bench by the path.

"Uh, we're sorry," said Jason, embarrassed. "We didn't know you were out here."

"No, that's okay," said Will. "We don't really have anything to hide here. We're just not quite past the high-school make-out stage yet."

Ace chuckled and stroked Will's arm. "Aren't we a couple, though? The punk rocker and the pilot."

"I thought something was going on between the two of you. I'm glad. You make a cute couple." Sally smiled.

"So I bet you're glad to have the new jet, huh?" said Jason in his best Southern drawl.

There was a long pause.

"What new jet?" said Ace in a strangled voice.

"You didn't know? Juice didn't tell you?" Jason's eyes widened. "I hope I didn't just blow his surprise or something. We got a new jet delivered this morning. I figured you would have known about it."

"I was . . . not on the base this morning," said Ace. "Please, show me."

Jason led them all to the hangar. Ace seemed nervous and jumpy and kept inching ahead, as if she wanted to cut loose and run all the way. She tugged at Will's hand insistently like an impatient toddler.

Sally looked at Jason with admiration, and thought to herself that she knew exactly how Ace felt about missing something important to her.

The tighter security procedures implemented since the Archmage began his conquest were evident at the hangar. Armed guards checked their IDs and spoke to them for several minutes in addition to requiring each of them to blow into a tube connected to a computer that read their DNA. Ace was quivering like a racehorse as the computer reported its results and the guards decided they were legitimate. The side door into the hangar swung open smoothly, spreading a widening arc of bright light from the interior.

Inside they found a gleaming jet which looked like a fierce avian predator at rest. It retained similar lines to Ace's erstwhile *Bettie*, but this plane was larger and had a heavier, armored appearance. Where the *Bettie* had been a transport jet with some combat capabilities, this one was clearly a fighting machine that could incidentally haul the team with it. Gun ports in its nose were clearly marked with stenciled warnings. Missiles hung in clusters under the variable-geometry wings, waiting to unleash different kinds of destruction. Tenderly airbrushed under the darkened cockpit bubble was a name in fine, swirling script.

"*Rita . . .*" read Sally aloud. "Hayworth?"

"Of course," whispered Ace. "She's beautiful!" She ran her hand lightly across the smooth hull of the jet.

Jason elbowed Will, who gasped in surprise. "Looks like you got some competition, Stratocaster."

"Glad you approve," said a new voice. They all turned to see Juice walking into the hangar. "I must admit, I feel like a father who just bought his teenage daughter a new car. I wish I had keys to toss you."

Ace opened her mouth but nothing came out.

Juice chuckled. "She's fully-fueled up. Why don't you take her out for a spin, Ace?"

"Are you serious?" The diminutive pilot looked shocked and eager at the same time.

"Very much so," said Juice. "I need you to be intimately familiar with the workings of this new jet, because I expect we'll be needing some skilled flying from you soon. The more hours you can log in that cockpit, the more likely we are to survive an encounter. Consider that an order, Ace."

She drew herself up and saluted smartly with military precision. "Yes sir."

"Now go on, get out of here before I change my mind." Juice laughed. "No parties, no booze, and call if you're going to be late."

They all had a good chuckle at his nervous father antics as they left the hangar, including Stratocaster.

"You're not going out with her?" asked Sally.

"Are you kidding?" said Will. "I've ridden with her before, remember? I'll let her work out the kinks on her own without any distraction from me puking all over the cabin."

In a minute, Ace fired the *Rita*'s engines. They whined with barely-restrained power as she taxied out onto the pad in front of the hangar. The wings configured themselves into several different and interesting arrangements, folding and unfolding like a dragonfly's wings as Ace checked the articulation. She locked them into place for a vertical takeoff and brought the engines up to full. With a roar that shook the ground and cleared every last speck of dust from the launch pad, the *Rita* flung itself upwards so quickly it looked like it was falling *up*. Soon it was just another bright light among the stars, albeit one that moved with fanatical speed and purpose.

Juice looked back at the others. "Let's get back to work. We have a war to win."

CHAPTER FOURTEEN

Hold out baits to the enemy to entice him. Feign disorder, and crush him.

-Sun Tzu
The Art of War

July, 2004
Rugby, North Dakota

The sun still lay below the horizon and made Mount Rugby a dark shadow against the incipient dawn. The front lines were quiet as most of the units waited on standby and the soldiers grabbed what sleep they could. In spite of it being mid-summer, a chill floated in the air, carried on tendrils of mist which flowed outward from the Archmage's unnatural fortress.

Just Cause arrived shortly after midnight on the *Rita*, cloaked by the best magic Stratocaster could work. The zone which interfered with flight avionics over the fortress had expanded to meet the battle lines, so Ace set her beautiful new plane down well back from the front line. As the jet's engines wound down to a standstill, the members of Just Cause offloaded six of the seven robotic horses they'd captured from *Los Vaqueros*.

Jason looked over them, his face twisted up into doubt. "This is really dangerous. I can't believe this is the best plan we could come up with."

"Relax, babe, it'll be just fine. It's easier than riding a bike." Sally leaped onto the back of her own horse. Each one had been fitted with a saddle and riding gear.

"Will, go ahead and gear us up," said Juice. "Then you'd better get to the protection zone."

"No kidding. Soon as I start playing, I might as well raise a neon sign ten miles high saying *here I am, come and get me*," said Stratocaster.

"You'll be protected," Juice said. "You've got the best and brightest heroes in the world ready to defend you."

"And me too." Ace checked to make sure her sidearm was fully-loaded.

Juice spent a few minutes on his radio, ensuring all the other heroes were in place. He nodded at Will. "Go."

Will struck up an unusual and intricate piece on his guitar. Bright energies swirled around Sally and the others as shimmering medieval armor appeared upon all of them. Juice and Jason looked magnificent in full plate with great Claymore swords resting across the backs of their robotic mounts. Switchboard's and Doublecharge's armor were of chain and plate, as was Sally's. Doublecharge discovered that she carried a longbow, while Switchboard bore a heavy spiked mace and had a large ram's horn slung at his side. Sally carried a standard with the Just Cause emblem and American flags hung from it. Sondra looked like she'd stepped right out of *Ride of the Valkyries*.

"Wow." Sondra fingered her metal breastplate in wonder. "I don't feel like I'm wearing anything at all."

"It's an illusion." Will finished his musical creation and let the final chord ring out across the open plains.

"Nicely done," said Juice. "How long until they come gunning for you?"

"No idea. Soon, I suspect."

"All right, people, let's move out." Juice kicked his heels into the horse's sides and it broke into a canter.

The others followed after him. "Defense Team, we are now on hot standby. Be alert for any incoming."

They rode quickly across the front lines and made for the base of Mount Rugby. As the sun peeked over the horizon, a sense of foreboding settled on Sally. The last time they'd approached the Archmage's home turf, they'd wound up lost in space and time; it was an experience she didn't want to repeat.

From the fortress above, they heard horns sound as the Archmage's troops spotted Just Cause. A few minutes later, they drew up against the foot of the mountain. Juice called a halt and nodded at Switchboard. "Call them out."

Switchboard took up his horn and looked at it uncertainly. "I'm no musician. What do I do?"

"Just blow on it," said Doublecharge. "It's an illusion too, but Will wouldn't give you a horn that you couldn't blow."

"I suppose that's true," said Switchboard, and raised it to his lips. A clear, bugling call issued forth from the mouth of the horn. He tooted it twice more for good measure.

A lone armored figure rode down the road toward them with a white flag flying from the head of his spear. With a start, Sally recognized the young Sheriff who had retrieved Jason when they'd first arrived in Rugby. His face looked completely lifeless, as if he'd been drained of all his vitality.

"State your business," he said without emotion.

Juice raised his visor and spoke with a clear, calm voice. "I am Juice, commander of the armies besieging your fortress. I seek to negotiate with my opposite among your number."

"Wait here," said the Sheriff tonelessly, and spurred his horse back up the road toward the castle.

The six heroes waited as patiently as possible, which was the purest kind of torture for a speedster like Sally.

She fidgeted and twitched with nervous excitement until Juice had to order her to remain still.

The sun gleamed behind the castle, casting a long shadow across the plains. A small group of riders came down the side of the mountain. Jack led the group. Sparks flew from the hooves of his great black horse as he led the group down from the summit fortress. The Sheriff was with him, as well as four other people. Sally examined each one for potential threats. All seemed to be people who the Archmage had turned to his cause: a soldier wearing fatigues under his armor, a woman wearing what might have once been a business suit, and two young Hispanics who would have looked far more natural in professional sports team gear and bling than the suits of mail they wore.

Sally's heart beat so fast and hard she was surprised blood wasn't shooting out of her pores with each contraction. Her perceptions rode on a hair trigger, and she barely kept them in check so she could still follow what was going on. If they zoomed up to top speed, everything around her would seem to stop and she could neither listen to nor talk to anyone else because of the widening variance between her personal speed and that of the rest of the world.

Jack neither raised his visor nor took off his helm, and crossed his arms with a clanking of metal. "Speak."

"All I see before me is a suit of armor," said Juice. "And no sign of the man I used to call *friend*. Is this some kind of trick? How do I know you are indeed the leader of these men?"

"I'll not remove this helmet," said Jack. "But listen to your gut, Juice. You know it's me."

Sally's breath caught in her throat as she imagined the wry grin on Jack's face underneath the black helmet.

"Now, I haven't got all day. Speak your piece and be on your way and perhaps we'll meet another time on the field of battle." Jack tapped the hilt of his great sword against the saddle horn for emphasis.

"An excellent suggestion." Juice stretched his neck to one side, then the other, and was rewarded with audible pops as his joints reorganized themselves. "*Let's play.*"

The code phrase, pulled from the movie *Desperado*, triggered a powerful spell which Will had embedded within the illusory armor. With a great squall of guitar histrionics, pure white energy arced between the members of Just Cause. Sally dove off her horse and moved to the middle of Jack's group. For a fraction of a second, she would be in the most danger because she was the only anchor for the spell, and during that time she would be frozen in place.

She felt the energies hold her in place as easily as if her feet were made of steel and someone had turned on a giant electromagnet in the ground. The spell's power formed a ring of energy with her and the others as edge points, and entrapped Jack and three of his people.

"What is this?" cried Jack as he brought his sword up in a threatening manner.

A magical vortex appeared in the center of the dome, similar to the one which had trapped Sally and the others and sent them back in time. This one was much smaller and completely under Stratocaster's control. The tug from it was weak enough at the edge of the dome that even petite Sally could resist it. Inside, it was a much different story as Jack and his three soldiers struggled to keep from being sucked into it.

"Attack them, you morons!" Jack yelled toward the two Hispanic boys, the only ones outside the field of magic. They drew their swords and spurred their mounts into a charge.

The ground heaved and buckled underneath their horses and threw the boys from their backs.

Sally heard Stratocaster's chuckle as if he were beside her instead of miles away.

The vortex spun faster. It shot off random sparks as it doubled, then trebled its pull. Unable to resist its fearsome power, Jack and the others disappeared into it.

The energy ring collapsed in on itself and exposed the Just Cause heroes to its pull. Sally steeled herself for a stomach-twisting ride and flung herself into the vortex. Within the magical gate, she felt her body turn and bend in strange and impossible ways. It wasn't painful, just terribly disorientating. She felt no sense of up and down; gravity was nowhere and everywhere at the same time. Lights flashed before and behind her eyes and a whine of feedback assailed her ears. The unpleasantness lasted for a few moments, and then the whirling stopped and reality resolved itself once more . . .

. . . into the confines of The Bunker.

Just Cause's underground training facility was already state-of-the-art. Nanotechnology had given it thick, energy-absorbing walls where the heroes could cut loose with their powers without fear of damaging anything. Normally, the stadium-sized room would be set up for some kind of training scenario, miniscule robots building up the setting one molecule at a time. Now it was empty, with walls and floor bare and the naked sodium arc lights high overhead. Arcane symbols were inscribed on the center of each wall, as well as the floor and ceiling. As the team arrived within them, a secondary spell linked into their armor activated. The symbols illuminated and burned with ghostly blue and purple flames, sealing the chamber from the Archmage's flow of power.

Stratocaster had labored for hours in preparation for this chamber to insulate Jack and the others from the reach of the Archmage's magic. Once inside, only the magic that Jack carried with him would still function. Without a link to the Archmage, Stratocaster hoped Jack's powers would wane quickly and they could break the hold over him.

The other heroes appeared in the same positions they had been in when the magical gate first enveloped them. The three soldiers with Jack looked around in shock. The members of Just Cause were better prepared and leaped into action.

"Switchboard, put them down," Juice ordered.

Switchboard focused his mind to force the Sheriff, soldier, and the business woman to slump forward on their horses, peacefully asleep. Jason and Sondra hurried to pull the the civilians and horses to safety.

Jack sparkled with his own magical energies as he raised his sword and charged. Juice leaped from the back of his horse, more comfortable fighting on the ground even though it put him at a tactical disadvantage against a mounted foe. As Jack's dark charger rode in, Juice's illusory armor vanished. Crackling electricity surrounded Juice as Doublecharge hit him with as much power as he could take. His strength and toughness escalated geometrically with the influx of electricity.

Jack's sword became limned with flame and cut downward at Juice, who ducked and rolled as the blade whistled over his back. Jack wheeled his horse around, bringing his sword up in an arc intended to cleave Juice in two. As his arm reached its zenith, Sondra flew past and delivered a hard kick to his wrist to knock his aim off. Overbalanced, Jack needed a moment to recover from his heavy swing. Juice braced his feet and swung a massive fist across the horse's face, which sounded like a ballplayer cracking off a home run hit. With as much electricity as Doublecharge had pumped into him, the blow could have knocked down a building.

Jack leaped clear as his mount tumbled to the floor to lay still. It burst into flame, burning into a greasy hunk of charcoal. *One challenge down*, thought Sally. *Four to go.* She had to wait for an opening to fulfill her part of the mission.

Jason body-checked Jack across the floor. Juice leaped on him in an instant and pinned his sword arm to the floor. Jason was right behind him as Jack thrashed on the floor with a strength he'd never possessed before. Jason flung himself across Jack's legs, adding his own strength and weight to Juice's until Jack was immobilized. As Juice worked at wrestling the sword out of Jack's grip, Sally darted in with a spray can in one hand.

She raised the nozzle and aimed it right at Jack's visor slot and depressed the sprayer. A thick stream of insulation foam shot out, expanding as it contacted the air. In her sped-up perceptions, the foam seemed to move with glacial slowness but she could clearly see it push into the helmet. The Archmage may have planned for the helmet to protect from physical or energy assault, but apparently hadn't anticipated a subtle insinuation as this. They'd argued at the planning session about this strategy Sally proposed, but even if it hadn't actually worked, the foam would still have covered the helmet and still made things more difficult for Jack.

In the moment's distraction from the foam filling Jack's helmet, Sally released every buckle which held the armor onto him. *Second challenge*, thought Sally. Jason and Juice, who had been unable to break Jack's grip on the sword, hurled him across the chamber. Jack impacted high on the far wall. Pieces of armor flew in all directions when he struck. The scattered parts flared into crimson smoke.

Still unhurt, he dropped to the ground and ripped off his helmet. He leaped back into the fray with superhuman speed and strength. His flaming sword whirled so fast it seemed like a solid disk of fire. Sally circled him as she tried to find an opening in his swirling swordplay so she could do something.

The sword flashed down and around, slicing into Juice's chest. He yelled in surprise and pain as he fell backward with blood spraying from the deep cut across his pectorals. Juice's supercharged toughness hadn't done more than provide a token defense against the magical blade. Jack squared off with Jason and pushed him inexorably back with flicks of the sword. Sondra dropped out of the air next to Juice. Besides Jason, she was the only one strong enough to easily move the big man, and she dragged him back to safety.

Jason dodged and ducked to stay out of range of that wicked blade. Sally saw his feet tangle in the legs of Jack's dead horse. The look on Jack's face was of murderous triumph as he brought the sword around for a killing blow. Sally flung herself across the room to hit Jack's sword arm with all her might. Somehow, impossibly fast, he twisted the blade in midair and suddenly the point was only inches from her sternum. She ducked under the edge and felt a line of fire across her shoulder and back as the blade cut through her costume and skin. It burned like acid, but she only cared that she'd deflected his attention from Jason.

Jason laid a massive uppercut inside Jack's guard. The impact lifted Jack up and away. His sword spun away to stick into the floor point-first. Then Jason was holding Sally, cradling her in his arms, trying to wish away her pain.

"I'm okay," she gasped. "Stop Jack before he hurts someone else."

Jason nodded and ran, leaving Sally to wince at fresh waves of pain.

Jack leaped back to his feet, his face red with fury. Clad in only a loincloth, his muscles stood out in sharp relief under the bright lights of the Bunker. Sweat glistened on his skin. His eyes were shadowed under his brow, but a gleam of hatred shone from each one. He looked like he belonged on a movie poster for some epic fantasy where women wore chain mail bikinis and heroes slaughtered orcs by the hundreds.

Except in this film, Jack was the bad guy.

He held out his hand toward the sword. It quivered, and then flew out of the floor to spin toward him. Sondra dove into its path and grabbed hold of the hilt in midair as it sailed past her.

"How dare you touch my blade, woman?" yelled Jack.

Sondra cupped her wings to resist the pull of the sword, but was forced to drop to the ground and brace herself with her sturdy legs. The muscles in her arms stood out in sharp relief as she tried to hold the sword back from Jack's will. "You can't . . . fight us . . . forever," she hissed through clenched teeth.

Jason reached Jack and wrapped him up in a bear hug, only to yelp in pain and surprise as frost suddenly rimed his arms and chest. He jumped back and slapped away the icy coating. Doublecharge flew over to help Jason as best she could; her electrical powers would be useless against Jack. Switchboard stood still with his fists clenched in concentration. Sally could practically feel the psionic energies he hurled at Jack, but so far to no avail.

Sondra's boots scraped across the floor as the force of Jack's will on the sword increased.

"Yield!" he shouted.

"Never!" retorted Sondra.

Jack made a waving motion toward Switchboard, who fell back with blood streaming from his ears. Sally tried to get to her feet, but the pain from her wounds made it impossible to do more than just sit hunched over in agony.

"Sondra, how can I help?" called Doublecharge.

"Get him to use up his power faster!" Sondra's boot soles squeaked against the floor as the sword pulled her closer and closer to Jack.

"Power?" laughed Jack. "I'll show you power." He flexed his fingers and the sword pulled Sondra off her feet. She extended her wings to keep from skidding across the floor and wound up gliding only a few feet off the floor.

Switchboard rolled over and squinted at Jack, concentrating so hard that his psionic output distorted the air between him and Jack, putting all of his power into a single telepathic spike to break through the magical shielding.

It all happened very quickly, even in Sally's sped-up perceptions. Jack's expression softened and he looked confused. "Sondra?" he whispered as she bore down on him, sword in hand. She couldn't turn or stop in time, and Sally watched in horror as the magical sword slid through Jack's torso and its flaming tip emerged from his back.

Doublecharge screamed for the paramedics.

"Hi, honey," said Jack to Sondra in a faint voice as his hands explored the sword stuck through him. The weapon wasn't burning any longer, but neither did it fade away like the bits and pieces of his armor and horse had. "I think I'm having a bad day."

"Oh, baby! I'm so sorry!" Sondra cried as she cradled his head in her lap. Her wings folded over them both like a feathery cocoon.

"Always said I was stuck on you," said Jack with the ghost of his wry grin.

A small army of paramedics descended upon the injured heroes. The five interns moved uncertainly among them. Carver and Octane hung back, knowing their powers were useless in a post-combat situation like this and they'd just be in the way. Ment went right to check on Switchboard, who was barely conscious. The paramedic feared he'd suffered some kind of brain injury. Ment took Switchboard's head in his hands and concentrated.

Sally knew from reading his file that if anyone could heal brain damage, it was Ment. She winced as a paramedic applied antibiotic burn cream to the long slice on her shoulder and back while another jabbed a needle into her arm attached to an IV bag. "Take it easy, would you?"

One paramedic started a bag of plasma and injected something into the IV while the other squirted medical-grade super glue along the edges of the cut and pushed the skin and tissue back together. The pain of her wound became more tolerable as whatever drugs he'd injected took effect. "This will probably leave a scar," said the medic behind her.

"Lovely." Sally made herself sit still and watch the proceedings involving Jack.

His invulnerability, long thought to be absolute, had at last showed its Achilles heel: he was vulnerable to magic. The medical staffers couldn't figure out how to remove the sword without causing further injury. "Even if we can get it out," muttered one of them, "we won't be able to repair any damage surgically because of his damned invulnerability."

"I can't feel anything at all," whispered Jack.

"I think his spine is severed," said another doctor.

Minerva stepped up to the group with Snowball in tow. She tapped Sondra on the shoulder. "We can help him," she said, "but you have to trust us."

Sondra wiped her eyes. "Do it. Let them work," she told the paramedics, who respectfully stepped away.

Snowball gulped as she saw the wound Jack had sustained. She glanced at Minerva, whose face was intense and shadowed under her helmet.

"Just like we discussed." Minerva said softly.

Snowball nodded and carefully straddled Jack. She placed one hand on the blade on either side of his body. "Hold him still," she said.

Cold white light illuminated the blade edges. The temperature in the Bunker dropped noticeably, an impressive feat considering it was approximately the volume of a dome stadium. Frost built up on the blade and around the entry and exit wounds. It was a slow, careful process, but when Snowball stepped back, ice coated the sword wound on both sides. Sally shivered; she could see her breath in the air. She couldn't imagine how cold Snowball must have made the sword. Jack's flesh had turned pale and he was unconscious. Sally couldn't tell if he was breathing or not; he looked dead. The air blurred around him. Sally thought it might be his remaining magical energy flowing away.

Minerva felt around Jack's torso and used her mysterious powers to somehow confirm what was going on inside him. "Good," she said to nobody in particular. She slid the sword out of him with her bare hands, but the superchilled metal didn't seem to faze her in the least. The blade made a scraping sound as it emerged from Jack's frozen flesh. Once it was clear, she tossed it away and it shattered on the floor as if it had been dipped in liquid nitrogen. She turned to Doublecharge. "Doublecharge, can you use your electricity to heat conductive metal?"

"Yes. What do you need?"

Minerva drew her own sword from the scabbard at her waist. "I need you to heat this until I tell you to stop."

"What are you going to do?"

"First I'm going to thaw the ice so I can work, and then I'm going to fix him. You have to trust me. I can save him."

Sally realized someday Minerva would likely be leading Just Cause. She carried a powerful, quiet strength about her that made one want to follow her direction.

Doublecharge weakened under the unwavering gaze of the girl half her age. "Okay, say when." She cut loose with a steady, crackling stream of electricity, directed at the blade of Minerva's sword.

Minerva watched the play of sparks thoughtfully, unaffected by the charge in the blade. "That's sufficient."

"Are you going to stick me again?" Jack's voice was faint. Sally jumped at the sound of his voice; she'd thought he was unconscious. But in spite of his pallor and bluish lips, his eyes were open.

"Yes, but only for a few seconds. You won't feel anything, I promise."

Jack cracked a smile, but it was only a ghost of his usual sardonic grin. "All doctors say that."

"When's the last time you were at a doctor, Mr. Invulnerability?" Sondra tried to smile through her tears.

Sally winced as Minerva slowly slid the heated blade into the frozen hole through Jack's chest.

Jack closed his eyes. "I'm going to have nightmares about this day for years to come. I wish I hadn't seen you do that."

"If you'd been more careful at the beginning of all this, I wouldn't have to do this at all."

Jack's brow furrowed as he tried to discern what was going on in the vicinity of his spine. "Anyone ever tell you your bedside manner leaves a lot to be desired?"

Minerva withdrew her sword, dripping with melted ice, wiped it on her cloak, and slid it back into her scabbard. "I'm not a doctor." She put her hands on either side of the hole in Jack's chest and leaned her head down close to gaze into the gaping wound.

"Uh . . ." gasped Jack. "What is she doing? What are you doing?"

Minerva glanced up at him. "Fixing you. Don't move. This will take some time."

"Don't move? Did she say *don't move*?"

"Yes, baby," said Sondra.

"Fine. Me and my severed spine will do our best to *don't move*." Jack grimaced at the discomfort.

Sondra laughed in spite of herself. That was the Jack they all knew and loved.

"Say, Minerva? Long as you're fixing everything, I've had my mind set on a tattoo . . ."

CHAPTER FIFTEEN

"I don't trust him." –Betty McCutcheon
"You know something? I don't think you could trust yourself."
–John Hull

> *-Deep Cover*
> New Line Cinema
> 1992

July, 2004
Denver, Colorado
Just Cause Headquarters

Doublecharge assumed command of Just Cause once more because of Juice's injuries. As soon as she was certain Jack had been secured and freed of his magical burden, she put in a call to the group defending Stratocaster and ordered an immediate retreat.

"That should keep him guessing." Will materialized within the magically-protected Bunker. His demeanor changed when he saw the Just Cause heroes receiving treatment for their injuries.

Doublecharge intercepted him with quiet but intense questions about the situation in North Dakota. He reported that four of the defense team heroes had suffered injuries severe enough to require emergency treatment. He'd transported them to the Institute of Parahuman Medicine in Paris, where they could recuperate under under the watchful eyes of Dr. Grace Devereaux. He also explained that they'd *lost* three more heroes.

"What do you mean, *lost*?" asked Doublecharge.

"Captured by the Archmage's forces," explained Will sadly. "I'm certain they'll be turned against us."

"Who were they?"

"Toxic, of the Young Guns and Chrome and Seahawk of the New Guard."

Doublecharge sighed. "Well, it could have been worse." She pulled out her phone and requested that the Command Center send her complete files on the three captured heroes.

"How bad was it here?" asked Will as he looked around at the evidence of the carnage from their battle against Jack.

"Bad," said Doublecharge.

Minerva spent a full day and a half putting Jack back together. She didn't stop to sleep, eat, or even to use the restroom. Jack passed out into a near coma according to the paramedics, who checked him as best as they could without disturbing Minerva's progress. The rest of the team stayed with them in shifts to see if she or Jack needed anything.

Nobody understood how she was fixing him, but his wound was unquestionably healing. "Hell if I know what she's doing," Will said to Sally as she relieved him for a shift. "It looks kind of like she's gluing him back together at a molecular level."

"Is it magic?" wondered Sally.

Will looked over at Minerva, who seemed fully aware of their presence but didn't stop her work. "I don't know. It feels kind of like magic, but I'm sure it isn't."

"Because the Archmage would be after her too?"

"Yes."

"Weird."

"Yes."

Will left to spend some time with Ace while Sally sat beside Minerva, her arms wrapped around her legs and her head resting on her knees.

"Sally? Sally, wake up." Minerva's voice was quiet. Sally started and looked around in confusion.

"Whuh?" In spite of her powers, she was never one to wake up at full speed, Sally's thoughts swirled in a muzzy haze.

"I'm finished." Minerva glanced down at Jack and made a slight smile. "Good as new."

"Is he going to be okay?" Sally pushed her hair back out of her eyes.

"Yes. He should awaken within the next few hours." Minerva yawned and let her hood fall back. Her shoulder-length brown hair was matted and stringy from being covered for a day and a half. "I think I need a nap. And a bath. And a toothbrush. And some ice cream."

"This is amazing," said Sally as she examined Jack's torso. She could find no sign of a wound; not even a scar. "Will he be able to walk again?"

"I suspect so, but we really won't know until he wakes up." Minerva staggered suddenly. Sally was next to her in a flash to support the small girl. Minerva felt like a fragile bag of bones.

"Let's get you out of here," she said, and nodded toward the paramedics who hovered near Jack like nervous midwives.

Minerva could barely stand, much less walk, but insisted on getting some food inside her before giving into sleep or submitting to a medical exam, which would have been Sally's first choice. Sally helped her to the elevator and then across the headquarters building to the cafeteria. Once there, Minerva flopped gratefully into a seat while Sally zipped around and filled a tray for the younger girl.

Whatever she had done to heal Jack had created a monstrous appetite within Minerva. She ate plate after plate of food until Sally's stomach groaned in sympathy. Along with all the food, Minerva also drained several carafes of soda and finally started to slow down with a fifteen-scoop sundae in front of her.

"Wow," said Sally. "Where do you put it all? Hollow legs? Wormhole in your stomach?"

Minerva shrugged as she licked a stray drop of chocolate sauce from the back of one hand. "I don't know. My powers usually leave me feeling kind of drained and hungry, but this is a first for me."

"If I ate like that, I'd weigh as much as Jason," giggled Sally.

"If I didn't, I'd waste away. My powers feed directly off my body mass."

"What? That doesn't make sense!"

"Actually it makes more sense than the way most superpowers work. Take Doublecharge, for example. Where does her electricity come from?"

"I don't know. I've never thought about it."

"It has to come from *somewhere*. That's physics. It's most likely she's a conduit for her power, moving it from wherever it is to wherever she directs it. On the other hand, if she generates her power, a reaction has to create it, and that reaction requires fuel of some sort. My powers emanate from within me, and they consume my body mass." Minerva took another bite of ice cream.

Sally looked at her with a critical eye, as if she were Juice. Minerva's cheeks had filled back in and her bones no longer stood out in sharp relief. "That's really weird. And actually, it's kind of scary."

Minerva smiled. "I've learned to adjust." She pushed her bowl over next to Sally. "I'm not going to finish all this ice cream. You'd better have some."

Sally reached for a spoon. "What exactly *are* your powers, Minerva? Nobody seems to really know."

The petite young girl leaned back in her seat and released a quiet belch as she primly covered her mouth with the back of her hand. "Excuse me." She yawned. "I think I could sleep for most of a week."

"Oh look, blueberries," said Sally.

Minerva looked around at the empty plates on the table in confusion. "Blueberries?"

Sally laughed. "*Blueberrying* is a term my mother uses. It's when you change the subject suddenly, presumably because you don't want to talk about whatever it is you don't want to talk about."

"Blueberrying." Minerva smiled. "Yes, I believe that's a very apt description."

"You don't want to talk about your powers?" Sally felt disappointed.

Minerva yawned so deeply it made Sally's eyes water. "Maybe another time. Right now I need to hibernate. Thanks for staying with me, Mustang Sally."

"You don't need to be so formal with me, Minerva. You can call me Sally like everyone else does."

"You can call me Minnie," said the younger girl. "But not in front of anyone else."

"*All active members report to the Bunker infirmary,*" said Doublecharge over their phones.

Minerva sighed with frustration.

"No, you go ahead and sleep," said Sally. "You earned it after fixing Jack. I'll cover for you."

"Thank you." Minerva trudged off towards the dormitory like her feet each weighed a hundred pounds.

Sally hustled back to the Bunker in a few seconds. Most of the team was already there. Juice had his bed tilted up, with a thick bandage stretched across his massive chest. Normally very expressive with his hands, he had to keep them still. Every once in awhile he'd forget himself and move them suddenly, after which he would wince and gingerly set them back by his sides again. The wound across his chest was deep enough that the medics had needed to use heavy-duty staples and repairs had been made to his pectoral muscles.

Switchboard was in the next bed over. He looked disheveled and looked like he was wearing a domino mask with the bruising around his eyes from internal bleeding. He had a medium-severe concussion and was hooked up to a brain scan. Psionic injuries were poorly-understood, and even the researchers at the Institute of Parahuman Medicine had very little practical experience with them.

Jack was awake and lay peacefully in his bed with Sondra by his side. She stroked his hair lovingly. He grinned and almost flirted with the nurse who was taking his temperature.

"All right then," said Juice. "We're a little beat-up, but we accomplished our goal and freed Jack."

Jack's grin was as authentic as ever, for which Sally was grateful. "Thanks for that. Believe me, working for that guy was no picnic."

"You were aware of it?" asked Stratocaster.

"Yeah I was. At least, at some level I knew what was going on."

"That's disturbing," said Doublecharge.

"Preaching to the choir, dear Stacey," said Jack.

Juice continued. "The reports I've seen from the front lines are encouraging. The Archmage has recalled all his extended troops and retreated significantly."

"It worked!" Sally grinned and reached over to high-five Jack.

"Sort of," Stratocaster said. "He's strengthening his current position. All we've done is cause him a setback."

"Which was our intention," said Juice. "And now we need to move on him while he's in disarray."

"Are you thinking of a full strike on his fortress?" asked Sondra. "That sounds ripe for failure if you ask me."

Juice shook his head. "No. I've been giving this some thought and talking it over with Stacey, Will, and Switchboard and we've come up with a plan which I believe has an excellent chance of success."

"Meaning it's got at least an even chance of not failing," interjected Jack.

"We're going to insert an agent of our own into the Archmage's organization," explained Doublecharge. "The agent will get close to the Archmage and will be activated at a critical moment, allowing us a strike right at the head of the organization."

"Cut off the head and the serpent will die," muttered Jack. "Nice theory, at any rate. Who gets to be bait?"

"Me," said Sally suddenly, her intuition running at full speed.

Juice looked at her in surprise. "That's right. How did you know?"

"Well, it just makes sense to me," said Sally. "When the moment comes, speed will be essential, and nobody's faster than me. You'll need someone who can move faster than the Archmage can think or cast a spell or whatever he does."

"Go on," said Juice. "You're on the right track here, Sally. I know you've figured it out. Share with us."

"Um . . ." She faltered and Jason reached out and placed a supportive hand on her shoulder. Her thoughts whirled as she considered possibilities. "The Archmage will certainly use his magic to check me to make sure I'm not a spy, right? So then I'll have to be unaware of it, which means some kind of psionic and/or magical thingie in my brain. Glimmer laid a lot of that groundwork in my head back in Guatemala. I'm the logical choice."

Juice smiled. "If it didn't hurt so damn much to move my arms, I'd applaud you, Sally. That was brilliant reasoning. I'm proud of you."

Sally blushed to the tips of her ears. "Oh, uh, thanks. I guess."

"It's going to be a very dangerous assignment," said Juice. "And if you're not up to the task, say so now and we have a second and third choice in mind."

Sally looked around the room at the other heroes. She knew any one of them would gladly step up to do this job if she refused. But how could she honestly live with herself if she turned down the assignment and one of the others died in her place? She'd lost friends down in Guatemala and Shannon over a hundred years ago. They died so that she could live; it was time she returned the favor.

She nodded. "I'll do it."

Jason stiffened beside her. She didn't have to be psionic to know he feared losing her once more, and this time permanently. She reached out, took his huge hand, and squeezed it reassuringly. He gave her a small smile, but pain showed in his eyes. He bent down and kissed her, sharing a lifetime of passion in a few seconds of close contact.

Sondra left Jack's side and squeezed her tightly. Sally closed her eyes and inhaled the baby powder scent of her friend's wings. "We'll make sure you come out of it all right," she whispered in Sally's ear.

Jack winked at her from his bed. He looked like he was ready to jump up and go back to work but the doctor made it clear he wasn't going anywhere until twenty-four hours observation had passed. "You'll do us proud, kiddo."

Sally looked back at Juice. "What do I have to do?"

"Come with us," said Stratocaster. "We're going to turn you into a ticking time bomb, Sally, one to finish this conflict."

"What a lovely legacy I'll leave behind me. *Salena Thompson, Suicide Bomber.*"

Switchboard chuckled, but then grimaced at the pain from his injuries. "This won't be anything so permanent or devastating to you. We promise. We've been talking this over thoroughly. You're going to be our ace in the hole."

"That sounds better."

Ment hurried into the room, his long black trenchcoat flying behind him and a black do-rag tied over his head. "Sorry I'm late," he said. "I never heard the page."

Doublecharge opened her mouth to say something but Switchboard was faster. "Ment, glad you made it. I'm going to need your help with some complex psionics."

The young psi grinned and slipped on his sunglasses. "I'm your guy, dude."

"Wait a second, he's part of this?" Sally was beginning to have second thoughts. And third thoughts.

"I need him," said Switchboard. "I understand what we're doing, but I don't have the kind of ability to perform it. Ment has those skills, but needs my guidance. It's just another form of gestalt."

"Oh."

Stratocaster led her and the two psionicists to an empty examination room. "Don't worry. This won't hurt a bit. I promise."

"What exactly are you going to do to me?" Sally hopped onto the examination table and laid back.

"I'm going to hide a spell in you that will go off when you receive the proper key, and then Switchboard and Ment are going to erase your memory of its existence."

Sally swallowed nervously. "So I'm the mad bomber after all."

"Essentially," grinned Stratocaster. "The spell is the bomb. The key will be the detonator."

"And Switchboard and Ment?"

"They're the guys who get to convince you that you'll be richly rewarded in the afterlife. Seventy-two virgins and all that."

Switchboard frowned. "I find that remark to be in poor taste."

Will considered it. "I wear checkerboard pants and I have a purple mohawk. Poor taste is my stock in trade."

Ment rolled his eyes at Sally. *Old guys, huh?* She heard in her mind.

Will began to play. The tune seemed almost familiar to Sally. She found herself almost trying to hum along with it as it went through various stages and permutations. Each time she thought she had a handle on the direction of the music, it would change. Soon she was so caught up in the themes that she couldn't keep up, and let herself be carried away by the music, which seemed to permeate every molecule of her body. True to Will's word, the process didn't hurt at all; in fact, it was rather pleasant. The music flowed over and around her, as if it was a river. Soon, she could no longer keep her eyes open and drifted off into a deep sleep full of troubling dreams and the best, strangest soundtrack she'd ever heard.

CHAPTER SIXTEEN

Psionic abilities even today confound researchers. In spite of decades of investigation, we have a very limited understanding of the functioning of the human brain and how psionics affect it. And it's not easy to procure test subjects after the highly-publicized crimes of villains like Mento or The Scream Queen. How do you tell someone you'd like to experiment with erasing their memories?

-Dr. Grace Devereaux
MacNeil-Lehrer News Hour
April 20, 1987

July, 2004
Rugby, North Dakota

The *Rita*'s engines roared as the jet hurtled toward Rugby. The cabin felt empty without Juice's large, comforting presence, but he'd been forced to remain behind due to his injury. Sally sat with Jason, held his hand, and daydreamed of balloons.

Even though she knew they'd gone over the strategy in a planning session, Sally felt it had somehow slipped away. Oh well, she thought. She'd have plenty of time to figure out what was her part when the moment came. With her accelerated perceptions, she could almost always find time to put together the puzzle.

One piece that didn't fit was her missing horseshoe. When she'd geared up for deployment, she'd found that the extra horseshoe she'd found with Shannon's body, the one which had been her anchor to bring the team through time back to the present, was missing. She'd turned her entire suite inside out to find it, but couldn't find it. When she mentioned it to Jason, he got flustered and embarrassed, and covered it up with a deep, passionate kiss. She wondered if maybe he'd taken it. He wouldn't do anything like that to be mean. Not her Jason. He must have some kind of motive. Maybe he was going to present it to her as a gift, or had made something unique out of it. That would be more his speed. Whatever it was, she was sure it would turn up soon.

"Ten minutes to target," said Ace from the cockpit.

Doublecharge thanked her. "All right, everyone. Sondra, you and I are tactical air support. Get to the airlock and prepare to exit on Ace's mark. The rest of you, follow Stratocaster's orders once you're on the ground. We're only going to have one good shot at this and speed is essential. Sally, you know what that means."

"Uh, yeah," said Sally. "Speed is totally my thing."

Doublecharge nodded at her and then headed after Sondra for the airlock.

"Jase, baby?" Sally curled up in her seat and wished she was anywhere but about to head into another fight with the Archmage. "What exactly am I supposed to do? I'm not sure Doublecharge ever told me."

"You don't remember?" Jason's brow furrowed. "You're, uh, supposed to secure the perimeter of the assault team." He looked over at Switchboard as if confirming it.

"That's right," said the psi. "Nobody better on the edges than you, Sally."

Stratocaster smiled at her. She noticed a change to his guitar. A discoloration that wasn't there before. "What happened?" she asked, pointing at it.

"Just made an adjustment for the big battle," he said. "A little ace in the hole, you know?"

"Is it magic?"

"Of course."

"Three minutes," said Ace. "Multiple contacts inbound. Airlock opening in thirty seconds."

"Stand by for immediate dispersal once you touch down," said Doublecharge as electricity crackled between her fingers. Sondra slid a fresh clip into each of her pistols and thumbed off the safeties. She normally only carried two spare clips when going into combat; today she wore a harness with eight extra clips, and two spare guns were strapped under her arms in shoulder holsters. She winked at Sally as the internal door to the airlock slid shut.

"Ten seconds," said Ace. She counted down to one, and then opened the lock to let Doublecharge and Sondra out into the late afternoon sky. Dark clouds hung low and heavy, and lightning arced between them and illuminated the approaching dragons and gryphons. The *Rita* dipped sharply to one side as Ace shed forward velocity. "Evasive maneuvers. Stand by."

Outside the jet, Doublecharge added her own bright lightning to the sky. She toasted a gryphon into fried chicken with a concentrated blast of electricity. A row of bloody explosions along the flank of a dragon indicated Sondra had entered the fray as well.

Ace slid the *Rita* between plasma jets from the dragons, and then opened the throttle wide for a moment to catch a gryphon in the wash from the jet nozzles. The ground rushed up at them and Sally felt her stomach trying to leap out of her mouth.

"Touchdown in ten seconds," said Ace. "Prepare for rapid deployment."

"Remember your orders, everyone," said Doublecharge.

Sally's perceptions slid into fast time as the jet hit the ground; massive shock absorbers in the landing gear compensated for the impact. Ace opened the bomb bay door. Thunder echoed as Ace swept the incoming horde of fantasy monsters with the *Rita*'s belly gun. Sally clamped her hands over her ears.

"Lifting off now. Switching to monitoring. Good hunting," said Ace over their radios.

The *Rita* roared and the vectored-thrust nozzles of the engine spat flames. The jet lifted into the air on a column of burning exhaust to head for the safety of upper altitudes.

The Archmage's army had sprung from the imagination of someone who saw *Lord of the Rings* too many times. Sally saw scimitar-wielding goblins with patched-up armor, orcs with great swords as long as she was tall, huge leering trolls that needed neither weapon nor armor, and here and there residents of Rugby or National Guardsmen who had been captured and turned by the Archmage.

A large detachment of the army headed for the Just Cause heroes. Stratocaster played his guitar hard and fast. Uneasy energies swirled around them all.

"Wow," said Sally, "there are a lot of them."

"Easy, Sally," said Switchboard, who had eschewed his normal blue jumpsuit for a full SWAT team outfit and assault carbine.

An idea popped into her head like a searchlight on a dark night. "Too bad we don't have a balloon. We could just float over the top of them."

Switchboard looked at her sharply, then glanced at Stratocaster, who didn't seem to notice. "Best put that out of your mind, Sally. Our objective is to reach the base of the mountain. Hopefully Will's presence will draw the Archmage out into the open. He can form the wedge with his powers. Jason and Sally, you clear anyone who breaks the barrier. Let's move like we have a purpose, people!"

They closed with the Archmage's army. A cloud of whistling black arrows arced over the front lines, aimed to drop down among the heroes.

"Sally," said Switchboard. "This is your show."

She slipped into extreme fast-time and grabbed a discarded shield. As arrows began to fall among them, she danced around in a blur and swept away any that would have hit her companions with the shield. Instead of a hail of arrows, the team was pelted only with splinters from the shattered shafts.

As Stratocaster played, his magical wedge of force tossed aside goblins and orcs like blowing leaves. Switchboard kept his carbine at shoulder height and swept the sides, popping a single shot off at any non--human denizen of the Archmage's army that managed to somehow penetrate Stratocaster's enchantment.

Sally dispensed with the shield by hurling it like a discus at one of the trolls. It whizzed through the air like a Frisbee and whipped right through neck of the monster, who had enough time to look surprised as its head sailed away like a gruesome balloon. She unhooked her horseshoes from their clips at her waist.

She was ready to fight.

An orc with sharpened teeth thrust its way through Stratocaster's tenuous magical shield. Jason ducked under the whistling blade and swung a heavy fist into the orc's forearms. The creature yelped as its arms folded the wrong way and its sword went flying. Exhibiting a bit more grace and finesse than he normally did, Jason spun around and swept his leg into the orc's midriff. The orc flew backward into a cluster of its compatriots, who snarled as they tried to penetrate the shield.

Switchboard snapped a new clip into his weapon. "We're not going fast enough," he yelled. "Pick up the pace!" He fired at a new target.

"Don't know if I can hold them back if we go faster," shouted Stratocaster. His fingers were torn from his intense playing and blood spattered the front of his guitar.

"We don't have a choice!" Switchboard concentrated momentarily, eschewing his carbine, and put a bespectacled man to sleep.

Overhead, Sondra and Doublecharge fought to keep gryphons and dragons from attacking the group. Stratocaster's faint magical wedge grew weaker and Sally, Switchboard, and Jason found themselves hard-pressed by those in the Archmage's army who broke through the shield. Soon greenish gore streaked Sally's horseshoes and Jason's fists. Switchboard used his psionics more and more to stretch out his remaining clips, and he was clearly tiring.

None of them were unscathed either. Jason's uniform shirt hung in tatters and four parallel scratches across his chest oozed blood where a troll had gotten a good swipe on him. Sally had been stabbed in the leg by a goblin and was limping. Even so, she was still faster than anyone else and holding her own. Switchboard caught an arrow through his right bicep and lost his carbine. Only Stratocaster remained untouched, but he had to fight off the Archmage's own magical attacks as they pushed closer and closer to the base of the mountain.

A troll pushed through the shield and went straight for Stratocaster. He switched to a different theme and blasted the troll to bits with a burst of energy from his guitar. In doing so, his magical shield collapsed against the Archmage's onslaught from the safety of his castle and the horde was on them. He managed to form a smaller shield to only encompass him and Switchboard, but Jason and Sally were stranded outside his safety shell.

Doublecharge's voice echoed over their radios. "Abort the mission! Ace, get us out of here!"

"About fucking time," grumbled Ace in reply, and from afar they heard the engines of the *Rita* approaching.

Goblins, orcs, and trolls swarmed over Jason and Sally. Jason fought with no regard for his own safety, taking blades and claws across his skin and trusting to his own natural toughness to keep him alive as he tried to reach Sally. "Sally!" he cried as she was surrounded.

Sally had run out of room to run, or hardly even to move. Her perceptions had accelerated to their maximum level and she seemed to be the only thing moving in a world filled with statues. She punched left and right with her horseshoes, desperate to reach Jason. She was better equipped to fight a group of opponents than most heroes because of her speed, but she was wearing down.

Jason roared in fury as he picked up a goblin and swung it like a grisly club. Sally could see him, only a few feet away from her, but surrounded by the Archmage's army. He fought to reach her, and even as she ducked under lethal blows aimed at her, she felt her heart swell with love for him. Then that love turned to fear as he was knocked down by several orcs and a troll piling onto his back.

"No!" she screamed.

Switchboard tried a wide-area psionic attack to give Jason the chance to get free, but to no effect.

A great thundering chatter surrounded them all as Ace strafed the area with the *Rita*'s guns. The Archmage's forces exploded into wet shrapnel as fifty caliber bullets tore through them. The engines screamed in protest as Ace dropped the jet into the heroes' midst, bomb bay doors gaping wide. Doublecharge's lightning blasts provided counterpoint to the chatter of the guns as she and Sondra worked feverishly to keep the dragons and gryphons off the Rita long enough for Ace to perform an extraction. Sally took a bad step on her injured leg, lost her footing, and fell. As she went down, she saw Jason battling toward her, but for every step he gained, he was pushed or pulled back two. She felt bodies pile on top of her as the army overwhelmed her and screamed in terror and frustration.

As a troll lifted her triumphantly in the air, Sally caught a brief glimpse of the *Rita* as Ace lifted it clear of the combat zone. As the bomb bay doors closed, she saw Jason being restrained by Stratocaster and Switchboard, tears of fury and frustration running down his face as he tried to reach Sally one more time. She tried to smile at him, to let him know she'd be all right, but it was such a brief, fleeting instant that she didn't know if he ever saw. She knew her friends would eventually come for her the way they had for Jack. Right now they were outnumbered and wounded and this was for the best.

The *Rita* lifted straight up into the air as Ace opened the jet nozzles to full. It rose like a balloon, but it was the wrong shape and the wrong color. Sally spared a moment's reflection to wonder about her sudden obsession with balloons. Then somebody threw a heavy blanket over her and she was spun around and wrapped up like a burrito. The foul stench of the thick cloth assailed her nostrils and made Sally's stomach churn. She couldn't move and could barely even breathe as she was carried.

For a moment, the person held her perfectly still and Sally wondered if she was about to be released. Then she felt a sudden jerk followed by a rolling, twisting motion, and she realized she was airborne, probably being carried to the castle at the mountain's summit by a dragon or other magical beast.

Just when she didn't think she'd be able to take it any longer, she crashed down onto a hard surface. Hands spun her around to unwrap the blanket from her. She tried to get herself under control so she'd be able to act if the moment called for it. With any luck, she'd be able to move against the Archmage directly if he chose to gloat over his latest capture.

Except she couldn't move at all.

She was made to sit in a high-backed chair by two women whose waitressing outfits had been modified into dancing-girl costumes. They stood patiently to either side and behind the chair in which Sally was held fast by unseen forces.

"What a marvelous present your rulers have made to me." The Archmage stepped out of the shadows.

Sally strained against the invisible bonds but couldn't move even a fraction of an inch. She wished she could float away like a helium-filled balloon.

"I'm keen to know what you hoped to accomplish by your foolish attack."

Sally could do nothing but glare at her captor. Unable even to blink, her eyes began to water, which made her furious because it looked exactly like she was crying.

"What, tears already, my dear? But I haven't even begun to torture you yet." His mocking laughter echoed throughout the chamber

One mistake, thought Sally in her fury. *One slip and you're mine.*

"But wait . . . I've thought of an even better use for you than torture. As I'm sure you know, I recently lost the General of my armies."

He loves to hear himself talk. Sally was reminded of an old bit of Mafia wisdom she'd read somewhere. *Let a man speak; when he is finished, let him speak some more.* Sooner or later he'd talk too much, say the wrong thing, and then she'd have him.

"I'm somewhat familiar with your exploits." The Archmage flipped a hand idly and an internet browser window opened in midair. Sally was astonished to see her personnel profile from the Just Cause central computer displayed. "I suspect you're more powerful than even you believe. Certainly you're the most powerful member of your pitiful little club."

Sally couldn't believe what she was hearing. He had to be playing her somehow, trying to get inside her head. All blond jokes aside, she tried to make her mind all empty, like a balloon.

"You'll make a fine addition to my forces, suitable for command." Wolfgang Frazier stepped closer to her and looked her over in a way that made Sally's skin crawl. "And yet . . . you're so very beautiful. Perhaps you can serve me in other ways as well."

A horrible gnawing sensation filled Sally's belly. She wished for control of her mouth for just one second, long enough to spit in his face.

"It can be lonely at the top. Ruling the world isn't nearly as fun without someone to share it with. At some point, I'll need to provide an heir. Or two. Or more. Because even I can't live forever. At least, not yet. Perhaps that will change when I take Stratocaster's magic."

Still paralyzed, Sally could do nothing but think an unending string of profanity at the Archmage.

Frazier laughed at himself. "Ah, but I do go on, don't I? I suppose I've been cooped up here for too long without true companionship. Well, except for my faithful Seth, of course. Seth?"

"Yes, my Lord." The older man that Sally remembered from her last time in the Archmage's castle stepped from the shadows, a simple wooden flask clutched in his hand. She was positive that she didn't want whatever was in that flask. Seth passed it to Frazier, who gestured at Sally.

Unable to resist, Sally felt her head tilt back and mouth open. Her tongue pressed downward to open her throat. *No no NO!!* she screamed in her mind as the Archmage brought the flask over her lips. He upended it and Sally felt the horrible burning liquid slosh down to her stomach. She wanted to gag and vomit it back out, but even her internal organs seemed to have been paralyzed by Frazier's magic.

She felt the energetic liquid quiver in her stomach like a living thing. It seemed to stretch out beyond her stomach and sent tingles down her limbs all the way to her fingers and toes. It frightened her that the sensations weren't unpleasant. It felt as if she relaxed like in the moment right before falling asleep. Shreds of her resistance leaked away like air from a punctured balloon. Something important hovered on the fringes of her memory, something about balloons, but she couldn't focus on it, and then it went away.

The Archmage bent down and looked deeply into her eyes and Sally felt her heart fill with love for him. She would lay down her life in an instant if he requested it. She would lead his armies, bear his children, be his anything and everything.

"How do you feel, my dear?" he asked her, and she found she could move again. Why had she been unable to before? She couldn't remember. It certainly wasn't important now that he was here and had freed her.

"Wonderful, my darling." She threw her arms around his neck and kissed him deeply.

CHAPTER SEVENTEEN

"The difference between false memories and true ones is the same as for jewels: it is always the false ones that look the most real, the most brilliant."

-Salvador Dalí

August, 2004
Rugby, North Dakota

Sally wandered through Wolfgang's castle. She felt a little lost and disconnected without the love of her life beside her. He was busy preparing the next batch of conscripts. He had explained to her how he was bringing peace to the troubled lands beyond his borders, a mile at a time. His forces worked very hard to keep from killing the innocents from the enemy army. Instead, they fought to capture them and bring them to the sanctity of the castle, where Wolfgang labored to free them from their conditioning and make them free-thinking individuals willing to fight for his cause.

The enemy had been camped outside the castle for as long as she could remember. Wolfgang was constantly reminding her of the dangers they presented, with their guns and jets and tanks and missiles. He was careful to fight them with weapons of old, using troops he'd pulled from the very bones of the earth itself. The conscripts he brought into his fold were more than happy to lay down their previous masters' weapons of war in favor of the swords and bows that Wolfgang preferred.

Her love had spent a day carefully measuring her for a suit of armor that would protect her when she led her first assault on the enemy host. She had thrilled to feel his hands on her skin, and wished desperately he had time for more attentions. Unfortunately, his duties often called him away before she could do much more than buss him across the lips. And it was his manservant Seth who came to remind him of those duties, usually giving her an evil glare as he passed her.

She didn't like Seth; and she knew he hated her with a passion she didn't understand.

The clock in the great hall chimed and she knew it was time to eat. She walked through the corridors toward the dining room atop the tall central tower of the castle. Her thoughts seemed very cloudy these days. She found it difficult to recall details of the past. As far as she knew, she'd always been part of the Archmage's entourage. Or perhaps she was one of the converted, a soldier from the barbarian army beyond Wolfgang's magical wards. Perhaps he'd freed her from her slavery. Unbidden, images of brightly-colored floating spheres filled her mind. This happened frequently, and the illusions were real enough that more than once she found herself reaching out to touch them even though they weren't present.

She didn't understand why she kept seeing them. They certainly weren't anything she'd seen in the castle, or from the army beyond. Wolfgang hadn't cast any spells that showed her such things. Deep in her mind, in the part that occasionally screamed wordlessly at her and gave her the nightmares, she knew there was something very important about those floating spheres. And yet, she was loath to mention them to Wolfgang. She didn't want him to think there was something, well, *wrong* with her. She strove to be perfect for him, because she loved him so much.

Every so often, it seemed that the world around her stopped moving altogether, and she found herself wandering through a castle populated by statues instead of people. When this happened, she would run from room to room, searching for her love in the hope he could help her regain her sensibility. Once she'd found him and he was just as frozen as everyone else, and it terrified her. Seth eventually found her, huddled in a corner of a disused chamber, moaning and crying since she thought she'd somehow lost everything. It was like the nightmares that tormented her constantly. Every night she ran in great terror from beings that sought to murder her; a dog-faced man, a bolt of lightning shaped like a woman, a walking pillar of strength, a vicious clawed harpy, and the Musician

The Musician was her greatest fear, but he was also Wolfgang's obsession. He was training her for the mission to bring the Musician back into the castle. The Musician directed the enemy army's attacks on the castle, and Wolfgang explained to her that his capture would result in the end of the war. She nodded as she brushed away tears she didn't know had escaped her eyes, and smiled at him.

Lunch was, as always, a repast worthy of kings and emperors. Wolfgang sat down wearily at the head of the table. Seth moved to his side quickly and gave him a vial of a cordial to help his strength return. Sally knew her position was to wait until Wolfgang had been served and began eating before seeking her own nourishment. The food smelled wonderful, and looked incredibly delicious, but somehow her appetite had waned of late and she could barely stomach even a crust of bread.

Wolfgang loaded up a plate with meat, potatoes, cheeses, and succulent vegetables, and filled a great flagon with his favorite spicy wine. He looked down the long table at Sally and smiled. "You look as fantastic as ever, my dear."

"Thank you, my love." Her heart swelled with joy as feelings welled up inside her to push aside even the constant images of balloons.

"I have good news," said Wolfgang. "I've completed your armor. You'll be able to lead the troops tomorrow."

Sally's breath caught in her throat. Was she really going to be able to prove her love for the Archmage at last? "Oh, Wolfgang!" she cried. "That's wonderful!"

He allowed himself a condescending smile. "Yes, it is rather special, isn't it?"

"Might I try it on tonight before bed?"

"Of course. We should make sure everything fits."

"And perhaps later . . . I could join you in your chambers?" Sally asked hopefully. She had yet to be allowed in to spend any time with Wolfgang without his retainers present. She wasn't sure why, but it was certainly for her own good.

A new, unholy glint appeared in the Archmage's eyes. "Yes, I think that would be satisfactory."

Seth sidled up next to Wolfgang. "I don't think that's wise, my Lord. Let her prove herself to you first before you risk being alone with her."

Sally glared at Wolfgang's aide. *How dare he?*

The Archmage sighed and drained his cup of wine. "Yes, you're right, I suppose. I can always trust you to have my best interests at heart, can't I, Seth?"

Seth lowered his eyes. "I exist to serve you, my Lord." Sally heard a slight cynicism in the man's voice, but it was apparently lost on Wolfgang.

They finished eating in silence, Wolfgang lost in his thoughts and Sally daydreaming of herself in his armor.

Soon the meal was finished and the servants began clearing the table. Wolfgang wiped his mouth fastidiously with a napkin and stood. "Come, Salena." He held out his hand to her.

She was by his side in a flash and tucked her eager arm inside his. He led her through the castle to his workshop. She caught occasional glimpses of Seth behind them in the shadows. His quiet stalking made her a little nervous, as if he awaited an opportunity to slip a dagger in between her ribs. She swore to herself resolutely that he'd never get the chance.

The workshop was brightly lit by torches along the walls. Her suit of armor floated without any apparent means of support over a raised platform in the middle of the workshop. Her breath caught in her throat as she took in the beautiful creation.

The necessity of her freedom of movement and speed had guided the armor's design. She wouldn't be overly restricted by the overlapping plates of cerulean blue armor trimmed by ebony chain mail. "Oh, Wolfgang!" she said. "It's beautiful!"

He smiled at her. "I would be honored if you would try it on, Lady Salena. I'll give you some privacy while you dress."

Sally was going to say she didn't mind, but before she could, Seth drew Wolfgang away into an adjoining chamber. The dark look he shot her made her spine tingle. She tried to put her nervousness about her true love's majordomo out of her mind as she shucked out of her gown. She stared at the armor for a minute, because it floated several inches above the floor, as if it was some kind of strange balloon, and she forgot her anxiety and smiled. The only problem, she thought suddenly, was that it was the wrong color.

It ought to have been red, not blue.

Her feet slipped into soft leather ankle boots with straps that crisscrossed up her legs. Plates of steel protected the tops of her feet and the thick, soft soles would give her plenty of purchase. Her legs remained bare to allow freedom of movement. A leather belt fastened around her midriff and a soft thong creased her buttocks. A skirt of flexible chain hung around her waist, connecting to a large ring that centered over her navel. *I should get that pierced, he'd love that*, she thought. The unwarranted thought was immediately followed by strong guilt as she suspected the *he* in question wasn't Wolfgang, which made no sense to her. Her breasts were sheathed in a leather bikini with a chain mail overlay. It also connected to the ring at her navel. Blued steel guards covered her shoulders, and bracers wrapped around her upper arms. A thin steel helmet lined with cotton and topped with bright peacock feathers perched atop her head.

Sally stared at herself in the mirror. She looked amazing and yet, part of her mind kept screaming it was completely wrong in every possible way. A powerful wave of mixed emotion rolled over her and she felt like laughing and crying at the same time. A single tear wound its way down her cheek. She wiped it away quickly with a flash of anger at her lack of control.

"Wolfgang? I'm finished."

The door creaked open and he stood in the hallway and regarded her with open-mouthed awe.

"You look fantastic."

She spun around gaily and flipped her hair like a flag. "Why thank you!"

He stepped into the room, followed by a slinking Seth. The older man drifted off to a shadowed spot along one wall and seemed to fold himself into a ball of hatred and distrust. Sally glanced in his direction before Wolfgang drew up to her and gently grasped her arms. He bent down to place a kiss on her forehead.

"I'm ready to lead your armies, my love," she said with pride.

"Not quite yet. I'd be amiss if I sent you into battle with naught but the armor on your shoulders."

He raised his hand, palm toward the ceiling and fingers curling up and around. A bluish glow filled his hand, and then lengthened into a long haft of finely-grained wood inlaid with silver tracings. A tuft of silky fur dangled from one end, and from it sprouted a wickedly barbed point which shimmered like water in the sunlight.

A spear, thought Sally. *That's not right*. Nevertheless, she reached up to take the offered weapon in spite of the wrongness of its shape and size.

"Go on, try it out," said Wolfgang.

Seth stiffened noticeably from where he lurked. Sally ignored him. She stepped back from Wolfgang to give herself enough room to operate.

She whipped the spear around experimentally to get a feel for it. It was incredibly light, and she made it whistle around her as she twirled it like a quarterstaff. She brought it around behind her smartly and then snapped it butt-first down to the floor with a sound like thunder. Cracks radiated outward through the stone floor from the point of impact. Sally's chest heaved, not so much from exertion, but from the excitement of using the weapon that seemed to meld itself into every move she made. She grinned at Wolfgang, who applauded.

"Brilliant, my dear. You're a natural." She swelled with pride to hear his words. His smile turned dangerous. "Perhaps we should test you under more adverse conditions."

He snapped his fingers and suddenly they were in the courtyard. Sally noticed he hadn't transported Seth along with them and that knowledge gave her a secret thrill. Wolfgang trusted her at last. It was a turning point. Sally knew it was only a matter of time before she'd be allowed to share everything of herself with Wolfgang.

The Archmage waved his hand at the cobblestones and a group of spectral minions rose up from the ground. They looked oddly familiar to Sally, but she couldn't imagine where she might have seen such strange people before except perhaps in her dreams: two huge, hulking men, one black as night and the other with a dog's face; a cackling harpy with talons and feathered wings; a living bolt of lightning in female form; a laughing rascal of a demon; an amorphous blob with stringy tentacles which reached hungrily for her head.

And amid them all was a shadowy representation of the Musician.

"They displease me," said Wolfgang. "Destroy them for me, Salena. Prove yourself worthy of the gifts you have received."

Sally didn't hesitate. Swinging the spear fluidly, she waded in among them. The harpy screamed at her and threw knives from both hands. Sally dodged them easily, batting them out of the air with the haft of her spear. As the living lightning bolt cast itself at her, she spun the tip of the spear around and spitted the glowing specter neatly through its chest. The creature disappeared in a flash of ectoplasmic residue. Sally reversed the spear and swung it hard to cut through the harpy's wings. The monster fell to the ground, still screaming, and Sally pinned it through its chest. With her spear firmly planted, she leaped up and kicked out at the leering demon, smashing its face in. It vanished in a puff of smoke. Tendrils wrapped around her head suddenly, blinding and suffocating her. She lashed out, spinning the spear in a wide arc. The tendrils vanished as quickly as they had formed, leaving her only to face the two monstrous men and the Musician. With one mighty blow of the magically-sharp spearhead, she cleaved the black creature in half and it vanished in a puff of smoke. The dog-faced demon wrapped her up in a bear hug, but wasn't fast enough to entrap her arms. She reversed the spear and thrust it behind her just past her hip. As it gored into the spectral being behind her, she gasped from a feeling like she'd done something horribly wrong. But she couldn't dwell on that now; she still had the Musician to face.

But before she could move against the Musician, Wolfgang dismissed him with a desultory wave of his hand. The spirit vanished off to whatever realm it called home and left the two of them alone in the courtyard once more.

"Wonderful," said Wolfgang, rubbing his hands together. "I know now that you will be successful. I am proud to make you the leader of my army. Tomorrow morning we move against the Musician, and by tomorrow night we celebrate his defeat."

"But tonight you should rest, my Lord," wheedled Seth from the tower entrance. "You'll need all your strength tomorrow. *All* your strength."

Wolfgang sighed. "I suppose you're right, old friend." He turned to Sally. "One more night apart, my dear. Tomorrow night you shall join me in my chambers and I will make you my queen."

Sally felt herself quiver with repressed desire and frustration. It seemed like she'd never be able to quell the ache deep inside her. She sighed. "One more night, my darling. I look forward to finally sharing your bed."

The look of pure hatred that Seth shot her almost made her regret her words. In that moment she knew she would have to kill him.

CHAPTER EIGHTEEN

"War, war is still the cry, 'War even to the knife!'"

-Lord Byron

August, 2004
Rugby, North Dakota

Sally couldn't sleep.

The excitement of the approaching battle made her toss and turn in her bedchamber in the castle's south tower. She wished for a moment she had a clock so she'd know what time it was. Then she laughed at herself for such a ridiculous thought. The sun peeking through her window would be clock enough for her.

She got out of her bed and wrapped a blanket around herself against the chill of the night. She'd asked the Archmage about the unusually cool weather considering it was the middle of summer. He'd explained that the Musician's powers were altering weather patterns and that he'd be able to restore the natural balance once their opponent had been vanquished once and for all. The fire in her hearth had died down to a soft glow. She could have thrown another piece of wood on it, but it was hard enough to sleep without flickering firelight on the rounded walls of her chamber. She stepped over to the window to look out across the darkened lands far below.

The lights of the enemy burned with their unnaturally steady glow as they made constant circles around Wolfgang's lands both in the sky and on the ground. They constantly tested his defenses day and night, but she saw no battles being fought at the moment. The enemy troops seemed content to wait in their encampments. Nearer to the base of the mountain, she could see Wolfgang's own armies, their camps lit by cheerful fires and lanterns. She could see the remains of a few vehicles burning away the last of their flammable parts, grim testaments to the power of her love's soldiers.

Tomorrow she would be leading those very soldiers into battle.

She sighed happily and thought perhaps she was getting a little drowsy after all and should go back to bed. She closed her eyes and imagined the thrill of combat in her love's name. Her mind filled with the images of floating balloons the color of fresh blood and she shook her head angrily. Why did those visions keep tormenting her?

She heard the slightest of clicks from the latch of her chamber door, and time seemed to stop around her.

Her heart pounded in fear as she threw off the blanket. The blanket hung in midair, not yet affected by the pull of gravity. She hurried over to her bed and thrust a couple of pillows underneath the sheets. It didn't really look like someone asleep, but perhaps in the darkened room it would be enough to give her a momentary advantage. She ran lightly to the hearth and grabbed the poker; it was the only weapon she had readily available to her. She moved to stand in the slight alcove by the door with the poker raised in preparation.

The blanket she'd dropped settled to the floor.

The latch turned quietly and the door swung open. The corridor beyond would normally be lit by torches, but now it was dark. A figured swathed in black slipped into the room. The dim light glinted off the naked blade of a dagger clutched in his hand. Even in the near-darkness, there was no mistaking that look of disdain. Seth had come to kill her in her sleep.

Sally's ire rose. *What nerve to attack me under Wolfgang's protection!*

He started to turn. In a flash, Sally brought the poker down across Seth's wrist to shatter bones and tear sinew. The knife clattered to the stone floor.

Seth didn't scream; instead, he grunted and staggered away from her.

"How dare you come in here like this?" She brandished the poker.

"You are an impostor," he spat. "You'd harm my master. You'd kill him."

"I love him!" She didn't care if she woke the entire world with the admission.

"You only think that. He makes you love him."

"No, that's impossible!"

"He won't look past your beauty, but I know better. You're a traitor somehow, and I won't let you hurt him," Seth hissed.

"I'd never hurt him. I *love* him!"

"You are only a toy to him, but he's like a son to me. I raised him from birth. You don't know him like I do!" In spite of his badly-damaged hand, Seth leaped at her.

Sally sidestepped his awkward headlong rush. He crashed into a table which shattered into splinters. Sally swung the poker hard across his back and he fell to the floor to writhe in agony.

"Stay down," she said, "or I will kill you."

He glared back over his shoulder. Blood leaked from his mouth and hatred ran rampant across his face. "Fucking traitorous bitch."

"What is going on here?" thundered a voice. Wolfgang appeared out of thin air in the middle of the room.

"Your manservant—" Sally spat the word with vitriol. "—came to kill me in my sleep. I was forced to defend myself." Her eyes became cold slits. "With your permission, my love, I'll finish what I began."

The Archmage spoke a single ancient word, and Sally was frozen in place. "You will do no such thing. Seth, is this true?"

Sally strained to argue her case, but even her tongue and jaws were paralyzed. Her eyes began to burn as they dried out.

"Yes it's true!" cried Seth. "She's dangerous, my Lord! You said so yourself that you couldn't see into her mind. Doesn't that suggest she's hiding something?"

"Ridiculous," countered Wolfgang. "Her mind is weak. Her personality fragmented when I took control of her. I couldn't see into it because there was nothing left to see. All she is now is what I have made her."

"She is a spy, sent to you by our enemies. Mark my words, if you keep her alive and near you it will be your downfall." Seth struggled to his feet.

Energy flowed from the Archmage's hands to envelop Seth's injuries. "We talked about this, Seth. Don't make me repeat myself." His voice hardened. "You know I don't like that."

"Thank you, my Lord." Seth massaged his hand as if it still ached. "I apologize. It won't happen again."

Wolfgang smiled. "Oh, Seth. My oldest friend . . . what would I do without you and your counsel?" He circled Sally as he spoke. "I've been watching this one. She is incredibly powerful in her own way, truly one of the Great Powers of this age. Even she hardly begins to suspect the range of her capabilities." He crossed in front of her again. "She has it within her to defeat each and every one of the defenders that fool Stratocaster can bring to bear. She will be the key to our victory."

"And afterward? She's too dangerous to keep around."

"Perhaps. But she's very beautiful." Wolfgang stopped before her. Sally felt a growing horror inside her; something was going wrong. She couldn't breathe.

"There are many beautiful women, my Lord. And you'll have your pick of them once this battle is ended."

"You're right, Seth. Indeed . . . I would be lost without you." Wolfgang waved a hand and Sally collapsed and gasped for air. She was too stunned to immediately bolt for safety. She looked up at him, tears in her eyes. "Well, we can't have you remembering that, can we?" He smiled at her, and as his eyes bored into hers, all her fears and doubts vanished and once more she found herself gazing up into the face of the man whom she loved.

"Wolfgang? I'm . . . I don't . . . what are you doing in here?" She felt confused, like she'd been sleepwalking.

He held out a hand to her, which she gratefully accepted. "You had a nightmare, my dear. Seth and I came to make sure you were all right. Are you?"

"I . . . I think so." Sally looked around the room. It seemed unfamiliar, even though she knew she'd spent her entire life in it.

"Then back to bed with you. You have a busy day tomorrow." He embraced her.

Sally let him lead her back to her bed where he tucked her in. She smiled at him as he bent down and kissed her forehead. "Thank you, my love."

She fell into a deep sleep, punctuated by dreams of red balloons.

When Sally opened her eyes, she saw Wolfgang standing over her with anticipation and eagerness plain on his face. "Good morning, Salena."

Sally smiled up at him and shyly pulled the blankets up to her chin. "Good morning, my love."

"There's time for a quick breakfast before the battle is joined." He turned his back while Sally left her bed to take refuge behind a dressing screen. She wrapped herself in a heavy cottony robe. She hurriedly braided her hair into a thick rope which hung down the center of her back, and then splashed some water from the jug on her face. Feeling suitably refreshed, she emerged from behind the screen.

Wolfgang beamed at her. "Today we shall take the battle to the enemy. Today the Musician shall fall before us. We shall destroy his instrument together."

"I can't wait!" Sally skipped along beside Wolfgang as they made their way from the south tower to the dining hall.

There was no sign of Seth at breakfast, only the Archmage's ghostly servants which drifted in with food and drink and left as silently as they had come.

After awhile, Wolfgang pushed his plate away. A servant slipped it from the table and vanished. "I've done everything in my power to tilt the balance of the battle in our favor. Your objective is simple. You are to spearhead a phalanx of my strongest warriors, leading them directly upon the Musician. The warriors accompanying you will keep opponents away from you while you battle the Musician's guardians. I have cast a spell that will prevent him from teleporting away. He will have to physically travel away from the region before he can disappear. You will reach him before he can get to that point, and when you do, you will touch him with this."

A gorgeous, finely-wrought silver bracelet with a large green stone appeared in midair before Sally. She reached up and took it in wonderment. It snapped itself around her wrist with a *clack*. "What will happen when I do?"

"The two of you will be instantly transported back here. Once he is inside this castle, I can overcome him and bring this conflict to an end."

"And then we can be together forever," breathed Sally, hoping it to be true with all her heart.

"Yes, of course. Now, it's time to go. Your armor is waiting for you in your chambers."

Sally jumped up and dashed over to him to buss his cheek, and then ran like the wind back to her bedchamber to find her armor floating in the middle of the room. She peeled her robe off and tossed it away. A cold breeze from her window made her shiver. She looked out to see dark yellowish storm clouds swirling low over the surrounding plains. Circling winds were kicking up a great cloud of dust. She could see the vehicles and soldiers of the enemy as darker shadows marked by their unnatural lighting. Overhead, the morning sun was a faint, tarnished coin whose glow could barely penetrate the thick overcast cloud cover.

She wiggled into her armor. It wrapped around her like a living thing and fastened its buckles and catches even before she found them with her fingers. She saved the helmet for last, and savored the moment as she placed it over her head. It made her feel powerful and invincible. The spear Wolfgang had made for her floated upright by her bed and called to her with a voice she couldn't quite hear. Energy crackled around her hands as they closed around the haft. She took a deep breath and turned to face herself in the mirror. She stared at herself as she tried to understand why the reflection didn't match her self-image at all. But when she tried to feel for that self-image, to bring it forward from the murky depths of her befuddled memory, it danced tantalizingly out of reach.

No matter, she thought, *it is time to go to war.*

She made her way through the castle down to the front gate, where she met an honor guard of captured and turned troops. Wolfgang had opted to watch the proceedings from the battlements above. Sally waved up to him. He nodded imperiously at her before turning his attention to the various cantrips he was casting that would enable him to closely monitor the coming battle.

Sally could have sprinted down the path from the castle gate in a few seconds, but it didn't feel right to her to leave the company of troops behind. Instead, she opted for a quick march. The soldiers fell in behind her and followed her pace exactly. The sound of a hundred feet striking the ground in unison with each step gave her chills.

At the base of the mountain more troops joined her company, and yet more, and within a few minutes she led a full battalion of the seemingly endless hordes of the Archmage's creations. Human soldiers gave way to goblins with wickedly-barbed short swords and the larger orcs with their maces and scimitars. Spaced evenly around the edges of the group were trolls wielding heavy clubs. A flight of dragons and gryphons circled overhead. Sally felt completely protected.

Something in the helmet she wore pointed her unerringly in the direction of the Musician. She could feel him out there as he prepared magics of his own to use against her and her army. She smiled at the thought of him trying to stop her and Wolfgang with his puny power. It would be like a single stem of grass trying to turn the course of a mighty river.

"*Your orders, milady?*" asked a spectral figure beside her. He would relay her commands to his minions, who would in turn pass them along to the army at large.

"Send a wing ahead to either side. Trolls in the front with orcs and goblins supporting. Force a corridor to the Musician's personal guard. Use dragons and gryphons to clear enemy vehicles. I want enemy combatants subdued, not killed. Bring them back to the castle where they will be re-educated. All human troops are to stay with me because the enemy will be less likely to fire upon their own. A sizable portion of the main force must remain within the phalanx as we move further into enemy territory. We cannot allow ourselves to be cut off from the castle."

"*And what of the Musician's personal guard?*" asked the specter.

"I will deal with them myself. Return to my side when you have passed along my orders."

The figure bowed to her and dissipated into nothingness. Moments later, two wedges of her army pushed forward against the enemy lines. She heard the guns roar and saw orcs and goblins fall. The trolls' heavy armor and thick skins were proof against the bullets of the opposing force, but she couldn't afford to take too many losses of her line soldiers.

"Air support," she said. "Clear those lines."

Dragons and gryphons wheeled overhead, then streaked for the distant points. Enemy soldiers ducked and dove for cover as the airborne monsters rushed in upon them. The dragons spewed flame and the gryphons slashed with claws and fangs.

The enemy broke ranks in disarray from the swift air attack, and Sally's troops rushed in. They overwhelmed the soldiers and relieved them of their unnatural firearms. Trolls crushed the rifles and pistols into unrecognizable shapes, while orcs and goblins subdued their opponents and passed them back to the rear guard where they would be taken to the castle.

The offensive strike moved forward rapidly, and Sally was pleased. Her troops formed a protective shell around her and she stayed untouched as they pressed forward and headed toward the shining figure of the Musician in the distance. His personal guard surrounded him as her own force drew closer. She felt her heart pound in anticipation of combat. The noise of battle around her deepened in intensity and she could feel the Archmage's magic in the air.

She saw the opening for which she'd been waiting. The world seemed to stop around her, and she moved.

Sally ran through the break in the enemy soldiers and swung her spear left and right. Every time it touched an opponent, that person fell, stunned from the powerful magic. She could see the Musician as he stood on the back of a vehicle, unafraid of the arrows and spears of the Archmage's army; they flashed into nothingness within a few yards of him. He played his nefarious instrument and used it to blast her troops into columns of ash. Beside him, a petite woman with dark hair fired a rifle, and each time she did one of her soldiers would drop. Overhead fought two more of his protectors. With guns and blasts of electricity, they carved a path through the army. Two more stood their ground below, a smaller man with a rifle and a giant boy with only his fists. The boy fought like a wild dog and seemed oddly familiar to her. Somehow she knew that she had faced him before, and that he was exceptionally dangerous.

Sally didn't hesitate to engage the guardians. She ducked underneath the gunfire of the man dressed in blue and brought her spear soundly across his temple. His feet flew out from under him and he crashed to the ground, unconscious. Before he had fully settled, she was already flanking the boy in gray who frightened her. He swung a leg at her. She leaped lightly over it as her spear whistled around in a tight arc. The flat of the head connected with the boy's ribs and flared brightly with the impact. He staggered and dropped to his knees.

Using his body as a ladder, Sally put a foot on his shoulder and jumped high into the air, flipping over a burst of lightning from the warrior-woman in black and white. She brought the spear up in a rising arc, catching one foot with its tip. As the lightning-caster fell, Sally twisted her own body in midair and used the falling woman's body to push herself even higher. She came down on the back of the winged woman. In a swift maneuver, she reached around the woman's head and pressed the haft of the spear against her throat. The winged woman slipped from the air, unconscious, which allowed Sally to tumble forward and land upon the vehicle's engine compartment. Her bracelet glowed with emerald light as she reached for the Musician.

"No!" cried the dark-haired woman next to him, and she grasped his arm. Sally felt a hand close around her ankle as she stretched out her hand and brushed the Musician's leg with the bracelet.

With a swirling sensation of rapid movement, she materialized in Wolfgang's Great Hall. Besides the Musician, the transporting magic had also brought the dark-haired woman and the boy in gray, who still held her ankle.

The heavy wooden shutters framing the windows of the hall slammed shut, and the ironclad doors at either end swung closed with a resounding boom. The torches in the wall sconces and the candelabra in the center of the large table jumped to life and filled the hall with flickering firelight.

Wolfgang's voice spoke a single word of power and paralyzed everyone except Sally. The Archmage drifted out from behind a pillar. He floated several inches above the floor. Sally's heart swelled with love for him and she moved beside him and wrapped her arms around one of his legs. He smiled down at her.

"You've done well, my dear. You shall be rewarded." His eyes narrowed. "But first, these minor, trivial annoyances will be dealt with."

CHAPTER NINETEEN

"Hit the bastards where it hurts and then kick them while they're down."

-Lady Athena
1975

August, 2004
Rugby, North Dakota

Wolfgang gestured and elevated the three prisoners to their feet. Sally smiled to see the three of them straining against the magic. Wolfgang motioned again and unlimbered their mouths. The three prisoners began yelling and cursing at him. "Silence," he whispered and although their mouths moved, no sound issued forth.

"Quickly, my Lord." Seth stepped from the shadows. "There is no time to waste. Kill Kramer, and take your rightful place as the Heir to All Magic."

Wolfgang waved at him with serene indulgence. "All in good time, my old friend. First we'll have a bit of sport with them." He gazed fondly down at Sally, her arms still wrapped around his leg. "What do you think, my dear? Shall we amuse ourselves with the others first?"

"Whatever you wish, my love."

The large blond youth stopped straining against his unseen bonds upon hearing Sally's quiet reply. A look of horror crossed his face.

"What's this?" The boy's reaction had not gone unnoticed by Wolfgang. "Can it be you have feelings for her? She has given herself completely over to me, boy."

"C-completely?" the boy whispered, his voice audible once more with Wolfgang's permission.

The Archmage only laughed at his discomfort. "He believes that you love him, and he still loves you in spite of whatever you may do. Salena, my dear, I think we'll start with this poor, disillusioned youth." His voice turned ugly, but not to Sally's ears. "Take up your spear."

Sally stepped over to where her spear hovered motionless and took tight hold of it.

"My Lord, what are you doing?" Seth's voice was full of misgivings.

"Amusing myself, and you'll mind your tongue, my dear Seth."

Seth drifted back into the shadows to grumble to himself with acidic words.

"What would you have me do, my love?" Sally looked up at Wolfgang.

He waved his fingers toward the muscular blond youth. The boy staggered and nearly fell to the floor before regaining his balance. He flexed his fists uneasily, unsure of what to do now he had been freed from enchantment.

A smile devoid of humor crossed Wolfgang's face. "Toy with him. Hurt him. It will please me."

Sally glared at the nervous boy. "Anything for you."

"Sally?" asked the boy uncertainly.

She charged at him with her spear whirling traceries of blue energy in its wake.

He shouted in surprise as she slipped inside his guard and poked him in the arm with her spear. He yelped as the magical tip pierced his unnaturally tough skin. Sally danced out of his range before he could grab her. He retreated. She moved in again, reached up and clubbed him on the side of the head with the flat of the blade. He cried out and fell backward, an angry red triangular mark on his face.

Wolfgang laughed as he watched the boy scramble backward, unable to stay away from the girl half his size.

"Goddammit, let him go!" cried the Musician. "He's no threat to you! It's me you want!"

"Wait," whispered Wolfgang. "Your turn will come."

Sally had the boy in full retreat. She aimed a jab at his midsection. He slapped it away and grunted from the pain the magical spear left in his hands. She allowed the force of his slap to spin the spear around and pushed the blunt end of the haft into his instep.

"Stop it!" screamed the dark-haired woman.

Wolfgang clenched his fingers in the air and the woman was lifted into the air. "I'm doing nothing. He will survive to fight in my army."

The boy found his back against a wall. Sally lunged at him but he ducked and rolled to one side. Her spear cracked the stone wall with a flash of cobalt light.

"Sally," he whispered through his pain. "Baby, it's me. Stop hurting me."

He was rewarded with a thrust to his thigh which made him collapse to the stone floor.

Sally's heart was pounding and her blood roared in her ears. The torture she inflicted on the boy had quickened her breath, not from exertion but from pleasure. Causing pain to others was . . . exciting.

"Break him. Make him mine to command."

"Yes, my love."

The boy choked as she poked the spear into his throat. She jabbed again and again, faster and faster, until her attacks came in a blur. Each time, the tip penetrated his skin just enough to raise a welt and bring forth a single droplet of blood. He couldn't fight back when Sally could be everywhere at once. He hunched down like a turtle to protect his midsection from her lightning thrusts.

"Please stop! We'll do what you want!" The dark-haired woman cried openly now. Wolfgang ignored her plea.

A horrible, tortured wail came from the boy on the floor, a cry of surrender and obeisance.

"Hold," said the Archmage quietly, and Sally jammed the haft of the spear into the floor with a sound like a mountain splitting asunder.

The boy groaned and panted from the pain he endured. He wouldn't raise his head to look at Wolfgang. "Please . . . no more . . . I'll do anything . . . just make her stop." His voice shook.

"Come over here, boy. Crawl."

Sally watched as the boy crept slowly across the stone floor. Sweat ran off his face in rivulets. His gray and brown clothing was all but shredded. His skin was lashed with the marks left by her spear, but nowhere was he cut or bleeding. She felt not the slightest bit of pity for him and stared down at him as if he were a dog cowering from a beating.

"Bow before me."

The boy bent his forehead to the cold stone floor as tears squeezed from his tightly shut eyes.

"You are mine to command. Say it!"

"I . . ." The boy choked on his words, and then spat them out in a painful whisper. "I am yours to command."

A grin of triumph overtook all other emotions on Wolfgang's face. He turned to the corner where Seth watched. "You see, dear old friend? Did you really doubt any other outcome?"

"No, my lord," said Seth. "But it grows late, and your enemies are marshaling their forces. Would it not be best to end this amusement and claim your birthright?"

Wolfgang sighed. "Yes, I suppose you're right." He smiled fondly at his servant. "You have always advised me well, Seth. I shall reward you richly for your loyal and faithful service."

Seth bowed.

Wolfgang turned back to the beaten youth. The Musician and the dark-haired woman remained frozen in place. Their cries of anger had been replaced by horrified silence. "Boy, what is your name?"

"J-Jason, m-my lord."

"A heroic name. Hardly fitting for one such as you. Evermore you shall be known as Dog, for you are no better than one. Say it."

"My n-name . . . is Dog."

Wolfgang laughed. "It will amuse me to use the Musician's infernal instrument in his destruction. Fetch it for me, Dog."

Sally watched as the cowering boy went over to where the Musician strained against his unseen bonds. "Don't do it, Jason. Don't give in," he pleaded.

Wordlessly, Jason lifted the strange guitar over the Musician's head. Unable to resist, beaten, the Musician lowered his eyes. The boy slung the guitar around his own neck so as not to drop it, and trudged slowly toward the Archmage. As he passed Sally, he raised his head slightly, meeting her eyes with his.

Improbably, he winked.

Seth, ever vigilant, started to utter a warning, but he wasn't quick enough. The boy touched a spot on the guitar and something burst forth from it. It wasn't a bomb or magic spell; it was only a red balloon, inflated suddenly by a concealed gas canister. It drifted upwards and spun to reveal a bright yellow image of a chess knight on it.

A bomb went off inside Sally's brain.

Bright white light blinded Sally and tremendous sound echoed through her head as all her memories came rushing back like a tidal wave breaking over and through a levee. Her perceptions accelerated to the fastest they had ever been and suddenly it seemed as if the world had gone completely still. She realized she could see the light moving away from her, slowly and lazily as if it were thick molasses. It was coming from her, shining brightly in all directions. She saw the Archmage, flung backward by the force of the magical brightness, about to crash to the floor. She saw Seth, his hands outstretched as if he were trying to stop her act.

And she saw Jason changing his form in front of her. Instead of the boy who she knew she loved, and to whom she had done a terrible wrong, she saw a man with a sardonic grin and a purple mohawk.

Stratocaster.

Somehow he'd fooled the Archmage into thinking he was Jason, who hung paralyzed in the air beside Ace.

Time sped up again. The Archmage skidded across the floor, stunned by the burst of magical energy which had emanated from Sally.

"No!" Seth screamed, too late.

Stratocaster didn't waste a moment to thank Sally, and began to play, pressing his advantage while he could. His fingers danced a difficult toccata over the fretboard of the magical guitar. Blast after blast of magic poured forth from the strings. Each one hit the Archmage harder and harder. Stratocaster's face was terrible to behold; he was a man bent on murderous revenge for uncountable wrongs perpetrated by the Archmage.

Seth leaped at Stratocaster, screaming wordlessly, with his fingers arched into claws. The musician spared a single blast of magic to deflect away the hapless man. In that moment of distraction the Archmage recovered his poise. The next blast from Stratocaster's guitar split apart in front of the Archmage, curved around him, and blasted a crater in the wall behind him.

"A fine trick," spat the Archmage through a mouthful of blood. "I'd be impressed if I wasn't so pissed. Time to die, Stratocaster, like all the others."

Sally realized she still held the spear in her hands. In the space between breaths she covered half the distance across the Great Hall and forced the spear deep into the Archmage's ribs.

The spear penetrated easily into his body, but it was Seth who fell with a choking, bubbling scream. Blood fountained out of a deep wound which had appeared on his chest. It soaked through his fine clothing to spray the floor around him. Somehow the Archmage managed to transfer the fatal wound Sally inflicted upon him to his faithful servant. Even so, he appeared startled by the ferocity of the act, as if he'd never really expected Seth to fall in his stead.

"Seth?" he cried.

Sally yanked the spear free from his undamaged body and flung it away from her as if it were unclean.

The Archmage screamed out wordless anguish. A blast of foul-smelling corrosive liquid shot toward Sally from his hand. Even with her perceptions running full tilt, she barely dodged the jet as it splattered against the wall, dissolved stone in rivulets, and filled the air with acrid fumes. She ran and the stream of corrosion followed her, cutting through pillars and scarring the floor.

Stratocaster blasted more heavy power chords toward the Archmage, forcing him to break off his attack against Sally.

He doesn't fight multiple foes well, she realized, the insight striking so hard it almost made her stumble. *That's important, that's how we can defeat him.*

The wall of the great hall, overstressed and weakened by the Archmage's acid attack, buckled and collapsed. Large chunks of stone rained down and beams of sunlight poked through the dust. Sally ran to Ace and Jason—the *real* Jason. The paralysis the Archmage had imposed upon them seemed to be weakening, for they could move their heads and their fingers were twitching.

"I've got to get you out of here." Sally glanced over her shoulder at the escalating fight between

Stratocaster and the Archmage. They hurled massive spells against each other's protective shields. Energy and noise bounced away from the points of impact to wreak destruction across the hall around them.

"Take Ace first," said Jason through lips and tongue that could barely move. "She's more fragile."

"Now wait just a goddamned minute," began the Israeli pilot.

Sally knew Jason was right and she struggled to lift the woman up over her shoulders. She was thankful for the hours she'd spent in the gym under Jason's tutelage. A year ago she couldn't have swung Ace up into a fireman's carry. She staggered down the hall with her burden and made for the great archway at the far end. If anywhere would be safe in the area, it would be there.

"Wait here." Sally lowered the semi-paralyzed woman to the ground.

"And what? Watch you all die?" Ace struggled in vain to roll over.

"The only person who's going to die today is him." Sally glared back at the Archmage. "I promise you that."

Ace's mouth snapped shut in shock; she had never heard such bloodthirsty words come from Sally.

A puff of sulfurous air washed across the room to sear her lungs and send Sally diving for the floor. She wished she had her own costume on instead of this horrible armor Frazier had designed for her. Then she'd at least have her goggles and breathing mask. She squinted toward the two combatants through the clouds of dust and smoke which filled the hall.

Both Stratocaster and the Archmage had been wounded in the fight. Strat's face was cut and bled profusely; the hot droplets stained the top of his guitar, which was cracked and showed blistered paint. One string had snapped and hung loose, trailing sparks of green fire every time it swung. His mohawk had charred away to leave only sooty residue across his scalp. Still he played, countering every spell the Archmage hurled at him with one of his own. The Archmage was battered and bruised, and his left arm had withered into something resembling a dead tree branch.

Sally crawled rapidly back over to where Jason was. He had fallen over and was grunting with the effort of trying to bend his arms. "Baby," she said, "can you move at all?"

"Not enough," he admitted, his face purple from his efforts to force his body to overcome the magical paralysis. "I can't do much more than twitch."

Sally wrapped her small arms around Jason's massive shoulders and tried to drag him along the floor. It was like trying to pull a car on flat tires. She strained to move him a few inches, and then had to stop. The heat of the battle and the bad air had taken its toll, and her reserves of strength were nearly sapped. "I can't," she groaned.

Suddenly the air was full of whirling blades, directed outward from the Archmage. Stratocaster yelped as one of them penetrated his shields and opened a deep gash across his ribs. His guitar strap fluttered down in two pieces. Another blade whistled past Sally's head to bury itself in a pillar.

"Baby, you've got to leave me here." Jason looked at her with his great big puppy-dog eyes. "Go help Strat. It's the only chance any of us have."

"No!" she cried in anger, even though she knew he was right.

A great explosion rocked the hall and cracked the walls floor to ceiling. Stratocaster and the Archmage were both flung away from its epicenter. The shock wave sent Jason and Sally skidding across the jagged stone floor. Stratocaster fetched up against a column, which shattered when he struck it. The Archmage left a furrow of shattered stone along the floor where he hit.

The ceiling crumbled in one great mass. Sally ducked in reflex, even though she knew it wouldn't make a difference. In the space between heartbeats she grasped Jason's hand and squeezed it tight.

"No!" Purple light flashed around her and Jason and the falling stones slid to one side, deflected by an ethereal hemisphere that formed around them. Stratocaster managed to keep his wits about him and cast a spell to protect his friends. Sally saw Ace likewise shielded by a glowing dome.

The Archmage took advantage of the momentary distraction to summon a massive burst of pure magical energy and hurl it at Stratocaster. It overwhelmed the musician and knocked him back into the ruin of the castle wall.

His guitar spun out of his grasp to crash to the floor.

The Archmage shouted in triumph and pointed at it with his good arm. The guitar whirled around and shattered itself against the jagged base of a broken column. Pieces flew everywhere and the cracked and broken carcass of the strange and beautiful instrument landed at Sally's feet.

"This is how it ends, Kramer! This is how it all becomes mine! With you dying on the floor in front of your friends and me winning the world."

"Gloat all you want." Stratocaster coughed around a mouthful of blood. "They'll never give up. They'll never stop fighting you."

Sally glanced down and saw something incongruous amid the wreckage of Strat's guitar: her missing horseshoe—the one she'd found amid Shannon's bones all those months ago. Strange figures were inscribed along the iron curve in many colors, layered on top of one another giving the illusion of far more depth than was possible.

She reached down for it and as she did so, symbols illuminated all up and down her arm in a specific sequence, like a computer running self-diagnostics. With each symbol, she felt like a piece of a puzzle locked into place. Her entire body hummed and the horseshoe quivered in her grasp like a living being, eager to fulfill its mission. She looked at it, then over at the gloating Archmage, and suddenly she understood what it was she held. Her stomach twisted. She was no stranger to death, having seen friends and foes die during the past year, but she had never been directly responsible for ending the life of another human.

She didn't know if she could.

The final symbol illuminated and the horseshoe reshaped itself. The two ends became sharpened lances of crimson light. Bright yellow arcs of energy danced between the forks, and she knew she held the sole, ultimate weapon against the Archmage in her hand.

"I can stop them." The Archmage used his magic to hoist Stratocaster out of the rubble and made him hover in the air, arms outstretched as if he was being crucified. "Once you're dead, I can do anything I want." Frazier's withered arm thickened and strengthened until it was whole once more.

"What . . ." Stratocaster spat out a mouthful of blood. "What are you going to do, talk me to death?"

Energy gathered around the Archmage's hands as he prepared to blast Stratocaster into oblivion. "And so my reign shall begin."

"Wolfgang!" called Sally. He turned his head to look in her direction.

In the space between seconds, she closed the distance between them and hammered the horseshoe into his chest.

CHAPTER TWENTY

"By accident of fortune a man may rule the world for a time, but by virtue of love he may rule the world forever."

-Lao Tzu
Tao Te Ching

August, 2004
Rugby, North Dakota

A part of Sally's brain screamed at her that she'd just killed someone as the magical horseshoe plunged to the hilt into the Archmage's flesh. She couldn't believe it would be so simple. The best she hoped was to create a momentary distraction. Maybe it would give Stratocaster an opening, although she didn't think he could do his magic without a guitar. *Maybe I can go find him one*, she thought frantically. But even at her fastest speed, she reasoned, it would still take her a few minutes to find a music store in Rugby, if there even was one, and return with a suitable instrument.

Surprise was just starting to replace glee on the Archmage's face when Sally released the horseshoe. The symbols ran off her arm like dust in the wind, spiraling onto the glowing arc of iron which protruded from Frazier's chest, transferring their destructive power into him.

He looked down at the object in his torso, confused. His fingers explored it as he sank to his knees. "How?"

Tiny rays of light pushed out of the Archmage's body, the brightest from around the horseshoe itself. His head sank slowly to his chest and his arms dropped to the floor. The light within him grew brighter and dissolved his flesh into dust.

The world seemed to turn inside out and upside down. A tornado of whirling energy roared in place of the man who had dared to claim the title of Archmage. It consumed his remains until not even ashes remained behind. The castle walls evaporated around them and the mountain dove back into the plain as if it had never existed. Still the magic spun around, like an electrical storm seeking a ground.

It found that ground in Stratocaster.

Years' worth of magical energy Frazier had hoarded so greedily flowed into him. The sum total of the world's magical power rushed into him as if he were a void for it to fill. His wounds vanished, his hair grew back, and his clothing repaired itself. He closed his eyes, spread his arms wide, and drank in the power like a sun-worshiper on a Mediterranean beach.

The howl of the magic as it spiraled into Stratocasater was deafening, and Sally clamped her hands firmly over her ears. Spinning winds threatened to send her tumbling, but a strong arm wrapped around her waist and she caught the comforting scent of peach pie and knew Jason was with her.

The last of the stray tendrils of power vanished into Stratocaster, who shone like an earthbound star. He staggered, giddy, and held his head as if it might suddenly fly off of its own accord. All around them, Sally could see those people that Wolfgang had converted to his own troops, looking around and blinking in confusion like they had been awakened prematurely from deep sleep. Soldiers rushed in to take people to safety.

Sally saw Doublecharge approach, leading a mass of assembled heroes from several teams, and waved at her to let her know they were all right. Doublecharge ordered the other heroes to create a secure perimeter. She and Sondra dropped out of the sky by Sally and Jason.

Sally released her grasp on Jason so she could squeeze her winged friend and exult in the feel of feathers between her fingers.

"I'm so glad you're here," she whispered.

"Likewise, kiddo," said Sondra in a husky voice. "I've been worried sick about you. Hell, I've been *molting*."

Sally laughed. "I'm so glad you're all okay." She discovered she was crying, but didn't mind so much.

"Are you all right?" asked Doublecharge. "You've been through a lot."

"I'll be fine."

"What about him?" Doublecharge nodded toward Stratocaster, who hovered several feet above the ground, still glowing like a lighthouse beacon. He seemed transfixed by the play of energies around, between and through his fingers.

"I don't know," said Sally. "When we took down Frazier, the power all went into Strat. *Ooooh!*" She gasped and her hands flew to her mouth.

"What is it?" Doublecharge's voice was sharp.

"Strat and Frazier were the last two mages. Now Frazier's dead, and all the power is in Strat, and that makes him . . ." Sally couldn't finish; she didn't want to say what she knew was in her heart.

"The true Archmage." Doublecharge looked troubled.

"*The Archmage is dead. Long live the Archmage,*" said Sondra, her voice grim.

Sally swallowed hard. "I don't think he'd . . . you know, hurt anyone. He's not that kind of person."

"He has absolute power. All the magic in the entire world is at his disposal. We can't know what kind of person that will make him." Doublecharge clicked on her collar mike. "All team leaders, this is Doublecharge. Stratocaster is to be considered a top level threat until we clear him. Secure the perimeter and stand by for further orders. Do not let him leave."

The heroes moved in to encircle Stratocaster on the ground and the air.

Stratocaster staggered around and held his head in his hands as if he had a migraine. Strange flowers sprang from the ground around his feet with each step. He lurched suddenly and a sparkling pillar of crystal rocketed out of the ground to support him and sang with harmonic vibrations. He looked at it with interest, and then poked it with a finger. A stream of brightly-colored birds issued forth from the crystalline depths, flying in a long chain of follow-the-leader.

"Will!" cried a voice. "Let me through, goddammit!"

Sally looked to see Ace being restrained by Bullet from the Lucky Seven.

"Stay back, Ace," said Doublecharge. "That's an order. Don't make this any worse."

"ACE?" Stratocaster's voice rumbled with reverberations that shook the land, as if they were standing on a subwoofer. He cleared his throat with a noise like distant fireworks. "HEY. COOL. I SOUND LIKE DARTH VADER. *LUKE . . . I . . . AM . . . YOUR . . . FATHER!*" He broke into peals of laughter that built up into a feedback delay that soon had everyone wincing.

"Stop it, Will." Sally could hear the fear in Doublecharge's voice. They were all afraid; before them stood a man with the powers of a god.

"SCARING YOU? THIS IS NOTHING. I COULD SHOW YOU THINGS THAT'D STRAIGHTEN YOUR HAIR, STACEY. THINGS THAT WOULD MAKE YOU NEVER WANT TO SLEEP AGAIN. EVER." A swirling cloud of malevolence circled around Will's ankles, containing within it shadows and hints that would give them all nightmares for years to come.

As quickly as it had grown, it dissipated into nothingness. "BUT THAT'S NOT IMPORTANT RIGHT NOW. WHAT'S IMPORTANT IS THAT I WANT TO TALK TO MY GIRL."

Doublecharge pointed at him. "Will, this isn't the time or the place."

"WHY NOT?" He gestured expansively and a grove of trees popped out of the dusty earth; they shook out their branches like dogs after a long nap. "I'VE DONE EVERYTHING I WAS SUPPOSED TO DO. I TOOK CARE OF YOUR LITTLE PROBLEM FOR YOU. I THINK I DESERVE A LITTLE *GRATITUDE*!" With his final word, a powerful force pushed all of the heroes apart to leave Ace standing by herself.

Sally found herself nearly paralyzed. Unlike the magic that Wolfgang had used on them, Will's was somehow softer; she could move slightly if she used only the gentlest of motions and forced herself to slow down. From grunts of exertion up and down the line of heroes she could tell the others were similarly frozen in place.

Ace was having none of it.

She had her hands on her hips and tapped one foot impatiently on the ground. "William Kramer, just what do you think you are doing?"

"ACE?" Will sounded uncertain.

She stomped toward him, anger boiling off her. "These people are your friends, Will! Look how you're treating them!"

"I'M . . . I'M SORRY . . ."

"The Will I fell in love with wouldn't do this. The Will I fell in love with was considerate and kind. You're acting like a dictator."

"IT'S ALL THIS POWER . . . IT'S MAKING MY HEAD SPIN. I CAN'T THINK STRAIGHT."

"You call yourself a hero? This is not how heroes act, Will, surely. This is what we'd expect from Frazier. Did we just trade one evil for another?"

Will bowed his head. "YOU'RE RIGHT. I'm sorry." His voice shrank back to its normal timbre. Suddenly Sally was free, and so were the others. "I'm sorry, everyone."

Ace was now standing right in front of him and looked sternly up at him. "Oh, Will . . . what are we going to do with you?"

He took her in his arms, and held her tight.

Doublecharge murmured into her throat mike, "Just Cause, stay on alert. Everyone else stand down but don't go too far away."

Time passed.

Just Cause remained near Will as he consented to be checked out by paramedics. They pronounced him in perfect health. He offered to heal any wounds anyone else had suffered, to repair any damages, and even to wash and wax all the military armor. The commanders politely declined, instead focusing their attention on getting the civilians back to safety.

Doublecharge handed Sally her cell phone after talking into it for several minutes. "It's Juice," she said. "He wants to talk to you."

"Sally?"

"I'm here."

"Are you all right? I know we put you through the wringer once again."

She took a moment to inventory herself and was both surprised and pleased to discover she was more or less whole on a physical, mental, and emotional level. "I'm fine, sir."

"I'm very proud of you, Sally. You're a real asset to the team. In many ways, I think you're the strongest of any of us for what you've gone through."

"I don't know," she said and felt herself blush to the roots of her hair.

"Well I do," he replied. "And I'm putting an official commendation in your file."

"Um, thanks."

"See you back at headquarters."

Sally handed the phone back to Doublecharge just as a nervous-looking Army colonel ran up to them with a field telephone. "Uh, Mr., uh, Kramer? I have the President for you."

Will grinned. "Which one?"

The colonel looked scandalized. "Ours, of course."

"I'm just joshing with you." Will took the phone and leaned back. A large, overstuffed office chair appeared behind him. As he swung his feet up, a heavy mahogany desk burst into existence beneath them. A cord twirled out of the field telephone to connect to a unit which sprang into being on the desk. "Mr. President? Will Kramer, a.k.a. Stratocaster of the Lucky Seven. How the heck are you?" He covered the mouthpiece and winked at Ace. "Always wanted to say that."

Stratocaster nodded, grunted, and made lots of "uh-huh" sounds as the President talked his ear off. "Mr. President," he said at last after taking a sip from the giant cherry cola Slushee which he'd conjured into existence. "I can personally guarantee that Wolfgang Frazier is no longer a threat to this country, or any country." Once more he covered the mouthpiece and nudged Ace. "You think he knows I didn't vote for him?"

Sally's phone buzzed to notify her of an incoming message. As she pulled it out to check it, she noticed all the other Just Cause heroes likewise retrieved their own phones. The message was from Juice.

Per Homeland Security, detain Stratocaster for questioning. Be careful.

Sally looked at Jason in dismay. "Why?"

"How?" he muttered back.

Ace glanced around at the approaching Just Cause heroes. "Baby," she said. "Tell the President you'll talk to him later."

"Ace, move away," said Doublecharge softly.

Ace drew her gun and held it ready, but not pointing at anyone yet. "What is this?" she asked. "He's not doing anything to anyone."

"Mr. President, I'm going to have to call you back. We'll do lunch," said Stratocaster. His conjured office vanished into sweet-smelling smoke.

"Ace, put the gun down." Doublecharge made no threatening moves, but Sally could tell she was moments away from unleashing a blast of lightning. Doublecharge wouldn't hesitate to act if she felt it would be advantageous. "We're not going to hurt him. We've been ordered to detain him. That's all."

Tears tracked down Ace's cheeks and her gun wavered. "That's how it always starts," she whimpered. "Detained for questioning. I've seen it before. Military minds all think alike. Then you take him away and he disappears forever."

"Babe," said Stratocaster. "Look, I'm sure this is just some kind of a misunderstanding."

"Look at her!" screamed Ace. "She's ready to take you down right now!" She clenched her free hand on Stratocaster's arm. "Please, just magic us away from here. Please, Will."

Sally, said Doublecharge's voice in her head. Switchboard must have been facilitating telepathic communication. *Disarm her. Now.*

Sally felt like she was being torn in two between her duty to Just Cause and her loyalty to Stratocaster and Ace. She wavered in indecision. Doublecharge turned her head slightly toward Sally and glared at her.

The world ground to a halt as Sally's perceptions accelerated to maximum. She sprinted forward and thumbed on the safety of Ace's pistol. Then she popped out the cartridge and slid the bullet from the chamber.

"Sally, what are you doing?"

Sally shrieked at the unexpected voice. She whirled around to see Stratocaster slide his arm out of Ace's frozen grasp. His mohawk bobbed as he looked at her.

"I'm . . . I'm making sure nobody gets hurt," she said at last. "How can you see me when I'm moving this fast?"

"Magic," he said with a smile. "Parahuman powers are nothing compared to the sum total of all the magical power in the world. I've stopped time for the moment."

"You . . . stopped time?"

"Yep. It's easier than trying to balance everything else out while we talk. This way we can take our time and not have to worry about my trigger-happy girlfriend here or your short-fused boss." He nodded toward Doublecharge. "She's a good person, and a strong leader, but I just don't like her very much. I'd rather talk to you. I figure we've got a lot of history together." He laughed at his own joke.

"What do you want to talk about?" asked Sally.

"The fate of the world." Stratocaster gestured and a couple of couches materialized. "And my fate. Popcorn?" He offered her a bowl filled with the soft, buttery snack that hadn't been there a moment ago.

"No thank you."

"Suit yourself. It's awfully good, though. Now, what's this all about?" Stratocaster sat on a couch, put his feet up on the arm, and chewed contentedly on a mouthful of popcorn.

"Juice said we were to detain you on Homeland Security's orders."

"Why?"

"He didn't say. He just told us to be careful. I don't think he agrees with them."

"Juice is a smart guy. He knows what's at stake."

"Well, what *is* at stake?" Sally gave in and sat on the other couch.

Stratocaster shrugged. "I'm the Archmage now. Contained within me is the sum total of magical energy in the entire world. That's a lot of power for one man.

Look at what Frazier did, and he only had *most* of it. I've got it all."

"So what are you going to do with it?"

Stratocaster chewed thoughtfully on more popcorn. "I could do a lot of things. Just about anything I put my mind to, really. You want me to feed the world? Make the deserts fertile? Piece of cake. Destroy all the nukes? Child's play." His face hardened. "I could turn every terrorist into a pillar of salt, or make Washington into a glass pancake so America could start over again." His expression softened again. "I could bring Shannon back to life. It's so easy once you understand the power."

Sally's breath caught in her throat. Shannon's death still felt like an open wound on her psyche. She almost demanded Stratocaster bring her back right then, but somehow she knew that would only lead down the path that Doublecharge and everyone else feared. If he brought back one person to life, how could he say no to other requests?

A god can't grant every prayer.

"A god?" said Stratocaster aloud. He must have read Sally's thoughts. "Yes, I suppose that's a fair assessment. The God of Magic. Sounds better than Archmage, don't you think?"

Sally gasped; she didn't know what to say.

"You're right, of course," said Stratocaster. "I really am dangerous with this kind of power. No wonder the government wants their hands on me."

"They're afraid of you," said Sally. "And they're jealous. They want that power for themselves. They want to control you."

Stratocaster chuckled in a way that made her blood turn to ice water. "They might find that harder than they'd think."

"They'd figure out a way. Maybe they'd hold Ace as a hostage or something."

"There is no place they could hold her that I couldn't find and rescue her."

"Then they'd . . . I don't know. I don't think like they do, but I'm sure they'd figure something out. That's what governments do, isn't it?"

"Which leaves me with what as an option? Oh, I suppose I could leave."

"Leave?"

"Leave the world. Take my ball and go home. Although I don't know where *home* would be after that. Mars might be nice with a bit of atmosphere. Or Venus with some air conditioning. I could terraform either one. Only problem is it's kind of a long ways away. I'd miss this place. Well, maybe not North Dakota so much, but you know what I mean."

"Could you just let the power go?"

Stratocaster's mouth closed with a snap. "Let it go?" he managed after recovering from wide-eyed surprise.

"Sure. Can you just release the power into the wild or something?"

"It's not a wild animal, Sally. It's magical energy."

"Well, it had to come from somewhere, right? Where does magic come from?"

"Nobody really knows that. Even I don't know that, and I know everything there is to be knowed about it."

"If you . . . died . . . where would the power go?"

Stratocaster's brow furrowed as he considered. "Without an individual for the power to travel to, I guess it would just spread out until someone came along who could draw it in."

"What if there wasn't anyone?"

"I suppose the world would just eventually absorb it all, but there's no guarantee someone wouldn't rise up again in another thousand years to do this once more."

At last, Sally couldn't resist her appetite any longer and reached for some popcorn. It was delicious. "I was thinking, what if you just went back in time, way back before people, and just let the magic go free? Can you do that?"

A look of wonder crossed over Stratocaster's face. "Give away my power. Live a normal, mundane existence instead of being all-powerful. Tough choice."

Sally nodded toward Ace, still frozen in the act of holding onto Stratocaster's arm. "I think she'd rather be with Will the man instead of Will the mage."

Stratocaster smiled. "That's true. There might be something to that idea. Tell you what, Sally . . . Let's talk it over with the rest of the team and see if they agree before this gets any uglier."

"Are you sure?"

"No," said Stratocaster. "But it's got to be better than the alternative."

"What's the alternative?"

"I turn you all into woodchucks and be on my way."

CHAPTER TWENTY-ONE

*"My vocation is more in composition really than anything else
– building up harmonies using the guitar, orchestrating the
guitar like an army, a guitar army."*

-Jimmy Page

August, 2004
Rugby, North Dakota

"This is a bad idea," said Doublecharge. "I'm not sure I
can smooth this one over with Homeland Security.
They're sending someone to take charge." She looked
grimly at Sally. "I'm sure it's Goodwin."

Sally chewed on her knuckles and watched as
Stratocaster directed his magic. She'd explained her
idea to Juice and Doublecharge. Doublecharge had been
against it; Just Cause had pushed Homeland Security
about as far as it could and there would undoubtedly be
consequences of their actions. Juice had once again
overruled his second-in-command to give Stratocaster
the go-ahead to try to dissipate his magical power. "*I
won't be party to what amounts to a witch hunt,*" said
Juice. He said he would assume all responsibility for
whatever happened, and had the Command Center log
the order to proceed under his name. Whatever
ramifications came from Just Cause disobeying
Homeland Security's directives would be on his head.

A great stage grew from the dusty plains of North Dakota at Stratocaster's behest. As Sally watched, scaffolding unfolded out of itself to form an arch overhead. Lights sprouted from it like buds on a vine. Shadowy smoke formed into stacks of speakers. A riser at the stage's rear bubbled into a massively complicated drum set.

As he'd explained it, Stratocaster was going to treat them all to one hell of a concert as part of his spell. Sally knew it was more than just that; he was such a showman, he couldn't resist a performance like this.

In spite of his protests that it would be safe, National Guard troops formed a perimeter well back from Stratocaster's stage. He may have wanted to play for an audience, but they'd have to watch him from at least a quarter mile away. To compensate for the distance, Stratocaster erected monstrous video screens and speaker stacks to carry images and sound to the audience. The word had gotten out and a steady stream of curious onlookers flowed into the area. It may not have been a 21st Century equivalent of Woodstock, but people anticipated the performance would be a strong final movement to the symphony of magic which had been the biggest event ever in the high plains.

Sally reached out and grabbed a Frisbee before it could smack into Jason. Like every other outdoor concert, people were throwing them around, batting beach balls, and cheering. She gaped in surprise to see the Just Cause logo on the Frisbee, which morphed into a likeness of her face before it dissolved into tendrils of sweet-smelling smoke that blew away on the late-afternoon breeze. "He's really going all out with this," she said.

"He's wasting time and endangering people," said Doublecharge. "I wish he'd hurry up and get it over with before Goodwin or whoever gets here."

As she spoke, the stage lights dimmed. Sally hopped up and down a couple of times to try to see better. Jason laughed and lifted her up onto his shoulders. She curled up to nip his ear playfully and then toyed with his hair as the wail of a single guitar echoed across the plains under extreme amplification.

With a blast of sound, incendiaries went up on either side of the stage, shooting sparks and flames high into the air as the lights came up. Sally saw Stratocaster decked out in his finest rock garb: tight checkerboard pants tucked into Doc Martens; a sleeveless tank top with some incomprehensible symbol on it that constantly shifted and changed. His mohawk stretched to improbable heights and sparkled from base to tip. His guitar, a duplicate of the same one he'd built in the past with Nikola Tesla, hung low from its strap as he raised one hand in the traditional two-fingered rock salute.

"Hello, Rugby!" he called into the microphone.

The audience cheered. Sally felt herself swept up in the excitement and hooted right along with them.

Ill-defined, shadowy figures rounded out the band on the other instruments: drums, bass, rhythm guitar.

Stratocaster's fingers danced across the strings with a flourish of notes which could have made eardrums bleed as far away as Fargo. "Appreciate you all coming out tonight for this last stop on my farewell tour," he shouted. "I've got a few tunes to play for you now." And with that, he launched into a fast-paced virtuoso performance which made Sally want to get up and dance.

The concert progressed for what felt like hours, but each tune was so amazing in its complexity and sheer musical power that the fans cheered and screamed their approval with each new number. One piece was so haunting and beautiful that tears ran unchecked down Sally's face and she felt Jason's chest hitching with sobs. Another had such a sensuous, driving beat that she was ready to let Jason take her right there amid the audience.

She slipped off his shoulders, straddled his waist, and ground against him as they swayed to the beat. Tune after tune, each one a new sensory adventure in emotion.

During a slow ballad, a dark sedan nosed its way through the gathered crowd to stop by the Just Cause heroes. Three men in dark suits climbed out followed by a furious Christine Goodwin. "Jesus fucking Christ," she said after surveying the audience enthralled by Stratocaster's performance. "You men get to the stage and shut that shit down right now."

The three agents disappeared into the audience.

Goodwin closed a hand around Doublecharge's arm. "What the hell is going on here? I have an order straight from the Director to take Stratocaster into custody, and you're having a goddamned concert. I will have your ass, Doublecharge. Yours, Juice's, and everyone else's on your team!"

Doublecharge glanced down at the woman's hand on her arm. Electricity crackled between her eyes and at the ends of her fingers. "Take your hand off me."

"Don't you dare," said Goodwin with a finger raised in threat. "It is a federal crime for you to use offensive parahuman abilities against a normal human."

"Fine." Doublecharge laid an admirably-fast right across Goodwin's jaw. The woman dropped into a heap and lay still. Sally gasped in astonishment as Doublecharge hopped up and down, holding her hand in agony. "Son of a bitch, that hurts!"

Jason whooped with glee. "Tick tock!" Then he looked around, embarrassed at his exuberance.

Sondra knelt down beside Goodwin. "She's out cold." She grinned. "She's going to have one hell of a headache when she wakes up. God, Stacey, I didn't know you had it in you."

"I shouldn't have done that," said Doublecharge. She peeled off a glove and winced at her swollen knuckles. "But it felt really good." A smile creased her face.

"I'll take care of it," said Switchboard. "She tripped on a loose rock. Fell and hit her head. Lucky for her, Just Cause was here to take care of her."

"What about the other agents?" asked Jason.

"I don't think we need to worry about them, baby," said Sally, and pointed. "Look."

The crowd had raised the three suited men up and were bodily passing them back toward the heroes. They struggled to no avail against the massed hands that pressed them inexorably away from the stage. The crowd deposited them none too gently on the ground by Goodwin.

Switchboard did something to them. Their faces blank, they collected Goodwin, got back into the sedan, and pulled away from the audience. "They're going to take her to the hospital to get her head checked," he said.

Stratocaster finished a tune with a powerful flourish that made the aurora borealis gleam overhead. He grabbed the microphone. "*Thank you, Rugby! You've been great tonight. I've got just one more tune to play for you all and then I must be on my way.*"

People in the audience began to raise their hands, cigarette lighters extended. Sally felt something in her own hand and looked down to see a silvery lighter in her hand emblazoned with the horse-head logo she used as her trademark. Jason already had his hand up and a small flame flickered from a lighter. She shrugged, laughed, and raised her own in salute.

Stratocaster began his last tune. Where the other pieces had affected the audience's emotions, this one seemed to focus on the world itself. Reality twisted as it throbbed in time to the driving melody. A bright star appeared high overhead and started a slow descent. Sally watched as it grew until she realized it was a giant, glowing guitar dropping body first with its neck pointed toward the sky. Mystical strings vibrated across its face with each strum of Stratocaster's pick hand.

Like a rocket slowing for a landing, the eldritch instrument touched down upon the stage behind Stratocaster to tower a hundred feet over him.

He stopped playing, but the huge guitar continued without missing a beat. A portal opened in its base, filled with the purest white light Sally could imagine. Stratocaster stepped into the portal, only a shadow against the brightness. He reached out a hand and a petite female figure stepped up onto the stage.

Sally realized it was Ace and took a step forward. "Wait, what's she doing?"

"She's going with him," said Sondra.

Ace took Stratocaster's hand and together they entered the brilliant light inside the guitar. Steam shot forth from beneath it as it rose into the air like a majestic balloon, so bright it hurt to look at. Sally squinted at it and raised a hand in farewell. She hoped they could see her as the giant guitar flew higher and higher. The music reached a final crescendo with a massive drum fill and crashing power chord that peeled paint off parked cars and cracked windows but didn't harm anyone listening.

The guitar overhead flared bright like a supernova filling the sky. Everyone raised their hands to block out the glare. It vanished in a heartbeat, along with the stage, the music, and all the magical artifacts that Stratocaster had so liberally spread throughout the onlookers.

Sally blinked and looked around in astonishment. She felt like she'd just awakened from a dream. If so, she decided, it had been a good dream. She slipped her hand into Jason's to reassure him as he gaped at the uncertain crowd in the middle of an empty plain in North Dakota.

Stratocaster's final music still rang in her ears.

EPILOGUE

"Like a flash of lightning and in an instant the truth was revealed."

-Nikola Tesla

December, 2004
Just Cause Headquarters
Denver, Colorado

"Happy birthday, dear Sally, happy birthday to you!"

The gathered members of Just Cause and the Lucky Seven sang cheerfully off-key. Sally blushed and wished she could just disappear. It had been bad enough a year ago when it was just the Lucky Seven singing to her. Now it was all of Just Cause—even the new interns—and she felt quite overwhelmed at the attention.

Turning nineteen wasn't supposed to be this big of a deal. It wasn't like eighteen, or twenty-one.

Jack had taken charge of the party, as was his wont. He'd gone all out to decorate the cafeteria in gaudy red and yellow streamers. There were tasty appetizers, which Jason inhaled by the plateful, and gallons of punch, thoughtfully spiked by the intern Carver. Sally felt a little tipsy, but kept Jason close by her in case she started to sway. Juice turned a blind eye to the alcohol, but hinted in a short speech that anyone misbehaving from it would be called in for emergency drills early in the morning.

Sondra and Jack gave her a DVD collection she'd been wanting for a long time. She hugged Sondra and surprised Jack with a kiss that made him blush like a schoolboy. Jason gave her a cowboy hat she'd been coveting since she saw it online. She whispered to him she'd wear it for a special present she had in mind for him later. He grinned.

Then Juice stepped up and presented her with a pin recognizing her first year of service with Just Cause, marked with three gold stars for active deployments and exceptional valor. "Take a week off," he said. "A vacation. You've earned it." Jason stood up a little straighter and Juice laughed. "Please, take this overgrown puppy dog with you."

Doublecharge shook her hand. "It's been a crazy year, but I've been proud to serve beside you. You're a real asset to the organization."

A Just Cause staffer entered the cafeteria with a box and headed for Sally. "From my mom?" she asked, but it was postmarked from somebody called *Harbaugh, Scraggs, & Jessup*. "What is this? I don't know these people."

Juice looked at it. "That's a law firm down south. Pretty prestigious."

Sally swallowed a nervous lump. "I'm not being sued or something, am I?"

Juice laughed. "No, they'd contact Just Cause lawyers first. I'm curious, though. Open it up."

Sally slid a fingernail through the tape sealing the box. Inside she found a sealed envelope with a note attached. Mystified, she read the note. "*Dear Ms. Thompson . . . The contents of this envelope have been entrusted to this firm for many years, with the direction that it was to be delivered to you on this date of your nineteenth birthday.*" She looked at the others.

"Well, don't keep us all in suspense, girlfriend! Open it already!" said Sondra.

Sally pulled an old, yellowed piece of paper from the envelope. "It's a letter." The name on the signature leaped out at her. "Oh my God . . . it's from Stratocaster."

She read it aloud.

"*Dear Sally and friends . . . I hope this letter reaches you and that you are all well. I wanted to tell you what happened after Fairuza and I left North Dakota. We traveled back in time. Way, way back. Before the dinosaurs, before plants, back to when the Earth was empty of life. There I released as much magic as I could except for what I needed to return. It was amazing, glorious as the power flowed out to be absorbed by the planet below. Sometimes Fairuza and I like to joke that we may have started life on Earth with that very act.*

"*Once it was done, we planned to return, but knew we couldn't come back to your present, where I would be a fugitive from the government. Nor could we return to an earlier point of our lifetimes. After much discussion, we chose to return to an earlier point in time. We settled in Colorado Springs in 1900, where we reconnected with Nikola Tesla. With his help, I have divested most of my remaining magical ability into artifacts which we have spread throughout the world. It will prove very difficult for anyone to ever become an Archmage in the future without locating them all.*

"*Fairuza and I miss you all, and thank you for the chance to have a normal life together. It was an honor to work with you and to be a part of something greater than ourselves.*

"*Sincerely, William and Fairuza Kramer, August 7, 1925.*"

Sally sniffled a bit and the words blurred on the page. She checked the envelope and found two more items within. First was an old photograph of Will and Ace and Nikola Tesla standing outside a brick house. She almost didn't recognize Will without his trademark mohawk, but Ace's smile was radiant and Will looked as happy as she'd ever seen him. The other item was a small envelope sealed with wax. Sally carefully broke the seal.

Inside was a short handwritten note, which she read aloud as well. "*If for some reason you ever need me and my magical skills once again, strum any guitar with this pick and it will summon me. Stratocaster.*" A guitar pick slid out of the envelope into Sally's hand. It was inscribed with hundreds of tiny symbols and almost hummed with self-contained power.

Juice picked it up and examined it. "Sondra, I believe this should go into a secure case in the Archives, along with the letter and photograph."

"I'll see to it," said the winged woman.

"Do you think they're still alive?" asked Sally. She felt an odd mixture of sadness at the notion of more of her friends perhaps having died, but happy that they'd been together for so many years, and perhaps many more.

"Over a hundred years," said Juice softly. "I doubt it, Sally. We could find out their eventual fate. Perhaps they had children, and might even have descendants still living today. Would you like me to have Research follow up?"

"No," Sally said after consideration. "Not right now. They're still alive here, and I want to remember them that way." She tapped over her heart for emphasis.

Juice nodded.

The party was winding down a couple hours later when Jason and Sally made a discreet exit and wound up back in his quarters.

"Happy birthday, baby." Jason lifted her up.

She wrapped her legs around his waist, her arms around his neck, and kissed him like she hadn't seen him in a century. "Thanks, Jase. I love you, you big doofus."

"I love you too, babe. You're the light of my life."

Sally gasped at the simplicity of his romantic statement. It was like a balloon had inflated in her chest and made her float up toward the skies. She smiled and buried her face against his neck. "Strat and Ace wrote that letter twenty-five years after they landed," she whispered. "I'd love to be with you for that long. Or even longer."

"I'm okay with that."

"Put me down, big guy." Jason obliged and Sally reached up to perch her new hat at a jaunty angle on her head. "This cowgirl's ready to go for a ride."

Jason grinned. "*Yippee-kai-yo.*"

ABOUT THE AUTHOR

 Ian Thomas Healy dabbles in many different genres. He's an ten-time participant and winner of National Novel Writing Month and is also the creator of the *Writing Better Action Through Cinematic Techniques* workshop, which helps writers to improve their action scenes.

When not writing, which is rare, he enjoys watching hockey, reading comic books (and serious books, too), and living in the great state of Colorado, which he shares with his wife, children, house-pets, and approximately five million other people.

Ian is on Twitter as @ianthealy
Ian is on Facebook as Author Ian Thomas Healy
www.ianthealy.com

~~~

ABOUT THE COVER ARTIST

S. Bell is a comic book artist and illustrator who lives and works in San Francisco. She holds a BFA in Fine Art and an MFA in Illustration and is currently pursuing her MA in Arts Education. She is the author of the series *The Urban Fairytales*, the fourth volume of which is forthcoming.